THE KING'S COMMONER

The Tudor Saga Series
Book Two

David Field

SAPERE BOOKS

THE KING'S
COMMONER

Published by Sapere Books.

20 Windermere Drive, Leeds, England, LS17 7UZ,
United Kingdom

saperebooks.com

ISBN: 978-1-913028-85-5

I

Ten-year-old Tom Wulcy groaned as he looked down Edmund Pountney Lane and saw Thomas Howard and his escort of ruffians waiting for him. It was the second time this week, and he could guess why. He had to answer to for the special commendation he had received that morning from the Abbott of Blackfriars, during the daily Mass of Our Lady. It was hardly Tom's fault that his Latin was better than that of many ordained priests, but it seemed he had to pay the price for his cleverness.

Thomas Howard was the same age as Tom Wulcy, but there the resemblance ended. Tom was inclined to plumpness, and very disinclined towards martial arts, whereas Thomas Howard took his position as the son of the Earl of Surrey, and the grandson of the Duke of Norfolk, very seriously. Whereas the young Howard looked every inch the steely-faced knight that he would no doubt become in due course, Tom Wulcy looked more like an angelic altar boy than a knightly squire. Thomas was tall, dark and lean, whereas Tom was short, plump and light auburn in both hair and countenance.

'Cross yourselves — here comes a priest,' Thomas Howard yelled sneeringly.

'I am no priest yet,' Tom replied as assertively as he could, 'but I will even now pray for your soul, should you be about to perjure it by attacking a defenceless boy, with your stout entourage in tow.'

Howard's fox-like face darkened, and his eyes narrowed as he waved to his two companions with a dismissive gesture without breaking his glare at Tom. 'Stand off a pace. I can deal with this Papal pudding without need of any bodyguard.'

Tom stared him down. 'You will, as usual, dispose of me with ease, given that your power comes from the strength of your arm. But since mine comes from the depth of my learning, may I at least be permitted to place these books which I carry down on the ground? After all, for them to be of any value to you, you must first learn to read, and since you can barely do so in your native tongue, of what value to you would be a Latin discourse on the Stations of the Cross?'

One of Howard's retainers sniggered, then straightened his face immediately as his young charge whipped round with a threatening glare. Thomas turned on his heel and walked quickly towards Tom, red in the face. 'A pox on the Stations of the Cross! A pox on your fancy Latin, and a pox on you — butcher's son!'

With a single straight-armed punch from his left fist, he sent Tom sprawling into the mud, his valued books skidding across the wet ground in all directions. Tom slowly and painfully picked himself out of the puddle in which he had landed, wiping the mixture of cow's urine and sheep droppings off the seat of his tunic and the top of his hose as best he could.

Muttering to himself, Tom surveyed the damage to his clothing as he walked home, not that his attire was in any way grand; the sumptuary laws would have denied him the right to sport colours in his doublet such as the reds and blues that the Howards favoured. His short school doublet was — or rather had been, until it landed in a puddle of ordure — light brown, and his now stinking hose a darker shade of the same colour. Both were robust garments suitable for school wear, and they were made in the town from the fine wool worsted for which its craftsmen were famous.

Plain or not, his garments were not for playing in puddles with, and his mother would, when he got home, no doubt give him the benefit of another of her homilies on thrift. He looked up anxiously towards the jettied upper floor of his generously dimensioned family home, in case either of his parents was gazing out of one of the lead-mullioned windows to witness his return from school. Satisfied that he was unobserved, he slipped down the side passage to the external kitchen.

The pigs in the garden area were grunting and snuffling contentedly on the offal thrown from the kitchen door earlier in the day, and he could see his sister Bess bent diligently over the bench on which she was cutting out baked pastry into pie crusts, while young Dickon turned the spit on which the lamb carcass was basting nicely.

Tom's plan was to discard his soiled clothing in the kitchen, leaving Bess to hand it over to the washerwoman who called twice a week. He would then need to enter the main house by the scullery door clad in only his undergarments, slide stealthily up the back stairs to his upper chamber overlooking the rear garden, and present himself at the supper table freshly attired, in the hope that no-one, least of all his father, would notice the change in his dress from earlier in the day.

Unfortunately his parents had chosen that time to inspect the kitchen for vermin, and as he slipped quietly through the open door it was his mother who spoke.

'There you are, Tom, late as usual. And no doubt seeking some treat from Bess ahead of supper — little wonder that you grow so plump. And what in God's name is that smell?'

His father appeared from behind her with a knowing grin. 'Did you fail to make the jakes in time, boy?'

'No Father,' Tom confessed, realising that there could now be no pretence. 'In truth it is a fine mixture of cow's piss and sheep shit, which is to be found in abundance in the streets of this noble town.'

'Such vulgarity!' his mother protested, then in a more kindly tone, 'Did you slip over?'

'Nay, more like he was pushed,' his father observed as he took a closer look at the bruising around his son's nose and eye socket. 'Was it young Howard again?'

Tom nodded his confirmation as his father gave vent to his wrath.

'The Devil take these arrogant sons of earls and high lords! They besport themselves around the nation in their finery, holding themselves higher in their own esteem than those whose honest labour and wisdom in commerce brings much wealth into the nation. Where would my high and mighty Duke of Norfolk and his whelps be without the fleeces and finished garments that depart daily from St. Mary Quay bound for Flanders? Where would the Earl of Surrey and his impudent brat be without the leather goods that supply half the nobles of France?'

Fearful that his intemperate words might be repeated in less sympathetic ears by house servants who might earn a shilling by reporting them, Joan Wulcy attempted a change of subject. 'May we not complain to the bailiffs?'

Even Tom knew that this would be fruitless. Robert Wulcy might well describe himself as a butcher, if asked, but his real wealth came from less worthy activities, and he was more frequently the *source* of complaints to the town's two bailiffs than he was in the habit of lodging his own complaints with them. His pigs were forever escaping into the street, and the building two doors down from the Wulcy residence that he ran as an alehouse of sorts attracted the lowest sort of clientele, while its upper rooms were available for rent by the hour, and were infamous for their licentious assignations.

'The less we have to do with the bailiffs, the better,' Robert observed. 'Leave the matter with me, and let us discuss it further over supper.'

The determined look on his father's face as Tom sat down opposite his parents at the supper table, while their maid of all functions Alice fussed around them, left no-one in any doubt that the matter had been resolved, at least in Robert's estimation.

'I have in mind to remove you from the Grammar School as of this very day,' Robert announced as he cut himself a generous slice of lamb. 'Your learning shall continue here in this house, under the tutelage of an ordained brother from Holy Trinity.'

Tom smiled in appreciation. His best subjects were the classical tongues of Latin and Greek, and he had developed an avid interest in Divinity from the scholarly works he had studied in those tongues. There was an added advantage in a possible career in the Church, since it did not — so far as he was aware — involve riotous exercise.

His mother would have preferred Tom to be schooled more in the mysteries of commerce, since Robert would not live forever, and she wished to spend her final days in the same comfort she had enjoyed since marrying Tom's father. However, father and son seemed to be in happy agreement for a change, and so the change was agreed upon.

The following Monday, Dom. James arrived at the house in St. Nicholas Street with a selection of elementary Latin and Greek texts, which Tom had exhausted by the middle of the morning, sending the astonished monk scurrying back to the monastery's scriptorium for something more advanced. Three days later, almost in desperation, Dom. James sought an audience with his patron and confessed his dilemma.

'Sir, there is not a brother in our holy house who could compare with your son in the Classics or the more advanced theological philosophies. Say you he is yet but ten years of age?'

'Yes,' Robert confirmed. 'But if *you* cannot teach him ought, then who can?'

The monk thought hard. 'There is but one place I could recommend, and that is the University of Oxford, whose fees are not light.'

'The money is neither here nor there,' Robert replied sternly. 'When could he begin?'

The monk smiled back diplomatically. 'There is also the question of his age. I have never heard of a boy of ten being accepted, regardless of his brilliance. I can of course make an enquiry on your behalf, since I am conscious of the many and generous endowments that my humble house has received in the past, but...'

'Yes, yes,' Robert cut him off testily. 'And there shall be more yet, if you can secure a place of study for young Tom. Do not regard the matter of appropriate fees as a hindrance — either to your "humble house" as you call it, or to the university authorities. Just make it happen, Brother.'

On the first day of the Michaelmas Term, 1484, shortly after his eleventh birthday, and to the considerable amusement of fellow students almost five years older than him, Tom Wulcy took his seat on the study benches of Magdalen College, Oxford, at the start of one of the most distinguished careers as an undergraduate in Arts and Divinity that his tutors and professors could recall.

Four years later, as he presented himself at the Bursar's office for the preparation of the document that would record his award of the degree of Bachelor of Arts, he was asked how his name was to be correctly spelt. He thought for a moment, before advising himself that someone as learned as himself, who intended to rise to great eminence in the Church, deserved a more fitting name than the one he had borne thus far. At the same time, he owed his father everything.

'Wolsey,' he replied, then spelt it out for the Bursar to copy it onto the vellum.

He walked back out into the May sunshine and recalled the day when Tom Wulcy had been slammed into the mud by an ignorant oaf whose father was now lying in the Tower of London under an attainder.

'Tom, Tom, the butcher's son' was known throughout Oxford as 'the boy bachelor', and was about to become 'Thomas Wolsey, Bachelor of Arts' at the unheard of age of fifteen.

II

While Thomas Wolsey had been rising to academic pre-eminence, the fortunes of his old enemy, Thomas Howard, had sunk to a new low as the result of his family's poor choice of who to accompany onto the battlefield. Henry Tudor now ruled England and had expressed his displeasure at the support given to Richard III by Thomas Howard's father. The family's estates had been attainted and were now in the grasping pocket of a monarch seeking to replenish a bankrupt royal Treasury, while the Earl of Surrey himself was now a guest of the Constable of the Tower.

The newly-fashioned Thomas Wolsey, meanwhile, had no desire to return to his home town, even to witness the fall of an old adversary, nor did he have any developed idea as to where he might venture with his first degree, and he was therefore easily persuaded to spend more of his father's money in the acquisition of a Master's degree in Arts, which he achieved in 1491. He then took an appointment as a Fellow of Magdalen College, before accepting a post as Rector to the vacancy at St Mary's at Limington in Somerset.

In October 1500, Thomas donned the vestments of a priest of the Church of Rome, ahead of conducting his very first Mass. Underneath everything was his new white 'alb' gown, a symbol of the purity of every servant of God, fastened around his waist by a gold cincture. Draped across his shoulders, and lying directly on the alb, was a purple and gold stole that hung down on either side of it.

As Thomas raised his arms and intoned the prescribed blessing prayer, his two sturdy assistants lifted a heavy green chasuble over his head and into place on his shoulders; then finally a humeral veil was placed over his shoulders and back. It added considerably to the overall weight of the vestments that he was required to wear, but was essential for the raising of the Blessed Sacrament as the Mass reached its crucial moment. He nodded his thanks to his assistants, and bid them take their places at the side of the altar inside the church, where he would join them once he heard the choir begin the *Veni, Domini*. As they left the vestry with solemn faces, Thomas looked back at the overall effect of his appearance reflected in the window glass.

'No filthy hose here,' he muttered as he heard the opening anthem and walked out to impress the congregation with the richness of his apparel and the sanctity of his office.

A year later Thomas was in conflict with the secular authorities, in the person of Sir Amyas Paulet, whose family had effectively ruled most of the area around Yeovil for several generations from their seat in Hinton St. George. It began in June, when his lordship, who was also the local sheriff, sent a stern note of reproval to Thomas via his steward, following complaints he had received regarding the regular absence of Thomas from Sunday Mass, which was frequently conducted by one of his assistants.

It came to a head during the village fair to celebrate Harvest Festival. As usual, the apple harvest had been garnered some weeks beforehand, and there was a stall set up inside the fair on the village green at which local rough cider could be purchased for a groat. Thomas had many groats at his disposal, and had already developed a liking for the powerful local brew. When the stall opened, he was the first in line, a point not to be overlooked by the lord of the manor.

Paulet sent his steward to Thomas's side with a message, 'My lord says to remind you, Father, that this is his manor, and that he should be ahead of you in the queue.'

Thomas looked down his nose at the timorous steward. 'Remind your master that the apples come from God, and are best sampled first by His representative in this community.'

Later that afternoon, Paulet's revenge was sweet. It had been a hot day, and Thomas had consumed more cider than was advisable for an overweight man wearing a long black cassock. While wiping his brow for the tenth time that afternoon, he became light-headed and sat unceremoniously on his bottom in the recently scythed grass, to the excited chortles of several villagers. Paulet was attracted by the noise, and saw his chance.

He had earlier been plagued by locals to select a suitable target for the traditional fruit-throwing ceremony, in which a local 'worthy' was installed in the stocks on the village green in order that others might pitch over-ripe fruit in their direction upon payment of a silver penny for the local Poor Fund. The victim was normally one of Paulet's senior household, but this opportunity was too good to miss. Accompanied by the parish constable and two of his grooms, he strode over to where Thomas was sitting on the ground.

'I see we have a suitable candidate for this year's ripe fruit pitching. Place this man in the stocks, and let the festivities commence.'

Thomas glared up at Paulet. 'God will punish your sin should you allow over-ripe fruit to be hurled at one of His anointed while wearing his garment of office.'

Paulet took his sword from its scabbard, lowered the point and gently lifted the hem of Thomas's cassock, before bending forward to peer up it. 'This may well be, but He will think little of it should that man be clad only in his shirt and hose.' He turned to his retainers and grinned. 'Remove his cassock, and place him in the stocks clad only in his undergarments.'

Five minutes later, as the first of the browning tomatoes splattered down the front of his undershirt, and several of its seeds bounced onto his hose, Thomas asked himself whether he had really progressed all that far in his life. Once again he had filthy hose, but this time he vowed to make sure personally that one day the man responsible for that would pay dearly.

After recovering from his humiliation, Thomas sought out his superior, the Bishop of Bath and Wells, within whose diocese his parish lay. Once the bishop had suppressed his amusement at the mental picture he had formed of the portly and somewhat pompous young priest, clad only in his undergarments, being pelted with ripe fruit to the delight of his parishioners, he put a proposition to Thomas.

'I am much vexed by this man Paulet,' the bishop confided, 'who is forever bombarding me with letters of complaint regarding how my clergymen conduct their offices. He has also caused complaint to be sent to the Archbishop of Canterbury, no less, regarding two benefices that remain unfilled within my diocese. They are at Ilchester and Yoevilton, and since it would seem that your duties at Limington do not unduly tax you, perhaps you might also wish to join two more of my parishes?'

Thomas frowned, unsure of what was being proposed. 'It is your wish that I become a pluralist, my Lord? Surely, and with the deepest respect to your office, that will require the authority of the Primate of All England.'

'Indeed it will, Thomas, indeed it will, but how better to send a message to Sir Amyas that I will not be dictated to in the affairs of my office? Not only will I have formally answered his demand that the two empty benefices be filled, but I will be leaving him in no doubt that the choice of incumbent is mine, and as an additional rebuke for his insolence I will have done so by installing the one man who can inflame his wrath.'

'And you will intercede for me with his Grace of Canterbury?'

'No, Thomas,' the Bishop smiled. 'I shall send you in person to argue your case, but shall arm you with a note under my hand that you may present to Archbishop Deane in person, assuring him of your suitability for three benefices.'

Thomas lost no time in riding to Canterbury on a donkey that he had purchased a year previously at Yeovil Market, and which seemed to him most fitting, given that Our Lord had chosen a similar beast on which to ride into Jerusalem on his final journey to the cross.

He spent the night before his audience on his knees in his humble cell in the hospitium of a local monastery, praying to God to honey his tongue in the manner best suited to address the head of the Church of which Thomas was only a humble parish priest.

Archbishop Deane had a promising smile on his face as he put down the letter from the Bishop of Bath and Wells and indicated for Thomas to take a seat.

'It seems we at long last have priests of the same stern mettle displayed by my predecessor in office, who shared your Christian name. Thanks to Thomas Becket, the Church has always been afforded its rightful place — until now. The recent wars seem to have robbed men of their love for their fellow men, and as yet we have no way of knowing how far our new King Henry will be guided by Christ in his conduct of affairs of State.'

'I have heard that he is most pious,' Thomas offered tactfully.

'Indeed, he has demonstrated a desire not to interfere with God's holy ordinance during my meetings with him, although those have been mainly in my capacity as Keeper of the Great Seal. Closer to hand I am obliged almost daily to engage in disputes with the town authorities regarding the crowds that flock to Becket's Shrine.'

'These pilgrims no doubt bring great wealth to the town, as I'm sure your Grace regularly reminds the town bailiffs,' Thomas replied diplomatically, unsure where the conversation was leading.

'Indeed, had I the time, I would be constantly reminding them that without the cathedral, there would be no town,' the Archbishop confirmed. 'Unfortunately, as Primate of All England, and Keeper of the Seal, I have other matters with which to concern myself than the state of the local streets. Perhaps a man such as you could do battle in my stead?'

Thomas deflected his eyes to the floor in a submissive glance while urging his heart to beat less exaltedly as he took in the implication. 'You have God's work for me to do here in Canterbury, your Grace?'

'The Bishop of Bath and Wells advises me that you are ambitious, competent, diligent and most persuasive in argument. I am inviting you to become my chaplain, Thomas.'

Thomas could hardly draw breath to reply, which Deane took as a sign of uncertainty.

'Since you already have three benefices you should not look for any great financial reward here at Canterbury. However, the nature of the position I am offering you is one that would appeal to any man of your ambition. It will involve regular attendance upon me wherever I go, which these days seems increasingly to be the royal Court. Richard Foxe, the Bishop of Winchester and Lord Privy Seal, is ever seeking clerics who can negotiate matters of State without being overawed by nobility, and it may be that between us we can commend you to His Majesty for diplomatic duties across the Channel.'

'Your Grace does me great honour, for which I will swear before God to prove worthy,' Thomas mumbled.

'See that you do, Thomas, see that you do,' the Archbishop admonished him. 'And now your first duty must be to chase me to the bottom of this jug of excellent claret.'

III

Although not yet thirty years of age, Thomas was now, in material terms, comfortable if not quite wealthy. Given his taste for extravagance, this was perhaps as well, but once Archbishop Deane had formally granted the necessary dispensation for Thomas to enjoy the revenues from three benefices at the same time, while ministering to the prelate in a purely ecclesiastical capacity, Thomas was clearly in need of more than one house, which in turn would require a somewhat flexible and portable household.

He began with a modest four-roomed house in Canterbury itself, in which he installed a steward and a cook, while acquiring several ushers, footmen and servers locally from the town on a 'live out' basis. Given his need to occasionally show his face in one or other of his livings in Somerset, in order to justify their stipends while leaving the actual conduct of the services and other holy offices to lesser clergy upon payment of a pittance, he also required a house further north than Canterbury.

He chose a comfortable dwelling in Putney, close to the old bridge that would allow him to cross the Thames with speed should he be needed in Westminster when the Archbishop was in attendance on the King, while being only a mile or so down the road from Fulham Palace, the 'country' residence of the Bishop of London, regularly served by wherry from Westminster steps.

In this house Thomas appointed his own chaplain, a young man called Thomas Larke, a fellow East Anglian a few years younger than Thomas and the son of a Thetford innkeeper.

Thomas saw in Larke a kindred soul who did not possess the wit to rise as quickly as he had done, and therefore was no threat to his ambitions, but was perfectly competent to carry out simple clerical duties such as conducting Mass twice daily.

The choice of a house just outside London proved to be a wise one, since Archbishop Henry Deane seemed to be more in the King's service than he was in the service of God, and was almost permanently resident in one of the lesser suites of rooms in Richmond Palace, the favoured residence of Henry VII and his Queen, Elizabeth of York.

Here was installed a royal nursery for the princesses, while the princes Arthur and his younger brother Henry were, as tradition demanded, housed in Westminster, where Arthur in particular might be tutored for the regal role that he would one day occupy.

Henry VII was more inclined toward international diplomacy than he was the expenditure of vast sums of money on foreign wars, and he had sought to ally himself with the growing power of Spain by marrying Arthur off to the young Infanta of Aragon, Katherine. Katherine was welcomed into London by a massive crowd that threatened to sink London Bridge by its sheer weight, and proudly heading the triumphant procession was the young Prince Henry, already displaying the love for knightly display that would epitomise his later life.

The wedding was fixed for 14th November 1501, in St Paul's Cathedral, and was to be conducted jointly by the Archbishop of Canterbury and the Bishop of London. While the Archbishop was in attendance on the King, Thomas opted for a stroll through the gardens of Richmond Palace. Approaching him from the opposite direction was a young couple walking sedately arm in arm, and as the distance between them and

Thomas narrowed, he realised that he was about to confront his old adversary, Thomas Howard. Thomas smirked as Howard's face fell, and he couldn't resist the first word.

'Cross yourself — here comes a priest.'

Howard managed a pale smile in response, then turned to the elegant fair-haired lady on his arm. 'May I introduce my wife, Anne? Dearest, this is Thomas Wulcy, with whom I went to school. He was the finest scholar in our class, and as you can observe he has since taken holy orders.'

'Indeed he has,' Thomas replied, 'and were you to push him into the mud today, you would incur a penance of many thousands of *Pater Nosters*. You might also incur the royal wrath, since my master the Archbishop of Canterbury is even now in attendance upon His Majesty.'

'Not necessarily,' Howard replied with an ingratiating smile. 'I omitted to give my dear wife her full entitlement. She is Anne of York, the former Princess Anne, daughter of the late King Edward, the sister of the Queen, and therefore the sister-in-law of King Henry. That makes me a royal brother-in-law, as I calculate.'

'The last I heard, you were destined for the Tower,' Thomas sneered back ungraciously, invoking another superior smile from Thomas Howard.

'I was *never* destined for the Tower, and my father only resided there for a short while until His Majesty realised his mistake, and honoured him with the duty of putting down a rebellion in the north, by which process I became *Sir* Thomas Howard. I was knighted on the field by my father, who has been restored to his title of Earl of Surrey, a title that one day will of course be mine. Now, if you will excuse us, the Queen awaits us for an early dinner.'

As they moved past Thomas down the path, Anne Howard looking at him sideways with curiosity as he gave her a polite bow, he concluded, with some regret, that the arrogant young buck had probably got the better of their exchange. But nothing lost, he reminded himself. 'He that lives by the sword shall die by the sword', or so it was foretold in the Gospel of St. Matthew, and in these uncertain times a false word or an unwise alliance might result in death by the axe. Howard's reference to dinner had set Thomas's stomach rumbling, and he headed back towards the Great Hall.

Thomas was allocated a place in the nave of St. Paul's for the wedding ceremony and from there, as he stood craning his neck over the feathered bonnets and gable hoods of half the nobility of the realm, he watched the solemn procession of the bride. Prince Arthur was waiting with the Archbishop, the Spanish Legate and nineteen other mitred clergymen in all their ecclesiastical finery, for the ceremony that would make a fifteen-year-old Spanish girl the Queen-apparent of a nation of whose language she knew very little.

While the remainder of the congregation gazed in awe at the magnificence of the ceremony, the beauty of the bride and the solemnity of the wedding rites, Thomas looked in jealous fascination at the pectoral crosses on the chests of the bishops, their gilded mitres and their jewel-encrusted croziers. Was he not one of the foremost Latin and Greek scholars in the entire land? Could he not speak many of the languages of the nations immediately across the Channel? Did he not possess diplomatic skills honed in the settlement of petty parochial disputes between the parishioners whose causes he occasionally judged during his rare visits to his benefices?

Yet here he was, still a humble priest, dressed in a plain black soutane that contrasted sharply with the colours of the rainbow by which he was surrounded. If there was justice in this life, he should by rights be one of those on the raised platform, waving the incense and administering the Host with a jewelled hand upon which sat a fine gold ring of office.

Two days later, it was time to return to Canterbury, but when Thomas was admitted to the Archbishop's chambers in the Bishop's Palace, his patron was not alone. Seated across from him was a man who looked as if he had died some months previously, to judge by the skeletal set of his skull and the thinness of the frame under his simple ecclesiastical robes. Thomas stood uncertainly in the doorway until Henry Deane waved him over.

'This is the chaplain of whom I spoke earlier, Richard. Thomas, may I introduce Richard Foxe, Bishop of Winchester? He has need of your linguistic skills.'

'In what regard, my Lord?' Thomas enquired of the corpse-like visitor, whose mouth broke into a rictus smile that was both encouraging and repellent at the same time. He held out a parchment to Thomas.

'It is a despatch for the French Ambassador from King Louis, which in accordance with our normal practice has been intercepted and opened. We are currently engaged in diplomatic negotiations with Louis regarding his intentions towards Italy, in the hope of further ingratiating ourselves with Spain, and we wish to know what instructions the Ambassador has received regarding how to progress these negotiations. Take as much time as you require, and while you do so feel free to refresh yourself with some of this excellent Rhenish wine.'

Foxe beckoned to a page for an additional goblet to be placed at Thomas's disposal, and as he poured himself a generous measure Thomas read through the two-page vellum. After some five minutes he looked back up at Foxe and announced his conclusions.

'The Ambassador has been instructed to proceed slowly. See here — "*doucement*"? That means "slowly" in our language. However, he is not to positively obstruct any prospect of eventual agreement, simply to leave the door open wide, depending upon the outcome of his king's latest armed venture south of his borders. See here again, "*ne fait pas dilatoire*" — that best translates as "do not act in an obstructive way".'

Foxe's face relaxed into another sepulchral smile. 'It is as we had hoped. Our own King needs time to see the direction in which the wind blows. He will be most comforted by this, as indeed am I, since the King in one of his stubborn tempers is not a man with whom to discuss matters of fine diplomacy.'

Thomas looked across at the Archbishop. 'Your Grace, we must depart without much further delay, if we are to reach Canterbury by nightfall. Even then it will be a hard ride, and my old donkey is hardly the fastest mount on which to progress.'

Henry Deane smiled back indulgently. 'Bishop Foxe here has asked that you be allowed to remain, since there are other matters of translation upon which he would value your counsel. He is accommodated at Richmond, while you are comfortably housed here in Putney. I shall not require you again until Mass next Sunday.'

Thomas bowed from the presence, having promised to call on Foxe on the following forenoon.

For the next few days Thomas learned much of the devious machinations of King Henry around the thrones of Europe, the importance to England of its trade links with Burgundy, but the threat to it posed by the heir to the Holy Roman Empire, Maximilian, who was allied to Burgundy by marriage. Henry required to maintain good relations with Maximilian, and he was officially allied with him in seeking to keep the French out of Italy; at the same time, diplomatic overtures were being made to Louis XII of France in the hope of preventing him from further attacking principalities in Italy, since this would be likely to result in both Spain and the Emperor demanding that Henry commit English troops to a war with France, which he could ill afford.

Foxe was amazed by the alacrity with which Thomas grasped the essentials of this diplomatic puzzle, and by the second day of their discussions Thomas was even able to venture a few suggestions of his own as to how the impasse might be skirted around.

King Henry had a delicate matter for Foxe to negotiate. Henry had recently been obliged to put down a challenge to his throne by a pretender claiming to be the Duke of York, son of the late King Edward, and one of the 'Princes in the Tower' who Richard III had been accused of having murdered. His real name was Perkin Warbeck, and he had been given considerable support and encouragement by the Scottish King James IV.

King Henry was anxious to seal the northern door to his kingdom by means of a perpetual peace treaty with Scotland, possibly cemented by intermarriage between the two royal houses. Unfortunately, it seemed that James was reluctant to enter into any treaty directly with Henry, given that his army had suffered an ignominious defeat at the hands of the Earl of

Surrey. In the circumstances, any face to face confrontation between the two monarchs would seem, to the rest of the world, like a capitulation on unfavourable terms by a defeated monarch, and James was a proud man.

Richard Foxe, as Lord Privy Seal, had been given the thankless task of bringing James to the bargaining table, and had delegated it to the Keeper of the Seal, and his old friend, Henry Deane, with a helpful suggestion that he leave the actual organisation of it to his chaplain.

Within twenty-four hours Thomas had identified the most appropriate channel of communication, and organised a meeting, via their chaplains, with the Spanish Ambassador, Don Pedro de Ayala, who was also the accredited ambassador to the Scottish court, and could act as a speaking tube between London and Edinburgh without exciting comment.

Thomas advanced his plan while they sat in Don Pedro's suite of rooms in Westminster, drinking a fine Shiraz and sizing each other up.

'How would a treaty between England and Scotland benefit Spain?' Don Pedro began.

'Simply in this,' Thomas replied. 'Scotland has long been an enemy of England, and the need to secure his northern border against incursion necessitates King Henry keeping back many troops that might be employed elsewhere.'

'Where exactly?'

'France, for one. Scotland and France have a sad history of aligning against England. They call it the "Auld Alliance", and on many past occasions, when England has been at war with France, the Scots have harassed it from the north.'

'Then why should my master of Aragon not simply let the Scots stir the French? That way, England would need to wage war on France, which is what my master would have you do anyway.'

'Because, for the reason I just explained, any war with France would bring the Scots down upon us, necessitating that we withhold a sizeable number of troops from direct warfare with King Louis, troops that might be sent to assist the Spanish cause.'

Don Pedro thought for a moment, before nodding slowly, then taking the discussion to its next logical stage. 'And what seeks King Henry as the terms of such a treaty?'

'A vow of perpetual peace, and a marriage between the two houses. This might even result in Scottish troops being loaned to England to fight against France.'

'And who are to be the partners of this marriage?'

'King James himself, obviously, since he is currently unmarried.'

'And the English bride?'

'The Princess Margaret. She will be thirteen on her next birthday, which is not long away. She is well developed for a girl of her age, and doubtless would be in a suitable condition for the marriage bed before being allowed to travel north to consummate the peace.'

'No doubt this is the will of her father, but what mother would allow her virgin daughter to be sacrificed to a man with lusts such as King James is reported to feed?'

'You are a diplomat, my dear Don Pedro, and an excellent chess player according to my sources. You, above all others, know that on certain occasions it is necessary to lay a pawn in the way of a king. She will become a queen ere long anyway, and it is better that she become a queen whose throne can be united with Spain's.'

Foxe, and to a lesser extent Deane, were richly praised by a relieved King Henry for having brought about the resulting Treaty of Perpetual Peace, while being silently cursed by Queen Elizabeth, who feared for the health and comfort of her pubescent daughter at the hands of a wild barbarian whose legion of bastards were always on public display in the nursery of Stirling Castle. For Thomas, it was a triumph that would not be forgotten, and would shortly be rewarded.

IV

When Archbishop Dean died in February 1503, Thomas was genuinely mournful of his passing, since he owed him so much in his career thus far. He was now also minus a senior appointment and was therefore more than a little intrigued when Richard Foxe, attending the funeral at Canterbury, introduced him to Sir Richard Nanfan, Deputy Governor of Calais. Nanfan was highly regarded by King Henry due to his involvement in the negotiation of the Treaty of Medina del Campo that had resulted in the tragically doomed marriage of Katherine of Aragon to Prince Arthur. Unfortunately, Arthur had died of the sweating sickness only five months into their marriage, leaving ten-year-old Prince Henry as the heir to the throne.

Calais had suddenly become more important to the English than it had been for years. It was the last foothold for English forces in Continental Europe, and the sole remaining trophy of the years in which, under the now legendary Henry V, England had dominated France in the Hundred Years War. All but Calais had subsequently been lost by the witless Henry VI, but it remained as a secure landing site for English soldiers, should they wish to invade again. It was strategically crucial to English military ambitions in France, and was the most obvious port through which England's all important wool trade with the Continent could be conducted.

The governance of Calais, and the associated fortress of Guines with its prison at Hammes, all of which lay within the English occupied 'Pale of Calais', obviously carried with it a heavy responsibility, a great deal of administration, and the need for constant intelligence activity. Governors were chosen for their undoubted loyalty to the monarch they served, and Henry VII had, since his coronation, pursued a constant policy of employing men of lowly birth, whose loyalty he could purchase by elevating them to positions of authority in which they owed everything to their royal benefactor. Sir Richard Nanfan was no exception, but as he approached his fiftieth year he found the duties increasingly onerous, particularly those relating to intelligence gathering.

He was therefore more than interested when a man so close to the King as Richard Foxe, the Lord Privy Seal, recommended Thomas, as both a budding diplomat and a multilingual scholar, who could, in his spare time, minister to the ageing man's spiritual needs. Almost immediately after attending — and helping to conduct —Deane's Requiem Mass, Thomas was introduced to Sir Richard, and shortly thereafter joined his household across the Channel.

For the next two years Thomas familiarised himself with Calais and the border with Flanders, which was then being ruled by the Burgundians from their traditional lands further south. Towns such as Bruges and Ghent were important to the English wool trade, and successive Dukes of Burgundy had featured strongly in European power politics in recent years; they were also, by marriage, aligned with the Holy Roman Empire and could not be ignored by an English monarch with half an eye on defending his economic interests across the sea.

In his capacity as chaplain to the Deputy Governor of Calais, Thomas rapidly assessed every church, castle, religious house and inn in the entire Pale, until he could have found his way around it blindfold, should the need arise. His regular reports to Sir Richard were detailed and perceptive, and large portions of them were passed on to Richard Foxe, who was now King Henry's principal spy and facilitator. It had been Foxe and his 'ferrets', as the King called them, who had lured Perkin Warbeck to his doom, and had later manufactured the excuse to justify his execution. Foxe was the ultimate intelligence machine, and he in turn relied on men like Thomas Wolsey, who owed their preferment to him.

Foxe himself had risen from the yeoman class, had studied at Oxford, and had been a schoolmaster under holy orders when forced into exile with Henry Tudor in France, ahead of the invasion that had set the young Earl of Richmond on the throne. When Foxe's increasingly aching bones reminded him that the time had come for him to find a successor to himself as the King's chief bloodhound, he recognised in Thomas Wolsey a kindred soul, a base-born academic of the highest calibre who could hide the most confidential of matters beneath his ample cassock.

It was now 1506, and Sir Richard Nanfan had succeeded in obtaining a pension via the good offices of Foxe that would allow him to retire to his small estate in Gloucestershire. There was, however, one condition, and this was that he bring his chaplain back with him, and leave him at his Putney house with instructions to await further word from Foxe.

Thomas had barely had time to unpack all his vestments when word came that he was to report to Foxe at Richmond Palace, where he was in attendance upon the King, who had need of those best informed regarding how matters lay outside his immediate kingdom.

Thomas found Foxe in the antechamber, deep in conversation with a heavy-set middle-aged man, richly dressed and with an air of authority. Foxe rose and walked towards Thomas.

'Thomas, first let me congratulate you on the excellent and regular reports that Sir Richard was able to pass on to me from Calais. I would like you to meet Sir Thomas Lovell, the King's Chancellor, the Master of his Wards, and a man who knows the King's desires even before the King does.'

'You flatter me as ever, Richard,' Lovell responded with a smile as he nodded to acknowledge Thomas's obsequious bow. 'Well, you look the part — now let us hope you can play it to perfection.'

'*What* part, my lord?' Thomas asked.

Lovell looked back at Foxe, who shook his head.

'I have not yet had time to acquaint him with either the nature of his mission or the new role that he must play in the royal routine.'

Thomas's heart began to beat faster as he caught the inference of the words.

'His Majesty has need of a new chaplain, Thomas,' Foxe explained. 'It is most likely that you will exhaust yourself with nothing more, in his service, than the designing of mild penances for sins that owe more to the imagination than the commission. However, *we* — by which of course I mean the King's Council — have need of your filed tongue back across the Channel. The precise nature of your mission will be explained to you later, and you are here today simply that you may receive the royal approval.'

'I am to meet the *King*?' Thomas mumbled in astonishment.

'This very hour,' Foxe assured him. 'He is at present making a small board through that door, and once his dinner has been removed, we are to be admitted.'

'But,' Thomas protested, looking down at his second best soutane, 'I am hardly dressed as befits one being granted a royal audience, unlike you gentlemen in all your finery.'

Foxe smiled encouragingly. 'Fear not upon that score, Thomas. His Majesty judges men not by their dress but by their loyalty. He is already well appraised of your loyal service to him in Calais, and on our recommendation wishes you to put to best use your intimate knowledge of the people of Flanders and those who currently rule them. But for this morning, he simply wishes to become acquainted with the man who will guide his soul through the darker days that he imagines lie ahead of him. You must know that his health is not of the best, that he is plagued with a gout that makes him short of temper, and that this past winter has laid him low with a recurrence of his lifelong chest ailment. He does not expect to live long, and he wishes to achieve as much as he can in order to ensure that the throne passes both safely and richly to young Prince Henry of Wales. With all these things on his mind, His Majesty sees no-one of his Council except we two.'

Foxe looked up sharply as the dividing doors that gave access to the Presence Chamber opened silently, and a gentleman usher appeared in the opening.

'His Majesty will receive you now, gentlemen.'

Foxe and Lovell strolled in confidently. Thomas hesitated in the doorway, gazing for the first time at the King, a thin-faced, almost haggard man with sparse greying hair lying in thin strands upon his head, who was dabbing at his mouth with a kerchief, and clearly attempting to suppress an irritating cough. He looked past his two Council members and raised a beckoning hand towards Thomas.

'You are highly spoken of, Father Wolsey,' Henry reassured him. 'I trust that your penances are as light as your countenance is sleek?'

'Indeed, Your Majesty,' Thomas croaked in his first address to his king.

'Your main value to me will be as an ambassador in those places where a filed tongue and a sharp wit will stand a man in good stead. I will leave those details to Foxe here. In the meantime, be advised that I observe Mass upon my rising every morning, which is usually with the sun. The rest of the day will be your own, but on those days when you are abroad I shall require you to send another priest in your stead.'

'I shall do my utmost to serve Your Majesty with all my best endeavours, and in perpetual gratitude for the honour that you bestow upon me,' Thomas assured him.

'Save your flattery for foreign rulers,' Henry muttered, before lapsing into a fit of coughing, and waving for Thomas to leave the presence.

Thomas was followed out by Foxe, who drew him to one side.

'Do not be deceived by the show His Majesty makes of being a weak old man. It suits his purpose to appear so, while arranging for the fortunes of others to be tipped into his pockets. Match his mood with your own, and you will be well rewarded with public offices. Join me for dinner in my chambers, and the nature and purpose of your first diplomatic progress can be explained more fully.'

By early afternoon Thomas had learned that he was to proceed with all speed to the court of the Holy Roman Emperor Maximilian, and there assure him that Henry was eager to ally with him against Louis of France in order to prevent the latter from carrying out his badly-kept secret plan to attack Milan.

Thomas was handed a ring bearing two intertwined jewelled stones crafted into the emblem of the Tudor Rose, which would serve as confirmation of his authority. He was to lose no time in setting off, and raced back to his Putney home. He left instructions for an astonished Thomas Larke that he was to celebrate Mass for the King in his chambers at Richmond Palace at sunrise every day until Thomas's return, and he ordered one of his grooms to ride hard to Dover, where he was to arrange for fresh horses and a Channel passage boat to be waiting by the following morning.

Emperor Maximilian gazed with some amusement at the dust-streaked figure of the fat priest who knelt before him, and bade Thomas announce his business. Thanking God for the time he had taken to learn German, Thomas addressed Maximilian in his own tongue.

'My gracious lord, King Henry, would be united with you in the suppression of French pretensions to the townships in Italy that King Louis is rumoured to be planning to attack.'

'I knew nothing of this,' Maximilian protested.

Thomas saw his opportunity. 'It is as my master thought,' he replied, 'and he also thought it appropriate that the tidings be brought to the most powerful ruler in Europe, to whose army he would gladly commit men of his own, to ensure your success in warding off King Louis's intended sacking of Milan.'

'Tell your master that I am greatly in his debt, that he shares such confidences with me, and shows me such support before making use of this knowledge for himself.'

'May I assure my master that his offer of support has been accepted?'

'Most gladly,' Maximilian smiled down at him. 'You may also give him this gold chain, on which is the likeness of the Emperor Caesar Augustus worked by one of the finest smiths in my native Vienna, as a token of my constancy in this matter. And now, your business concluded, you must rest for the night and enjoy the hospitality of my modest house.'

'You are most gracious,' Thomas replied unctuously, 'but my bodily comfort is as nought compared with the anxiety with which my master awaits joyful confirmation that your causes shall be joined. If you will permit, I shall return to him post haste.'

'Your King is blessed to have men so well endowed with both superior powers of Statecraft and limitless amounts of energy. Depart with my blessing, Father Wolsey, and God speed your enterprise.'

Scarcely able to believe his good fortune, Thomas hastily rejoined his two grooms, who had the horses waiting, along with a saddle pannier full of meat, bread and wine that they had coaxed from the cook, and as they raced towards the rapidly setting sun, chewing vigorously and exchanging the wine gourd from rider to rider, Thomas said a silent prayer to the God he served as well as his King, both of whom were showering him with good fortune.

They disembarked at Dover and pounded directly through the lanes of Kent and Surrey until they reached Richmond at first light. Thomas demanded admittance to the royal apartments, and was just in time to see Thomas Larke, dressed in his finest soutane, emerge white-faced from the inner chamber and give thanks to God that he would not be required to conduct a third fumbling Mass to a monarch who coughed and shivered at all the inappropriate moments. Thomas was just thanking his personal chaplain for the service he had rendered him, when the King himself appeared in the doorway, a puzzled frown on his face.

'Wolsey,' he announced sternly, 'I did not submit to the furtive mutterings of this boy priest in order that you might spend longer in your bed. When is it your intention to travel on my business to the Emperor?'

'In truth, Your Majesty,' Thomas replied proudly, handing Henry the Imperial medallion on its chain, 'I have already been and returned.'

Henry looked thunderstruck as he took in the implications, then asked, 'What reply did he give?'

'That he is more than happy to unite with Your Majesty in the joint enterprise that you propose. Indeed, he was seemingly full of gratitude for your gracious offer.'

'Thomas, you have served me well. I ask only that you relay this information to Bishop Foxe and my lord Lovell, and then you may take what is no doubt your much needed rest. I shall take supper with you here in my chamber this evening.'

Thomas bowed, and when he looked up the King had retreated back into his chamber, and an usher had closed the door. Puffing out his cheeks in satisfaction, Thomas leaned on the shoulder of his bemused chaplain.

'Let us home, Larke, for I am both triumphant and exhausted. I have come to learn that being in the service of a king provokes a fierce thirst. I hope that you have not consumed all the Beaujolais that we brought back upon our retreat from Calais.'

The next day Thomas Wolsey took supper with the three most powerful men in the realm. He sat across from King Henry, who was toying fitfully with a slice of venison pie, while Bishop Foxe sat to Thomas's right, with Lord Lovell to his left.

'King Louis is no doubt already soiling his hose at the news that we are threatening to align with Maximilian,' Foxe observed with a sneer.

'How soon will he know?' Henry enquired.

'By sunset today, Your Majesty,' Foxe told him. 'My man at the French court is trusted, primarily because he is believed by

Louis to be *his* man. The information went by fast horse as soon as Thomas here passed it to me.'

Something still puzzled Thomas. 'If King Louis has been advised of what he will surely regard as treachery by England, will he not rise against our possessions in Calais?'

Lovell burst out laughing, while Foxe smiled indulgently at Thomas.

'His first ambition is Milan, is it not? And he is even now being informed that England has just aligned itself with the most powerful monarch in Europe. When one is standing up to one's neck in the sea, the last thing one needs is an incoming tide.'

Thomas persisted. 'And if Louis insists on laying siege to Milan, are we prepared to commit men to the side of the Holy Roman Emperor, as I promised him?'

Lovell, who had regained his composure, explained, 'Louis will *not* now attack Milan. That was the whole purpose of your visit to the Emperor, Thomas. Louis fears that should he do so, he will bring down two armies upon his head.'

It was Henry's turn to smile. 'You see how I am well served by my Council? The mere threat of our joining Burgundy, and Louis will hold his hand. By this means we have bought off the urgent entreaties of Spain that we take up arms against France. Everyone is satisfied, and we have no need to seek the grant of more taxes from Parliament to equip and dispatch our armies.'

'The Emperor seemed genuinely surprised to learn that Louis was planning to lay siege to Milan,' Thomas recalled. 'We were fortunate that we *did* know.'

'My man at King Louis' court again,' Foxe told him. 'The same man who will now warn him against it. All that is now required is that you, Thomas, advise the Spanish Ambassador of how Louis was frightened off, and Ferdinand of Aragon will hopefully cease his constant demands that we attack France, which would cost the Treasury dearly.'

'You can perhaps now perceive, Thomas,' the King added, 'why there was no time to be lost in your mission to the Emperor, with which I am most contented. There can be no question of my rewarding you directly, since Foxe here advises me that we have not the money. Nor would it look good were it voiced abroad that I bribed a priest in order to instil fear into the heart of the King of France. But there is another way in which I can put riches in your path. We have need of a Dean of Lincoln — would such a post appeal to you?'

'Indeed it would,' Thomas enthused, already in his mind ordering a new set of robes for his installation, 'but Your Majesty is over generous, I fear.'

'I do nothing for nothing, Thomas,' the King replied. 'You were a schoolmaster for a time, I believe?'

'Indeed, Your Majesty, it was my great pleasure and privilege, while the Head of Divinity at Magdalen College, to tutor the three excellent sons of the noble Marquis of Dorset, the stepbrother of your most gracious late Queen.'

'So you are well experienced in tutoring those of noble blood?'

'Yes, Your Majesty.'

'I wish you to begin to attempt to instil some book learning into the young Prince Henry. He is an indifferent scholar, since his main delight is with knightly show and dangerous sports. If the firing of arrows at retreating deer, the rattling of opponents' heads in the tiltyards, the launching of hawks into the sky and the tupping of eager ladies-in-waiting gave a man learning, then young Hal would be the foremost scholar in Europe. As it is, he knows as little of Latin and Greek as he does the internal workings of the human body, and he cares even less. If he is to take his place upon the throne of England then he must be swiftly assisted to make up for lost time. See to it, Thomas.'

With that, the King rose from the table and retreated through the door to his bedchamber. Thomas felt Foxe's reassuring hand on his shoulder.

'Courage, Thomas. Prince Henry is indeed the wildcard of the suit, but you will have daily access to the man who will soon be King, and who will be in awe of your learning. When he claims his throne, if he be his father's son, he will choose to have about him those in whom he can trust. This is how Lovell and I attained our high office.'

Two days later, in Prince Henry's chambers in Richmond Palace, Thomas appreciated how much luck he was going to need. Henry, an athletic, handsome youth of seventeen, had the scholastic attainments of an average nine-year-old. Whenever Thomas tried to engage 'Hal', as he preferred to be called, in the language of the Classics, he would find some way of diverting the conversation into one on heraldry, hawking or armorial bearings, which were more to his interest and a complete mystery to his frustrated tutor.

However, Thomas had learned enough about the ways of the Court to realise that there was something to be gained from every learned fact, if employed to advantage. He quickly came to appreciate that Henry was headstrong, wilful and totally committed to his own desires, and wanted nothing to do with affairs of State. He would shortly become a young, pleasure-driven king with a vast Treasury at his disposal and, as Foxe had advised Thomas, he would wish to leave the affairs of State in the hands of those he trusted, while he went off hunting, jousting or whoring. All that Thomas needed to do was to ensure that he was trusted, and the world would fall into his cassock pockets.

There was only one topic upon which Hal seemed to require Thomas's guidance at this stage in his life.

'Does not the Church say,' he asked Thomas one dismal November afternoon, 'that it is a sin to lie with one's brother's wife?'

'Indeed it does,' Thomas replied, slightly taken aback. 'The Book of Leviticus.'

'And yet my father insists that I wed the Spanish dumpling?'

'He does so for reasons of State, Hal,' Thomas advised him in hushed tones. 'It is to England's benefit to be allied with Spain, and it was doubly unfortunate that your brother Arthur died when he did, leaving Katherine a widow at so young an age.'

'Did Arthur manage to tup her, think you?'

Thomas dropped his pious gaze to the richly carpeted floor. 'I am an ordained priest, Hal, and such matters are not within my experience. Still less am I party to such intimate secrets.'

'He would need to have been desperate to do so, even were he capable of raising his flagstaff for the purpose. She smells of olive oil, did you know that?'

'Indeed I did not, and how would I?'

'You do not hear her confession?'

'Only your father's. I can, however, advise you that marriage to the Dowager Princess of Wales would be something against which the Church would counsel. But I am also obliged to advise you, privily, that for every sin there is an absolution, and for every contemplated sin there is a dispensation.'

'It seems to me that your Church is as flexible as a wet rope,' Hal smirked back. 'Your Church is one of convenience, Thomas.'

41

'It is God's church, Hal,' Thomas muttered.

'I wonder if God would agree with that,' Hal replied. 'But at least I know that I can always come to you for a convenient pathway out of any sin I may be contemplating, or may have committed. For the right price, of course.'

'May we continue with this translation, your Highness?'

'No, we may not,' Hal replied with a stubborn set of his lip. 'We may continue with your opinion of this latest sonnet. And please call me Hal, if we are to remain friends.'

In the early months of 1509, King Henry's health took a frightening turn for the worse. Thomas was constantly at his side whenever the physicians had finished fussing around him. At times when Henry was lucid, Thomas administered the last rites, just in case this might be Henry's last day on earth.

Then came the day when the royal physicians finally agreed that Henry would not see another sunrise. Foxe and Lovell muttered between themselves, the physicians came and went with their potions, and Thomas yet again administered the last rites, almost off by heart this time.

Late in the afternoon Prince Henry appeared at the foot of the bed, wreathed in sweat and mud from some royal park or other, and averted his gaze as if reluctant to be reminded of the mortality of human life. As Thomas finished the last service he would ever perform for the monarch who had raised him thus far, he lifted his head and met the eyes of the scared young prince. With an almost imperceptible gesture of his head, he indicated to Hal that he wished to speak with him outside the death chamber, and the young man needed no further encouragement.

'Is he marked for death this day?' Hal asked.

Thomas shrugged his shoulders. 'This day or the next, the outcome is not far away, Hal. I shall soon be calling you "Your Majesty".'

'You will continue to call me Hal or I will have your head,' the prince joked weakly, 'but I would have your counsel as to what I must do next.'

Thomas drew him to a bench in the hallway close to the chamber doors, and they both sat down. Thomas took a deep breath, said a short prayer for guidance in his choice of words, and placed his hand on Hal's shoulder.

'I am your friend, Hal, and would be your counsellor at this solemn time. But you must know that the throne is unpopular with the people, due to your father's misguided reliance on two men who between them have lined their pockets at his expense while letting the blame therefor rest with him.'

Hal's eyes widened. 'You speak of Foxe and Lovell?'

'No, I speak of Edmund Dudley and Richard Empson, who have plundered the wealthy and taxed the poor. Should they remain in office — or indeed in this world — then I fear a popular uprising against the throne, led by the London mob.'

'What must I do, Thomas?'

Thomas jerked his head towards the chamber doors. 'I will return in there shortly, and seek to persuade all those with knowledge of your father's death, when it comes, to speak nought of it for two days. In those two days you must secure the arrest of Dudley and Empson on charges of treason and have them conveyed to the Tower with great public show. Then you must yourself retreat to the Tower, for your own protection against any mob. I will come and go regularly, to keep you advised of how matters progress. No-one will suspect a humble priest going about his business, and within two days we may begin to plan your coronation, with great splendour. The common people love spectacle.'

It was Hal's turn to grip Thomas's shoulder, then he looked up expectantly as the chamber doors swung open, and the doleful face of Richard Foxe appeared. He looked down the corridor to where Thomas and Hal were sitting.

'It is time, Thomas. And a defining moment for you — Your Majesty.'

As Thomas and Henry rose glumly to their feet, Henry turned again to his mentor.

'I will find some way to repay your good offices, Thomas.'

V

Edmund Dudley and Richard Empson were arrested within an hour of King Henry's death and were already secured within the Tower before the new King reached it, along with a select royal bodyguard. By the time that Thomas joined him, Henry was seriously concerned about the will of the people.

'Is there yet any sign of rebellion, Thomas?'

'Fear not, Your Majesty. As yet, the people are unaware that your father is dead, and hopefully they will remain in ignorance for at least another day. As to any challenge to your throne, we shall have to await any rival claimants.'

'There can be none, surely?'

'Only from those few who remain within the pack of Yorkist dogs, of whom the most worthy claimant, your Plantagenet cousin Edmund de la Pole, has long been confined within these very walls, and according to my sources of information has all but lost his reason. But that does not exempt you from making your own claim to rule England stronger than it is at present.'

'What must I do, Thomas?'

'First, you must disclaim the policies by which your father grew rich. He has left you a healthy Treasury — much richer than it was when he won the crown from Gloucester — but it has been at the expense of the wealthy merchants and the nobility, most of whom would throw their hats in the air were you to proclaim that there will be no more taxation.'

'But how will I survive?'

'The taxation granted by Parliament is only one source of your revenue. You also acquire much by way of traditional feudal entitlements, the grant of monopolies, and trading profits from certain ventures that your father established with my assistance. Believe me, Your Majesty, you will not starve. Talking of which, I have ordered that your supper be brought forth shortly, and with your gracious leave I will join you at board.'

'Gladly, Thomas, gladly! There is so much upon which I need your guidance, if I am to be best placed to enjoy my inheritance. For example, how may I ensure that the people love me?'

Thomas thought deeply for a moment, then waved in the servers who stood hesitantly in the doorway behind the pages and footmen who hastily assembled the board. Platters of meats, loaves of freshly baked bread, tureens of soup and several jugs of wine appeared on the table as if by feats of conjuring, and as he dug heartily into his supper Henry appeared more relaxed, which was precisely as Thomas wished him to be before launching into the more delicate advice he had to impart.

'Your people are simple folk, Hal, and they require only peace, prosperity and security. Give them those, and they will hail your progress through the streets as a hero, a champion, almost a God. Peace and prosperity you can already give them, by putting down any rival claim to your throne, and by relaxing the burden of taxation upon them.'

'And "security", Thomas? What did you mean by that? A powerful army with which to repel foreign aggressors?'

'That certainly. You must always demonstrate your ability and willingness to lead a strong army into battle. But there is also the certainty of succession.'

'Meaning what, precisely?'

'Forgive me, Hal, but it means siring heirs — legitimate male heirs, that is. Once the people are assured that the throne is not only secure for the present, but that its peaceful continuation is assured by the existence of a healthy male royal heir, then they will feel secure for the foreseeable future. That is why your father took so much care over your safe upbringing once your brother Arthur died.'

Henry's face set in resignation. 'I must marry the Lady Katherine, say you?'

Thomas nodded as he took a mouthful of wine. 'That would be the most obvious policy at this time, Your Majesty. You were once betrothed to her anyway, although you renounced that, much to your father's anguish, when you attained your fifteenth year. But she is still available, still anxious to be Queen of England, and richly connected to the house of Spain, with her sister Joanna ruling Castile alongside their father in his lands of Aragon.'

'They say Joanna is mad,' Henry pointed out.

'Indeed they do, and with some justice, so I hear. But her father Ferdinand rules as her Regent, which is another pertinent argument in favour of your marrying Katherine. She is not uncomely, she is pious and gracious, and she is no doubt highly fertile, in that way of devout Catholic women of all Southern European nations.'

'Shall I need a dispensation from the Pope?'

'Indeed you shall, but your father thought of that, too. It was granted some years ago, and it covers *both* possibilities regarding whether or not her marriage to your brother Arthur was consummated.'

Henry sat deep in thought before announcing his decision. 'It shall be as you advise. Presumably there will be no objection should I also take mistresses?'

Thomas shrugged his shoulders. 'As an ordained priest, I can hardly be heard agreeing to fornication outside of marriage. In any case, that were a question best put to your wife.'

'Can you order a splendid ceremony, with the Archbishop of Canterbury presiding?'

'Only you can order that, Your Majesty, although I can manage the finer details. But speak you of your wedding? If so, might I respectfully urge against it? The splendour should surely be reserved for the coronation, and any magnificent ceremony ahead of that would detract from the glory of the actual crowning. If I might suggest a quiet wedding, followed by the most glorious of joint coronations?'

Henry nodded. 'It shall be as you say, and as ever I shall rely on you to make it all happen.'

'Very good, Your Majesty. And thank you for your trust in me.'

'If I cannot trust you, Thomas, in whom *can* I trust? Will you consent to join my Council?'

'In time perhaps, Your Majesty, but for the moment I would advise that you make no changes in that regard. It is as well to retain those men in whom your father trusted, while sending a message to your people that these are worthy men, and that there are to be no great upheavals in government.'

'Who were the most trusted?'

'Bishop Foxe, most certainly. And Sir Thomas Lovell. In his last days, your father trusted none other than those two, although I would advise that you add others of high degree — trusted men who will do your bidding.'

'Who would you recommend?'

'The Archbishop, perhaps? It is customary for him to also be appointed Chancellor, and from what I have learned William

Warham is a biddable man, although he begins to feel his advanced years of late.'

'None of those we have mentioned so far is a man of warfare, Thomas, save Lovell in his youth. What say you to Thomas Howard? He is loyal, his father the Earl of Surrey is a great military commander, and Thomas and I have shattered many a lance together in the tourney.'

'Perhaps, then, the Earl of Surrey himself, rather than his son, who is merely my age, and in my experience somewhat hot of temper?'

Henry smiled. 'Howard tells me that he once used to bully you at school. Do you still fear him?'

'No, Your Majesty, I pity him. But I merely suggest that, should you wish an accomplished and current soldier to be a member of your Council, then his father Surrey would be more appropriate. It will also serve as a reward to a man upon whose skill in battle you may one day come to rely.'

'Again, wise counsel. It shall be as you advise, Thomas. Shall we call for more wine, say you?'

'For myself, Your Majesty, I have had sufficient, and must now, if you will excuse me, depart for my own house. It is some miles away, in Putney, as you may know, and I must needs take a wherry down to Fulham steps.'

'Take the royal barge, Thomas. In fact, feel free to call upon a royal barge at any time that you are engaged on my business. But we must find you a house closer to Westminster and the Tower. They tell me that Edmund Dudley has a fine house in St Brides, which he will no longer require, so I would wish you to occupy it. That way, you will be closer to hand. I am also in need of an Almoner — would you consent to accept the post?'

Thomas suppressed a smirk of satisfaction and did his best to look humble. 'You do me great honour, Your Majesty, but I regret that such a position calls for a man much higher in the Church than I.'

'How high?'

'Traditionally, it is a post that has been occupied by a bishop, and sometimes an archbishop,' Thomas mumbled back, hoping that he was not reaching too high at this early stage.

'That is easily achieved, Thomas,' Henry replied. 'The first bishopric that becomes vacant shall be yours. *Then* will you consent to be my Almoner?'

'I have already consented, Your Majesty,' Thomas beamed back at him. 'It is simply that I did not wish so honourable a position to be in some way diminished by my lowly clerical rank.'

'Consider yourself appointed, Thomas. And since I appreciate that you must depart forthwith, please attend upon me in the forenoon tomorrow, that I may take up the dull drudgery of learning once more at your hand. I am but a poor scholar, I acknowledge, and I must rapidly acquire more learning if I am to acquit myself on the stage of Europe. But there is one more matter, ere you take your leave.'

'Your Majesty?'

'That. You call me "Your Majesty", when I have let it be known that I prefer you to call me "Hal". Do you presume to disobey me already?'

Thomas smiled unctuously. 'Forgive me, Hal. It is simply that you grow into kingship with such alacrity that your very bearing and demeanour demand regal respect. It would not be fitting for me to call you "Hal" in the presence of those who must needs call you "Your Majesty", and I would not wish it spoken abroad that I demean your royal dignity by being so forward in my address.'

'We shall compromise, Thomas. You may call me "Hal" when we are alone, but "Your Majesty" whenever you deem it appropriate due to the company we keep. Would that suit?'

'Admirably, Hal, and thank you once again for an excellent supper and such engaging company withal. I shall return at ten in the forenoon.'

In the days and weeks that followed, there were only two topics that engaged the King and his newly-appointed Almoner. The first was the completion of Henry's education in those areas of the Classics, the English language, Divinity and Science that were deemed — by Thomas — to be necessary. If Henry had been an indifferent pupil in the past, he now made up for it in his enthusiasm to grow rapidly into the role that heredity had destined him for, and Thomas noted that underneath the bravado was a perceptive mind eager for new knowledge, a fact that he tucked away for future exploitation.

The second topic to dominate their daily meetings was the preparation for the wedding and the coronation. By consent, the wedding was to be conducted almost in secret, and Thomas had no difficulty in persuading the Abbot of the Franciscan Priory at Greenwich to conduct the low-key ceremony, attended only by close members of the family and a few selected nobles of the realm. The priory had been the object of royal patronage since its foundation in the years immediately before the fall of Richard of Gloucester, and Henry VII had proved particularly generous.

A radiant, glowing and somewhat surprised Lady Katherine had been 'humbly' advised by Thomas that it was the young King's wish to honour his marriage pledge. Thomas subtly suggested that the marriage had come about through his diplomatic intervention with Henry, thereby ensuring that he was highly regarded by both King and Queen.

King Henry also had a surprise awaiting him. The 'Spanish Pudding', as he had dubbed her, proved to be an eager and energetic bed partner, and had exchanged the aroma of olive oil for that of rosewater by the time that they celebrated their nuptials. She fell pregnant almost instantly, and was already carrying the royal seed in her womb when the happy couple alighted, on Midsummer's Day 1509, at Westminster Abbey on the occasion of their joint coronation.

As the royal feet progressed sedately down the carpet, it was, in accordance with established tradition, torn up behind them and cut up into lengths by an ecstatic crowd for both souvenir and sale. Archbishop William Warham anointed and crowned each of them in turn, in the presence of every prelate within the realm who was in sufficiently good health to attend, and as Thomas beamed and nodded from the front row of the nave, he was mentally accounting for those who were missing, and whose dioceses he might therefore anticipate inheriting upon their deaths.

VI

For some time now, Thomas had been tutoring Queen Katherine in English. She had proved to be an eager student, and King Henry was delighted with her progress. Despite the misgivings of his early youth, Henry had rapidly warmed towards the marriage born out of diplomacy, and there was a deepening affection between the royal couple that Thomas chose to exploit to the full. By tutoring the Queen in the language of her adopted country, he ingratiated himself with her while earning the ongoing gratitude of the King, and the bonus was his constant attendance at Richmond and Westminster, or wherever else the Court might be.

'Tell me, *Tomas,*' Katherine began by way of a conversation opener for their English language lesson, 'how is your new house?'

'Very comfortable, madam. As usual, your husband the King has been most generous, and since he allowed me not only the house but also its furnishings, it was simply a matter of transferring my servants from Putney to Bridewell.'

Thomas had moved into the house across The Fleet, and just outside the city walls, several weeks previously, and it certainly had advantages in keeping close to the royal couple, either by means of a short wherry trip upriver to Westminster, or one further upstream to Richmond.

'I have never understood,' Katherine said with a furrowed brow, 'how you men of God remain so wealthy, when you have all taken vows of poverty.'

'That is for monks, madam,' Thomas replied a little frostily. 'Those of us in the mainstream Church must ensure that the glory of God is ever on show for the inspiration of those who worship in our churches and cathedrals. And it would only demean the image of God in this world were His servants to go around resembling stable hands or kitchen scullions.'

'But from where comes this wealth of the Church?' Katherine persisted. 'Everywhere I go, the bishops and archbishops, not to mention lowly priests, seem always to be well fed and dressed in rich clothing, like high nobles. Comes it all from pious donations?'

'Not all of it, madam,' Thomas explained. 'In the same way that the nobles of the land enjoy their wealth from the rents and other dues paid to them by those who occupy land on their estates, so the Church, too, owns much land, which tenants pay for their right to occupy. It is by these means that the glory of God is displayed in the arches, high ceilings and rich hangings of our greatest cathedrals.'

'And on the backs of God's servants,' Katherine observed slyly, glancing at Thomas's soutane.

There was a rush of action in the chamber doorway, and King Henry blustered in before the usher could even announce his arrival. He strode swiftly across the rich carpet, kissed Katherine full on the lips, playfully rubbed her protruding stomach, and called for more wine and an extra goblet. Then he spotted Thomas, who had slid from his chair to his knees, and had his head down in supplication.

'Off your knees, Thomas,' he ordered. 'I have need of your counsel — and that of the beautiful Spanish Ambassador here.'

Katherine preened herself proudly, and looked adoringly into Henry's eyes while Thomas regathered his dignity. The wine was served, and the King drank deeply before belching discreetly and looking up at Thomas.

'Today I require *both* your counsels on the latest request from my esteemed father-in-law, King Ferdinand.'

'Majesty?' Thomas enquired.

'There is to be a new alliance between the most powerful nations in Europe against Louis of France,' Henry explained. 'It is to be led by the Pope himself, and will therefore be called 'The Holy League'. Pope Julius has succeeded in persuading the Emperor Maximilian to commit his troops, and he in turn, being related by marriage to King Ferdinand, has caused him to bring Spanish soldiers to his banner. Ferdinand wishes me to add to the mighty force that can thereby be sent to silence Louis, and end his ambitions in Italy. What say you, Thomas? Should we commit?'

Thomas was well aware that Henry's greatest dream was to conquer France, not only proving himself to be the great warrior that he believed himself to be, but also to retrieve those lands won by his hero, and distant Lancaster ancestor, Henry V. On the other hand, the English tradition established by Henry VII had been one of negotiation and treaty. Not only did this preserve English lives, but it cost less money, and there was always the risk of armed uprising at home if the nobles and leading merchants felt themselves over-taxed to support wars that were none of their making. This policy of conducting foreign affairs by treaty had been developed by Richard Foxe, and was now being enthusiastically supported by the current Archbishop of Canterbury, William Warham.

Thomas was deep in thought when Henry, as usual, cut in to place his wishes beyond misunderstanding. 'I would that we proceed, Thomas, and I wish you to make that happen. To that end, I wish you to take up your seat at the Council table in your capacity as my Almoner. With yourself and Surrey on my side, we shall restore England to its former glory, and I shall lead our victorious knights through the streets of Paris with Louis on a halter.'

'That would gladden my father's heart,' Katherine chimed in. 'He has long suffered the threat of the arrogant House of Valois against his kingdom. Would it not also place my dear husband among the leading, and most devout, princes of Europe, to fight under a banner blessed by the Pope himself?'

The reference to the Pope reminded Thomas that there were others apart from Henry from whom he sought preferment. To please Pope Julius II would perhaps be a step towards the scarlet robe of a Cardinal of the Church of Rome that he most craved. All the favourable indicators were towards a war with France in the name of St Peter, and who was Thomas to ignore the omens?

'It shall be as you wish, Hal,' Thomas agreed.

Henry clapped his hands in delight. 'Most excellent! The Council meets tomorrow, at ten of the forenoon, in the Star Chamber. I shall require you to lend the weight of God to my argument. Be prepared to take on the head of your Church should it threaten to become a battle of the scriptures. And now you may leave us — I am sure that my dear wife has suffered enough tutoring for one day.'

Thomas bowed from the presence and made his way to his new house in Bridewell. Seated nervously at a trestle table was his returned chaplain, Thomas Larke, and beside him sat a comely young woman. She was sturdily built, with a more than ample bosom and long light auburn hair that flowed down to her shoulders. She gave Thomas an open smile as Thomas Larke rose swiftly to his feet and welcomed his master home.

'We are but lately returned from the old house at Putney,' Larke explained. 'I must apologise for having tarried so long in the resolution of my father's affairs.'

'I have few sins to confess during your absence, so fear not on that score,' Thomas advised him as he looked pointedly at the girl sitting at the table, still smiling. 'But unless I misjudge the situation, you may have a sin of your own to confess to me — is she your wife?'

Thomas laughed. 'In truth, master, she is my sister Joan. My father's death has placed her in an awkward situation. The inn which my late father owned has been sold, and will henceforth be managed and staffed by the family of the new owner. This leaves Joan with no position, a maid of but twenty-two years of age with no protector, no employment and no roof over her head. If she is not to fall prey to evil or malignancy, she must perforce be offered some new station, and I was hoping that one might be found for her here, under my protection. She has considerable experience in the service of wine, since she worked for my father, and she is also a most admirable cook, besides being a skilled seamstress. Perhaps you might...'

Thomas stemmed the flow of words with a hand gesture, as he looked back at the eager face of Joan Larke. 'No more, Thomas. It shall be as you wish. We do now have need of more servants. Present your sister to the Steward, in order that he may best employ her.'

The next morning, with some trepidation, Thomas made the wherry trip to Westminster, where he was admitted to the Star Chamber to find that while he was early, he was not the first. The Earl of Surrey was staring at the ceiling, deep in thought. Thomas bowed slightly and took a seat across the table from him.

Surrey considered Thomas's glowing, scrubbed countenance for a moment, before breaking the silence. 'My son, Thomas, wishes his best regards passed on to you.'

Thomas nodded his acknowledgement, then raised an eyebrow. 'How did he know I would be here?'

'His Majesty advised me late yesterday. He also advised me that we can rely upon you to talk some sense into Foxe and Warham.'

'Will His Majesty be here to argue his cause?'

Surrey smiled. 'That will depend upon whether or not there is a hunt somewhere within a day's ride of London. But did it not occur to you that you are expected to sway the others?'

'His Majesty certainly indicated how he would wish to decision to go, but even so...'

Surrey leaned across the table and lowered his voice. 'Be in no doubt, Thomas, that the King wishes war on France, and has done these many months. The Holy League is his best opportunity, and we will not long remain in favour if we cannot sway the Council to his will.'

As he spoke, the chamber door opened and Foxe entered, deep in conversation with Archbishop Warham. Thomas rose from his seat and approached the Archbishop, then bowed in order to kiss the ring of office on the outstretched hand. Warham looked down his nose slightly at Thomas, then took his place next to Foxe, who raised a quizzical eyebrow in Thomas's direction, but remained silent.

A few moments later the King bustled in, dressed for the hunt, and the expression on his face left no-one in any doubt that he did not intend to remain for long. He opened the proceedings by expressing his desire to deal first with the request from Ferdinand of Spain that England commit an army to the Holy League against Louis of France, and asked for the initial views of those around the table. There was an ominous silence, broken by Foxe.

'Since everyone else in Europe seems committed to keeping Louis out of Italy, why should we join in?'

'Because,' Henry enthused, 'France has ever been our enemy, and we have this God-given opportunity to further secure not only our possessions in Calais, but also our other Channel ports.'

Warham added his dour opinion. 'A Pope-given opportunity, certainly, but I feel sure that Your Majesty's Almoner, in his capacity as Dean of Lincoln, would agree with me that this is no automatic guarantee that God has placed His seal on the proposal. It is, if anything, a Pope-given opportunity to tax the people in order to raise an army.'

'We cannot, at this difficult time, tax the people further,' Foxe agreed. 'My memory goes back to the days in which the merchants of London were driven to the point of rebellion by being over-taxed.'

'Over-taxed by Dudley and Empson, to line their own pockets,' Thomas observed as his first contribution around the Council table. 'This would be a tax to preserve our nation against any threat from France for all time coming, which in turn would discourage the Scots, who I am advised are currently sharpening their axes in anticipation of foraging south of the Tweed.'

'His Majesty's Almoner has obviously forgotten that we are at perpetual peace with the Scots,' Foxe replied, 'which is all the remarkable for the fact that it was Wolsey himself who negotiated that treaty, at my request. Were his efforts so feeble that even the fact that the King's sister is married to the King of Scotland cannot prevent them from harassing our northern borders?'

'If we ally with Spain and the Empire, could we not then call upon their assistance, should we be attacked ourselves?'

Thomas countered. 'As for the cost of fielding an army, in my role as Almoner I can confirm that there is sufficient in the royal Treasury to finance such a venture, without need to seek further tax revenue through Parliament.'

'Ferdinand of Spain is most desirous that we join with him,' Henry added, 'and this would not be a good time to lose favour with such a powerful ruler.'

'He will surely look favourably upon the birth of yet another grandchild,' Warham added, earning himself a foul look from Henry that caused him to drop his gaze to the table. He was playing with fire, since Queen Katherine had lost their first child when it was born prematurely, and spent half her waking life on her knees praying for the safe delivery of the latest in her womb.

Thomas saw his chance to attack the Archbishop. 'I am somewhat nonplussed that the Archbishop is not more enthusiastic to do the bidding of the Pope,' he announced unctuously. 'After all, victory *must* be ours, if the expedition has the blessing of Rome.'

'Tell that to those who died in the many attempts to reconquer Jerusalem under the banners of several ignominiously defeated Crusades,' Warham snarled back. He looked up suddenly and pierced Thomas with a stare that was intended to be intimidating. 'And I would remind the Dean of Lincoln that it is his place to respect the view of the leader of his Church.'

Thomas was prepared for this. 'The Archbishop is certainly *primus inter pares* — first among equals — in the summoning of convocations of the English branch of the Church of Rome. But the direct authority governing those who are not under holy orders in Canterbury itself comes from the Pope himself, through — in my case — the Bishop of Lincoln. While I have not had the opportunity to enquire of my lord of Lincoln, I must bow my head to the will of the Holy Father himself — whatever Canterbury may say.'

Warham shot Thomas a look that would have been fatal if accompanied by a real dagger.

Foxe leaned back in his chair and looked sideways at Surrey. 'My lord of Surrey, you have not favoured us yet with your opinion. As a military man, would you deem it wise to stick our nose into the honey pot while the bees are still buzzing in residence around it?'

Surrey smiled condescendingly. 'There is such a thing as safety in numbers,' he advised the remaining members of the Council. 'This would be the best opportunity since the glorious days of the fifth King Henry to gain back territories in France that have lawfully belonged to England since the age of the first Plantagenet. With the might of the Holy Roman Empire engaged in the fighting in Italy, while Ferdinand of Spain marches eastwards from his strongholds, we may march south from Calais and be at the walls of Paris within three days' march. Once Paris falls, France is ours.'

'And the cost in human lives?' Warham muttered.

'There would be less loss under this arrangement than were we to attack France on our own,' Surrey assured him.

'How many men would you require?' Foxe enquired doubtfully, as he saw the debate swinging in Henry's desired direction.

'Ten thousand at most, should we be joined with Spain, with the Imperial forces to our south,' Surrey replied. 'Wolsey can no doubt advise how much this would cost in financial terms.'

'We can afford it,' Thomas insisted, his fingers crossed under the table.

'Shall we put this to the vote?' Henry suggested, eager to be away before the full heat of the day.

As predicted, it was three votes to two, the King having only an equal vote with the remainder of his Council, but with Surrey and Wolsey in his camp.

Thomas was elated at having assisted Henry to get his own way at his very first Council meeting. After a hearty supper, and the best part of a jug of the Beaujolais, he went early to bed.

He was dozing fitfully when the door to his bedchamber opened, and Joan Larke slid into the room carrying a pile of undergarments intended for Thomas's clothing chest. She stood for a moment, highlighted by the still flickering nightlights without which Thomas was unable to sleep, then when she realised that his eyes had opened, she explained her business.

'Beggin' yer pardon, master, but these clothes needs to be put away.'

Thomas grunted an acknowledgement, and waved his hand for her to get on with it. Undeterred, she approached the bed and stood in full view of Thomas's head as it lay sideways on his pillow. She unclasped her gown from the back of her neck and let it slip to the floor. She was naked underneath, and Thomas looked for the first time on a pair of full young breasts. He raised his head from his pillow and stared stupidly at the sight before him, as Joan reached down, pulled back the bedcovers and slid in beside him.

What followed was something that would require a great deal of penance for an ordained priest.

When he awoke the following morning and found that she had gone, he hoped for a moment that it had all been a dream sent by the Devil to test him. Then he discovered several long auburn hairs on the pillow, and realised that it was no dream, and he was in urgent need of confession. But his confessor was the last man on earth to whom he could admit what had happened, particularly when it happened the following night, and every night for a fortnight.

Seven weeks since the sinning had begun Thomas had convinced himself that he could hear his own confession. He presented himself daily to Thomas Larke with his usual confessions of pride and gluttony, and received the customary penances in *Pater Nosters*, which he mumbled under his breath in his private chapel in the rearmost room of the Bridewell house, adding fifty more for each blissful night between the sheets with the sister of his confessor.

This went on for almost three months until one morning, while numbering his ongoing occasions of sin in the form of pride and gluttony, Thomas became aware that his chaplain was looking sideways at him in expectation. As he finished, Thomas Leake coughed and said, 'Is there nothing further, master?'

'Meaning?'

'More sins. Lust, perhaps?'

Thomas was about to deny it indignantly when he caught the suggestion of a knowing smile on the man's face. 'Has Joan perhaps spoken with you?' Thomas asked, red in the face.

'She has indeed.'

'What am I to do?' Thomas asked despairingly.

'Think you that you are the only one in need of God's forgiveness in this regard?'

Wolsey's eyes opened wide in disbelief. 'You have also sinned in this manner?'

'Yes. With a female cousin on my late mother's side. And, more recently, with the girl Amy, in the stillroom behind the kitchen.'

Thomas thought for a while. 'As I understand the office of confession, we may hear each other's, then be absolved. I have been penancing myself with fifty *pater nosters* — is that sufficient, think you?'

'It is sufficient for me, although if Joan speaks truly your rosary will be worn through ere next Epiphany.'

'I can soon acquire another rosary, Thomas,' Wolsey assured him, 'but another woman like your sister? Never.'

VII

In June 1512, the Marquess of Dorset led a twelve thousand strong army, intent on invading Guyenne which, along with Gascony, had once been part of English-ruled Aquitaine until the French had won it back. They disembarked at Fuenterrabía, on the border of Spain with France, and had awaited the arrival of Spanish troops in vain. They then learned, through scouts sent out far and wide, that while the French had detached a sizeable portion of their army to meet the English invasion, the Spanish had used the occasion of the English landing to bluff their way into Navarre, the inland portion of the Basque region on the Franco-Spanish border. They had done so under the pretence of protecting it from the consequences of becoming a battlefield for the two mighty armies of England and France, but when no fighting eventuated the Spanish King Ferdinand coolly claimed Navarre for himself, and the English were left jilted.

By the end of August, the Marquess had a full scale mutiny on his hands, and was obliged to set sail back to England with what was left of his army. Ferdinand of Spain sought to divert blame for his own selfish actions by publicly denouncing their departure as cowardice, and even Henry realised that he had been betrayed. Henry was now experiencing his first doubts regarding his Spanish family connections, and — as was to become the custom — it was Thomas who rescued him from a downward spiralling depression by diverting him towards an all-out war with France.

For weeks after the ignominious return of Dorset, no-one dared approach Henry except Thomas. Even he was at considerable risk from the royal temper that had begun to reveal itself from under the party-loving exterior of the young King. Henry not only felt betrayed and humiliated in the eyes of Europe by the dismissive actions of his father-in-law, but he was growing anxious regarding the matter of a male heir to further secure his grip on the English throne. While Katherine seemed to conceive with ease, she seemed less capable of delivering a healthy infant; their first — a daughter — had been born prematurely, while a boy born in January 1511, named Henry after his overjoyed father, and anointed as the Duke of Cornwall, did not survive long. When the royal physician announced in the spring of 1513 that Katherine was yet again with child, it was not only Katherine who spent long hours before the altar in the royal chapel, praying that it might be a boy, and that it might survive longer than the other children that had been delivered of her womb.

Thomas adroitly judged the royal mood, and added extra layers of honey to his tongue as he continued to assure Henry that God would smile upon his willingness to protect Rome from the French, and would reward the crown of England with a worthy successor to its most devout King. He also avoided the blame for the recent fiasco in Spain by ascribing it to the ageing Marquess of Dorset, the man who had generously given him his first ecclesiastical appointment, but who was no longer central to Thomas's ambitions. Thomas flatteringly suggested to Henry that since Dorset, as the half-brother of Henry's own mother Elizabeth of York, belonged to a former age, it was only fitting that the next English army be led by the greatest contemporary warrior in Europe, Henry himself.

'Be that as it may, Thomas,' Henry replied as they stood staring out of the windows of Richmond Palace, 'have we the finance, without seeking further taxes from the people?'

'Once we are over in France, Hal,' Thomas assured him, 'we may live at the expense of the French whose lands and castles we plunder. If you summon your leading nobles to your banner under their ancient feudal obligations, they must bear the costs of the troops they bring to your cause, and the Treasury may be richly recompensed from the plunder that I will supervise, and have each item either sold back to its former owners or brought back to England for sale to the highest bidder.'

'And can you guarantee that our enterprise will thrive?'

'With you in its vanguard, Hal, it cannot fail. Louis of France fears you more than he does Ferdinand of Spain, or for that matter the Emperor Maximilian. You are the heir to that glorious Henry who made France his own, and you command the same love and awe from your army today as he did when he triumphed at Agincourt.'

'Should I lead my troops in person, say you?'

'How else will you ensure that they are inspired to conquer all before them, and that the banner of St. George flies high on the flagpole of every major castle between here and the Italian border?'

'What hear you of the Scots? Will they not take advantage of my absence to pillage from the north?'

'You forget that King James of Scotland is married to your sister, by whom he has his own heir to the throne. Also, with Your Majesty at the head of our troops in France, it will be possible to leave Surrey behind with men with whom he may defend our northern borders, perhaps under the overall instruction of your dear Queen, as Regent in your absence?'

Henry frowned. 'She is again with child, Thomas, as you know, and I would not wish any cares to be thrust upon her that might imperil a safe birth this time. Perhaps Foxe or Warham should be left in command in my absence?'

'Warham were best left to pray for your safe delivery, and that of your expected child, while ensuring, in his role as Chancellor, that law and order are maintained in your absence. As for Foxe, Your Majesty must have noticed for yourself that he grows frail with his advanced years, and it would be a kindness not to burden him with the management of an entire kingdom when he cannot even maintain control of his own bodily functions.'

Henry smiled. It was as he had wished all along, and he was too vain to realise that Thomas had simply acted as a deft mirror to his all too obvious desires. 'Very well, Thomas. See to it. But this time I wish you to accompany me.'

Thomas had not expected that, and had been planning to dominate the Council in the absence of the monarch, but it was high time that Thomas ingratiated himself with others closer to the Papacy, and he consoled himself with the realisation that the Holy Roman Emperor Maximilian was high on that list.

His natural flair for pomp and display was to prove Thomas's greatest asset as he stage-managed what followed. Ship after ship was commissioned in the royal dockyard at Portsmouth and hastily filled with food, fresh water and heavy ordinance. At the last moment, heavily armed knights under the battle banners of their lords were embarked and transported to Calais, which rapidly became the most bustling assembly point that English military forces had ever travelled to.

Finally, Henry himself was disembarked onto the quayside with a fanfare and a flurry, while the vessel behind his was carefully unloaded under the supervision of Thomas, who had brought along over a hundred of his own entourage, some of whom had been hired in the dockside streets at the last moment, in order to swell the number and add to his apparent importance.

It was hardly to be expected that all this could occur in secret, and Louis of France was advised of Henry's landing only the day after it occurred. He halted his southern progress and dispatched his steward, the Duc de Longueville, with a sizeable force, to meet the threat at the English held Pale of Calais.

Once ashore, and with Henry's leave, Thomas lost no time in riding to Bruges, where he once again found himself bowing before the Emperor Maximilian.

'I am advised that your master King Henry has greatly added to his army at Calais,' Maximilian announced in a slightly accusing tone. 'I assume that we are still at peace with England?'

'Indeed you are, my lord, and about to witness the final capitulation of France to the might of the Holy League, of which the Holy Roman Empire is the defining core.'

'Does Henry intend to take on France all by himself, and thereby enjoy the fruits of conquest, not to mention the glory, without any assistance from me?'

'Far from it, my lord, hence my appearance at your Court. King Henry sends his fondest and most loyal regards, and invites you to join in the suppression of your mutual enemy for all time.'

'You are presumably aware that half my army is at present across the Alps, assisting the Swiss to break the siege of Milan?'

'Indeed, my lord, which is why King Henry is seeking to divert the French from their aggression in the Italian city states by obliging them to race back and defend their own lands around Paris.'

'This is not simply a private war between Henry and Louis, in which England seeks to regain those lands it lost generations ago, and which were best left lost?'

'Indeed not, my lord. It is a further indication of my lord King Henry's commitment to the Holy League, and his determination to prevent the Pope from falling into the hands of the French. As an ordained minister of the Church of Rome myself, I have chosen to accompany my king in order to render what humble assistance I can to his Holiness's cause.'

'Since I hardly think that the mere sight of your incense and holy water will be sufficient to the task,' Maximilian replied, 'I assume that your visit this day is to request that I lend further troops to your banner?'

'With your seasoned fighting men alongside the English king's battle-ready heavy knights, flanked by his unrivalled archers and supported by his newly-cast ordinance, there can be no doubt of victory, and an end to French pretensions on the borders of your own lands.'

'I am perfectly capable of defending my own lands, Father Wolsey,' Maximilian responded with the hint of a sniff. 'Why then should I assist your master in his private squabble with Louis?'

'Forgive me,' Thomas replied. 'I was led to believe that we all fought on the side of his Holiness the Pope, and that between us we are seeking to prevent Louis reaching the Holy See itself. While he is defending his back yard from wolves, he can hardly act the fox in his front yard.'

Maximilian smiled at the eloquent imagery, and waved one of his nobles to his side, before engaging him in a whispered conversation that Thomas was unable to overhear. Then the

Emperor looked back at Thomas. 'I will commit some of my best ordinance to your master's cause. But I will do so as a hired mercenary bringing in a band of paid *coulevriniers*, rather than as Holy Roman Emperor. For this service I shall require your master to pay all my men their appropriate dues — not only my men, but myself as well. I personally require one hundred ducats a day to support my table.'

Thomas looked around the crowded chamber uneasily, and then back at the Emperor. 'Might we talk more privately, my lord?'

The chamber was rapidly cleared of all but a few obviously trusted advisers, as Thomas sought to achieve his mission at the minimum cost to the Treasury, employing the same strategy by which Ferdinand of Spain had secured Navarre.

'It shall be as you request, my lord, but I may privily advise that King Henry seeks only a token victory with himself at the head of the army. Perhaps a couple of small but significant towns in Normandy or Flanders, then I may perhaps persuade him to withdraw. The main advantage to yourself will be the distraction afforded to King Louis, whose forces in Northern Italy will be rendered more vulnerable to your southern armies by the need to send half his army back north.'

'Your master does not seek to lay siege to Paris?'

'At present he does, my lord, but I undertake to persuade him otherwise. I advise you of all this privily in order that you may be in no wise prepared for a lengthy diversion from Bruges.'

'It would seem that you know your master's best interests more than he does, Father Wolsey. Very well, let us seal this bargain with some of our excellent new wine crop.'

Several days later, Henry rode out proudly at the head of his army. To his side, sombrely dressed for once, and with not the slightest intention of becoming involved in the slaughter to come, was Thomas Wolsey, fresh from his successful negotiations with the Emperor, but tight-lipped regarding how much it was likely to denude the English Treasury. The King wanted his day in the sun of European conquest, and Thomas was determined that he would get it.

Thomas had, however, taken the elementary precaution of arranging for almost the entire force of light horse under the command of Henry Percy, Earl of Northumberland, to ride out before daybreak to a position south of Therouanne, which had been under siege for some time by English troops under George Talbot, Earl of Shrewsbury. The siege had reached the stage at which the townsfolk within were at starvation point, and it was known from reports brought in by English scouts that a considerable force of Frenchmen was somewhere to the south, from which it was expected to attempt to break the siege.

It would be Northumberland's task to head them off, allowing King Henry the notional glory of finishing off this insignificant little settlement before moving further east towards the more strategically important Flemish town of Tournai; in this, Northumberland would be assisted by a battery of bombards and culverins supplied by Maximilian.

By the time that the French cavalry under the Duc de Longueville became aware that their path to Therouanne was blocked by English knights on coursers rather than the heavier destriers, it was already too late. Suddenly they came under fire from a hail of arrows fired from the side by English bowmen and showers of missiles from Imperial cannon. They first halted, then fled. The English cavalry pursued and overtook many of them, hacking to death those whose livery did not suggest that they would attract a substantial ransom, and roping behind them those whose monarch or families might be persuaded to pay dearly for their return.

Six days later, a triumphant Henry was accompanied into the captured township by Thomas and George Talbot, and he made a great speech on the steps of the town's only church in which he graciously made a gift of Therouanne to the Emperor Maximilian, unaware that his Almoner had already arranged the transfer of the first payment for the services of his 'ally'.

Before the victorious monarch could finalise his plans to move east and take Tournai, he received other heartening news. His brother-in-law James IV of Scotland had proved as treacherous as had been feared, despite his marriage to Henry's sister Margaret, and had taken advantage of Henry's absence across the Channel to attack south of his border, honouring the long-established 'Auld Alliance' tradition with France.

Thomas Howard, Earl of Surrey, had been waiting for him west of the border at Berwick, and the two armies had met at Branxton, near Flodden Edge, where they clashed for three hours, at the end of which the ten thousand Scots dead included their King, and most of their leading nobility. The English army had been under the notional command of Queen Katherine, who celebrated by having the blood-soaked coat and gauntlets of the fallen king sent across to Henry, with an invitation that he use them as a battle banner in his next encounter with the French.

Then it was on to Tournai, which yielded up its gates on 23rd September after an eight day siege. As Henry rode proudly through the heavily dented gates of the town in the front line of English knights, dressed more for ceremony than for battle, his eyes lit upon the cluster of Romanesque towers of the Cathedral de Notre-Dame, and he turned to Thomas.

'We have captured several leading French nobles, whose ransoms will no doubt help to replenish our royal coffers, and there is clearly much within this noble town to pillage and take back with us. But what of you, Thomas? As a man of God, you will not, of course, seek material reward, but how say you that I make you a gift of this magnificent church?'

Thomas smiled in what he hoped was a self-deprecating manner. 'With the deepest of respect, Your Majesty, the building itself belongs to his Holiness the Pope. While your armies have bravely conquered the remainder of the town, and may now set about removing therefrom anything of value, they cannot carry away the spiritual grace with which this noble edifice has been endowed over the years. Nor can its bishop yield so much as a gold candlestick, since all that lies within belongs to his Holiness.'

'It has a bishop?'

'It most certainly must have,' Thomas replied, gazing upwards in envy, 'given the richness of the building, which is clearly a cathedral. Every cathedral has a bishop, and there can be no Episcopal see without a cathedral.'

Henry caught the wistful look on the face of his Almoner, and was in a generous mood. 'And it is the Pope who appoints bishops?'

'Yes, Your Majesty.'

'And will this new Pope be grateful to the King of England for forcing the French to scurry back north, where they were slaughtered in their hundreds?'

Thomas thought for a moment when he realised where the conversation was heading. In February of that year, Pope Julius II had died, and had been replaced by Pious X, who was a totally different pontiff from his predecessor. As Giovanni de' Medici, he was the head of a wealthy Florentine family much given to excess in the matter of art, and as far distant in Papal policy from the former 'warrior Pope' as it was possible to get. But even he looked with fear and apprehension at the gradual conquest of the Italian city states by Louis XII of France, and while he might not maintain the fervour of his predecessor's Holy League he would nevertheless be breathing a little easier at the recall of French troops necessitated by Henry's breakout from Calais.

'Without warriors such as Your Majesty to protect his city state of Rome from marauding armies,' Thomas assured him, 'his Holiness would be reduced to the status of a mere parish priest. I can assure you, Majesty, that when news is conveyed to him of your magnificent triumph over Louis, he will be the very soul of gratitude.'

'He is not the only one to have cause to be grateful, Thomas. Without your most capable management, this army of mine would never even have reached Calais. Whatever it has cost, we will be rich in plunder and ransom ere much longer, but all I can offer you is the Bishopric of this somewhat ancient pile. Would that be sufficient reward?'

Thomas hid his elation behind his best unctuous smirk. 'Your Majesty does me great honour, and as ever you prove most generous in victory. But, with the greatest respect to your royal person, it will require the sanction of his Holiness, as I have previously explained.'

'Leave his Holiness to me, Thomas,' Henry replied. 'In the meantime I will give out word that the cathedral must not be touched in the general pillage that seems destined to commence within the hour. Leave me now, and see to your reward.'

Thomas dismounted and walked jubilantly through the main doors of the magnificent cathedral, accompanied by two of his clerics, one of whom had been acting as his confessor during their time abroad. He genuflected in the doorway, then walked slowly down the long nave until he came to the transept, where he knelt and muttered a prayer of thanks. After being assisted back to his feet by his companions, he walked through the choir and prostrated himself before the altar. The cool flagstones reminded him that he would soon be clad in richer vestments, and as he gazed up at the golden candlesticks, other thoughts came to him as he recalled his last conversation with Henry.

He turned to his two clerics.

'Richard, search out the Earl of Northumberland, give him my heartiest congratulations on his victory, and request that half a dozen of his best armed men be stationed outside here to prevent looting, on the authority of the King's Almoner. Gerald, you must return to our camp and collect six baggage wagons, and sufficient of those ruffians we recruited to our cause in Thames Street ere our departure, and bring them all to me here.'

Less than an hour later, a red-faced and highly indignant Bishop of Tournai glared angrily at Thomas, as teams of rough-looking English peasants set about removing plate, rich tapestries and ecclesiastical ornaments from the main hall of his Palace.

'What means this outrage?'

Thomas summoned up his best French. 'It means, my lord Bishop, that you shall shortly be conducting Masses with less wealth as a sign of your office. You will also cease to be the Bishop of Tournai once the Pope gives his blessing to my ordination in your place. But you will not starve, since it is my wish that you continue to perform Holy office within the cathedral a few doors from here. However, you will ensure that all the revenues from your see are transmitted to the King's Almoner in London. I am he, and unless it is your wish to minister to your flock in a humble village you will ensure that every franc is duly accounted for.'

'God will punish your treachery to the Holy Mother Church!'

'God perhaps,' Thomas replied with a smirk as he turned to leave, 'but his Holiness the Pope will in due course demonstrate how the best interests of his Church are served. *Pax vobiscum.*'

He swept from the Bishop's Palace in order to rejoin Henry for dinner in his marquee in the English camp.

'What say you, Talbot?' a beaming Henry enquired as he took another generous swig from his wine goblet, 'on to the walls of Paris?'

Talbot's smile disappeared. 'Your Majesty, the men are anxious to return home with their spoils. We have the Duc de Longueville in our baggage train, in addition to the Lord Clermont, who I am advised is King Louis's Vice-admiral, and others beside. Woe betide that they contrive to escape before we can secure the rich rewards for their ransom. It will also soon be winter, and then we shall not so easily live off French land as we have thus far.'

Henry's smile thinned as he turned to Henry Percy. 'My Lord of Northumberland, do you share Talbot's careful counsel?'

'I do, Your Majesty. I may also add that without the skilled *bombardiers* of the Emperor, we would not have fared so well in sending the French racing back to their lines. But we can ill afford to take them with us to Paris, given their daily wages.'

Henry froze with the goblet halfway to his mouth, and turned angrily to Thomas.

'We are *paying* Ferdinand's men for their services?'

Thomas winced. 'Thus far, yes, Your Majesty. But, as both your commanders in the field appear to be advising, there will be no further need of those services.'

Henry let fly a string of curses, and those around the board with him looked uncomfortably at anything other than his countenance. Northumberland silently mouthed an apology to Thomas for having revealed his hitherto secret commission to the Imperial forces, and by the time that Henry fell silent, Thomas was able to steer the conversation in another direction.

'There is also the matter of Scotland, Your Majesty. Now that James is dead, your sister Margaret becomes Queen Regent for her son, the new King James V. This might be a good time to march on Edinburgh and let it be known that we will tolerate no more aggression while our backs are turned.'

'A pox on Edinburgh!' Henry raged. 'I will deal with those upstart cock-suckers when it best suits me. As you point out, my sister Margaret will keep them in their places until she learns my intentions. But your reference to royal children reminds me that my dear Queen is near her time, and that we should be back at Richmond ere she takes to her lying-in chamber. We shall break camp and make for home as soon as it can be achieved. See to it, Thomas.'

Two months later, there was much rejoicing as Queen Katherine gave birth to another boy, joyously named Henry. Then came the seemingly inevitable, as the royal physicians proved inadequate to the task of keeping the infant alive, and it was an apprehensive Thomas who answered the royal summons a week later. He found Henry in the Privy Lodgings, staring out of the window down at the oily-flowing Thames beyond the outer wall.

'Thomas, I have need of your wily counsel as how best to insult both the Emperor and my father-in-law of Spain at one and the same time.'

'Your Majesty?' Thomas asked, somewhat taken aback by the bluntness of the request.

'Come, Thomas,' Henry reassured him as he placed his arm across Thomas's shoulder, 'let us not pretend that we have not been belittled by both of our so-called allies in the Holy League of the former Pope. It was left to us to send the French packing, and to oblige them to withdraw from Milan. Maximilian only joined battle because we paid him to do so, and as for the Spaniards, they were presumably still tilling their vines and tupping their goats well to the west while we did the Pope's bidding. I have been publicly humiliated, Thomas.'

'Hal, there is not a monarch in Europe who does not fear you after your glorious victory and...'

Henry raised his other hand in a gesture to silence Thomas, and was clearly in no mood to be assuaged. 'Spare me the honey that drips from your jaws, Thomas, and earn your keep. How stand things between us, Maximilian and Ferdinand?'

Thomas thought for a moment before replying. He had his own spies in the ecclesiastical trains of leading clergymen, and had recently learned, via a friend of Thomas Larke who was in the service of the Archbishop of York and currently in Rome, that Pope Pius was anxious to establish peace with France in order to protect Rome, and his own native Florence, from Louis's rapid acquisition of Italian city states. This might be an opportune moment — for both England and Thomas — to support the Pope by allying with France and prevailing upon it to retreat from northern Italy. Thomas could also identify a way of slapping their former allies in the face in the process.

'Hal,' he suggested gently, 'you cannot even begin to contemplate any insult to Ferdinand of Spain while you are married to his daughter, and while his grandson Charles is betrothed to your own sister Mary.'

Henry snorted. 'As for the Queen, you might wish to ask Ferdinand if he has any other daughters who are capable of bearing sons. Joanna may well be mad, as they say, but at least her loins yield up live boys.'

Thomas diplomatically let the point hang in the air, and moved on. 'But the continued betrothal of the most eligible — and, if I might make so bold, the most beautiful — princess in Europe to the young man who Ferdinand no doubt sees as his successor, is hardly the best way to snub one's nose at Ferdinand himself. Were the betrothal to be called off, not only would you be cocking a snook at Ferdinand, but you would also be tweaking the beard of Maximilian, who is Charles's other grandfather.'

'Excellent, Thomas! However, that then leaves the matter of who to offer Mary's hand to. There cannot be an unmarried monarch in Europe who would not have her, but as I understand it, there is, unfortunately, *no* unmarried monarch in Europe at present.'

'There is Louis himself, Hal,' Thomas replied quietly.

Henry stared sideways at him for an incredulous moment, then burst out laughing. 'Thomas, there are times when you border upon genius! Not only do I kick the Emperor and my treacherous old fart of a father-in-law in the sweetbreads, but I also have the alliance of England's oldest enemy, and the gratitude of the Pope! How can I possibly reward you *this* time?'

'Lincoln,' Thomas replied with a triumphant grin.

'What about Lincoln?' Henry enquired.

'It is with some regret that I have to advise you of the death of Dr. Smith this past week,' Thomas replied. 'He had been in ill health for some time, and his passing was a blessing from God, given the bodily pains to which he was subject.' When Henry still did not seem to have grasped the point, Thomas continued. 'He was the Bishop of Lincoln, and his see therefore becomes vacant. Since his Holiness the Pope has not yet seen fit to confirm my appointment to Tournai, even despite your good offices, perhaps...'

'Perhaps *nothing*, Thomas. Pius shall be left in no doubt that if he seeks my influence as the brother-in-law of the man who even now threatens the Holy See with his warhorses and siege engines, then he must indulge me in my choice of Bishop of Lincoln.'

'You are most generous, Hal.'

'And you, Thomas, are most ingenious. I would have you at my elbow whenever a knotty problem besets me, and yet I am told that your journey upriver this morning was delayed by an adverse tide, and the need to skirt much wreckage floating downstream from the recent gales in Oxfordshire.'

'It is true, I'm afraid. Bridewell seems far from Richmond on days such as this.'

'Then you must seek to establish yourself closer to me when the Court is here in Richmond. You should also have a country house, away from the unhealthy miasmas of the Fleet.'

'At one time I had a house in Putney,' Thomas reminded him, 'and I must own that my health was much better when I could walk along the river bank without fear of cut-throats seeking my purse.'

Henry pointed out of the window, to his left. 'Upriver, not five leagues from here, is the old Hospitaller house at Hampton, which for many years was leased by Sir Giles Daubney, my late father's Chamberlain and a brave knight in many forays into France. He died some years ago, and I am forever receiving petitions from the Knights Hospitaller who seek either a new tenant or an outright purchaser of their estate. I have not seen it, but I am advised that its grounds sweep down to the river, and that from its steps it is but a few minutes' journey to Richmond by barge. I can, should it convenience you, have a royal barge stationed there at all times for your use.'

'You are, as ever, most gracious, Hal,' Thomas mumbled. 'If there is nothing further...'

'No, Thomas,' Henry replied sadly, 'unless you can double your prayers to God to grant me a male heir.'

VIII

On February 6th 1514, an elated Thomas Wolsey stood at the altar in the chapel of Lambeth Palace facing William Warham, Archbishop of Canterbury. Around Thomas's neck hung the *crux pectoralis*, the pectoral cross and the ancient symbol of high office in the Church of Rome, while the ring of office had just been placed on his gloved hand during his consecration as Bishop of Lincoln. On Thomas's head was the heavily jewelled bishop's mitre whose weight he would have to learn to endure if others were to witness him in all his splendour.

Thomas turned to face the small but very select audience in the chapel as the Archbishop raised a hand above his head and administered the final blessing.

'May almighty God bless you, the Father, and the Son, and the Holy Spirit.'

A murmur of 'Amen' rose up from the body of the congregation, and it was all over. The choir struck up the departing anthem as Thomas was led out by the remaining bishops to the smaller chapel belonging to the Bishop of London, in which certain preliminary ceremonies had earlier been conducted. As Thomas entered, the last in the line, Warham had already been disrobed by an attendant, and stood waiting for him, the ironic smile still on his face.

'Now that you are one of those under my Episcopal authority, Thomas, I shall expect more respect from you in Council.'

'You have always had my respect, Your Grace,' Thomas replied with a grin. 'The more direct question is whether or not you will have my co-operation.'

With some regret, Thomas allowed Thomas Larke to remove his chasuble and all the other clerical garments above his simple alb, over which he slipped his freshly laundered soutane before walking sedately to the Great Hall of the Bishop's Palace in order to host the small repast laid out along several boards down the centre. Henry himself had opted not to attend, so as not to steal the attention from his new bishop, but he had ordered several leading nobles to the ceremony, as a mark of respect. One of these was his personal favourite, and lifelong companion, Charles Brandon, Duke of Suffolk, who sidled up to Thomas as he poured himself a generous measure of Rhenish wine.

'Thomas, we must speak privily,' Suffolk urged him.

'Charles, my dear friend, nothing short of the death of the King could be so urgent on this day of days. Call on me tomorrow at Bridewell, and you shall have my undivided attention, as ever, but for today, please allow me to play the genial host.'

Suffolk withdrew, his face a picture of pain and anguish, and Thomas heard a mocking voice behind him.

'I trust that, at least for today, you are wearing clean hose.' Thomas groaned inwardly and turned to face the grinning visage of Thomas Howard, who continued, 'And before you tell me to cross myself because here comes a bishop, you should know that here comes an earl.'

'Of this I am already aware, Thomas, and I must congratulate you, not only on your father's elevation to the highest rank of nobility, but also the bravery of both of you in defeating the Scots while we took on the French.'

'I assume you took no part in the fighting?' Howard enquired with a sneer.

'No indeed,' Thomas assured him. 'I did, however, organise the feeding, deployment and spiritual comfort of fifty thousand men, while you presumably accounted for the deaths of a dozen or so.'

'Is it true that you have arranged for the Princess Mary to be wed to the King of France?'

'No,' Thomas replied with a shake of the head, 'I merely suggested it to His Majesty.'

'Then we owe you much thanks — our family that is,' Howard replied. 'Two of my nieces are to travel with the Princess Mary to the Court of France as her Ladies. Mary and Anne Boleyn, my sister's daughters. She is married to Thomas Boleyn, one of His Majesty's ambassadors to the Low Countries.'

'Delighted to have been of service,' Thomas replied. 'Now, if you would excuse me, the King requires my presence at Richmond ere nightfall. Your brother-in-law Boleyn may well find that matters diplomatic have been transferred to France.'

Thomas climbed out of the barge alongside the Royal Architect, and they both ascended the steps cut into the grass slope in order to survey the old Hospitaller farm building, from whose decaying roof rafters the crows took off in noisy protest as they walked closer. Thomas frowned as he surveyed the modesty of the edifice.

'Knock it all down and begin again, my Lord?' the architect enquired.

'Not necessarily,' Thomas replied as he visualised the finished product in his imagination. 'I have in mind a grand courtyard entrance, with guest chambers all around it in a quadrangle, like our finest university halls. A flight of steps at the far end of the courtyard, with stables to one side, and the steps leading up to a grand corridor, from which may be accessed the largest banqueting hall you have ever constructed.'

'And your private quarters? Shall they run along the upper level at the front, to command a grand view of the river?'

Thomas sniffed in disapproval. 'You and I have just had the misfortune to travel along that river, Sir Henry. It is, as your nose will have detected should it be as sensitive as mine, little more than a flowing guard-robe of other people's shit. I do not wish to throw open my casement in order to smell *that* when the wind blows from the south. My apartments shall be towards the back, and the vista shall be that of ornamental gardens, with perhaps a maze. Here at the front, more gardens, planted with herbs and flowers that will detract the more sensitive noble noses from the pestilence of what flows past lower down.'

'And the cost? Does your Lordship wish to restrict the expense to a particular amount?'

'No, his Lordship does *not*,' Thomas replied emphatically. 'Fear not for the cost, Master Architect, simply apply to my Steward when you have need of more money, and it shall be forthcoming. How soon shall it all be ready?'

The architect thought for a moment, then replied uncertainly, 'It will depend upon the weather, my Lord. We are at present blessed with a warm dry summer, but once the Autumn returns, with its gales and rain...'

'All the more reason to make a swift start, then,' Thomas retorted. 'I wish my new residence here at Hampton to be ready by this time next year, and once the roof is in place the internal fittings may commence regardless of the weather. Make this your first priority or the King shall hear of it, since it is my intention to entertain the entire Court here at

Midsummer's Eve. Now, who is this that disturbs our business?'

While they had been talking, they had become aware of three horsemen pounding down the grass slope towards them. They slid to a halt, and a tall, heavily bearded giant of a man leapt from his mount and strode purposefully towards Thomas, gesturing the architect aside with an imperious wave of the hand.

'My Lord of Suffolk,' the architect muttered deferentially as he bowed away backwards. Charles Brandon, Duke of Suffolk, slightly out of breath from his urgent ride, strode away down the slope, calling to Thomas as he did so.

'Walk with me a pace, Thomas,' he all but commanded, 'for we must talk privily.'

Thomas looked Brandon up and down with a slight air of disapproval once he caught up with him. 'I bid you call on me at Bridewell,' Thomas reminded him. 'As you can see, I am presently engaged in detailed discussion with the King's Architect regarding my new country residence. Can your matter not wait?'

'Can *any* affair of the heart wait, Thomas? Nothing you are presently engaged in can possibly compare with the sickness that my soul suffers as the result of your meddling.'

'And what meddling would that be, precisely?' Thomas enquired guardedly, although there could be no doubt what Suffolk was referring to.

Charles had been awarded his title — one of only three dukedoms in the nation — as the result of his father's bravery. William Brandon had been the standard bearer to Henry Tudor at the Battle of Bosworth, and had paid with his life when he became one of only two men standing between the terrified Henry and a berserk, axe-wielding Richard of Gloucester. The newly crowned Henry VII had not forgotten what he owed to the Brandon family, and William's orphaned son Charles had been raised in the royal nurseries at Eltham and Westminster alongside Prince Arthur, and after Arthur's untimely death Charles became a natural companion to the boisterous Prince of Wales, now King Henry VIII, seven years his junior.

This had rendered him something of a hero figure, and childhood romantic fantasy, to the royal princesses, and in particular the youngest and most beautiful of them all, the Princess Mary, who was now in her eighteenth year and about to be shipped off to France like a consignment of trade goods. It was no secret that the tall, dashing, muscular adventurer and the radiant and headstrong girl with the long and characteristic red-gold Tudor hair had been mutually attracted for several years, and that the development of their passion had only been restrained by the fact that Brandon was not of noble birth, while Mary was the most negotiable princess in Europe.

Suffolk was now beside himself with anxiety. 'You have traded the Lady Mary for some perceived advantage at the Court of France.'

'I have done no such thing,' Thomas told him cautiously. Brandon was still a royal favourite and confidante, and it was as well not to incur his displeasure, although in this matter it had been the will of the vastly more powerful Henry that had officially prevailed.

'Spare me the honeyed shit, Thomas,' Brandon glared back at him. 'Hal does whatever you tell him, everyone knows that.'

'I am certainly fortunate that His Majesty is graciously disposed to follow my counsel in some matters,' Thomas oozed, 'but it is hardly for a mere Bishop and King's Almoner to determine the destiny of the most eligible princess in

England. Particularly not one who is such a favourite of the King.'

'She is also a favourite of *mine*, Thomas, as you must know, and you do me no favour by wrenching her from my side to marry that old man who has a face like a pitted pear, who is plagued with the gout, and who is three times her age.'

It was time for Thomas to strike back, albeit diplomatically. 'Would you wish to marry her yourself, Charles? Do you therefore not still grieve for your late wife in Westhorpe?'

Brandon flushed with anger at the reproof, since his matrimonial escapades were the talk of the Court. He had first proposed marriage to Anne Browne, daughter of the Governor of Calais and his wife, a descendant of the once powerful Neville family. He had also got Anne pregnant before the nuptials could be celebrated, and had then thrown her over in favour of her aunt, the wealthy Margaret Mortimer. His marriage to Margaret was annulled at the instigation of the indignant Browne family, and Brandon and Anne Browne had finally tied the knot in a very public ceremony attended by King Henry himself. This was hardly the perfect track record for a romantic troubadour seeking the hand of a beautiful princess, and Brandon knew it, even though Anne Browne had died of the sweating sickness four years previously.

'You do me wrong to remind me of the impetuosity of my youth,' Brandon complained. 'My heart has ever belonged to the Lady Mary — is there nothing that can be done to change Henry's mind?'

'The preparations are well advanced,' Thomas advised him. 'She will sail from Dover on a favourable Autumn tide, under the protection of my Lord of Norfolk and accompanied by two of his granddaughters as ladies-in-waiting. She is already ceremonially wed to Louis, through the good offices of the

Duc de Longueville, and it wants only the final bedding across the Channel.'

Brandon shuddered. 'The mere thought of my beautiful Mary being pawed by that ugly old man, and I could run a sword through his innards! Does Henry care *nothing* for her, that he sends her to be violated by a scrofulous old goat?'

'Patience, my dear Charles,' Thomas urged him. 'King Louis will not live forever, and I am advised by one of Lady Mary's attendants that she has wrought from King Henry a promise that when Louis is no longer, she may then marry the man of her choice. She did not name you in that regard, but everyone knows where her true heart lies.'

'Truly, Thomas?' Brandon enquired breathlessly. 'This is not merely another of your honeyed reassurances, designed to deflect the arrows of displeasure?'

'Truly, Charles. It is, of course, little more than rumour through the mouth of a menial Court servant, but I had it from him while negotiating a mild penance in punishment for his lying with his cousin while drunk.'

Brandon placed a heavy mailed riding glove on Thomas's shoulder, and stooped in order to look him firmly in the eye. 'Thomas, I am, as ever, in your debt. If I might prevail upon our friendship further, and should Hal say anything more regarding the true alignment of Lady Mary's heart, do you remember me kindly to her brother.'

'Rest assured, Charles,' Thomas replied, as he wriggled out from under the heavy hand, 'you are forever at the forefront of my thoughts, and I will ever work for your happy advancement, as I feel sure I may also rely upon your good offices.'

'Indeed you may, Thomas, indeed you may,' Charles reassured him as he walked back to his companions and remounted his courser.

The doors to the Queen's Audience Chamber swung inwards, and Thomas walked serenely into the presence, dressed in his bishop's regalia and doing his best to look unconcerned. Since he was no longer tutoring the Queen in English, there was no obvious reason for the summons he had received via one of her grooms, but his spies told him that Katherine was in a foul humour of late, and he believed he knew precisely why.

Katherine sat in a high chair, her needlepoint on her lap, piercing Thomas with a steely glare as he walked towards her and bowed obsequiously. The Queen's ladies slid away on cue, and Thomas raised an enquiring eyebrow.

Katherine gestured for him to take the chair beside her. 'And take off that ridiculous hat, *Tomas* — you are not here to say Mass.'

Thomas dutifully removed his mitre, glad to be rid of its weight, and laid it ceremoniously on the floor beside his chair.

'Why are you conspiring against me, *Tomas*?'

'Me?'

'Yes, *you*. And do not reply to my questions with questions of your own.'

'In what way does Your Majesty consider that I am conspiring against you?'

Katherine 'humphed' loudly, unimpressed by Thomas's attempt at evasion. 'The Princess Mary was intended as a bride for my nephew Charles — to marry her to Louis was an insult to my family.'

'That was your husband's decision, Your Majesty, not mine.'

'No doubt under your guidance as ever, *Tomas*. Why do you persuade my husband to so insult my royal family?'

'I did not persuade him, Katherine — he persuaded himself. And on the subject of insults, it ill pleased him that your father failed to come to his banner — twice.'

'So he punishes my father by taking away his grandson's bride — is that how diplomacy is conducted in this country, by playing upon matters of the heart?'

'You forget that English troops under your direction took the life of James of Scotland, the beloved husband of the Princess Margaret.'

'That is not the same thing, *Tomas*. James chose to take the field of battle. And I will not have my mind diverted by your skilled tongue. Answer me truly if you love me, *Tomas,* has the King taken a mistress?'

The directness of the question left Thomas with his mind reeling. So far as his information gatherers at Court were to be believed, Henry had not once strayed from his marriage bed, which for a leading courtier in those times was a remarkable sign of respect and affection. Thomas lowered his eyes as if scandalised by the mere suggestion. 'Has His Majesty given you grounds for believing that his affections have been wandering?'

'His affections may wander where they will, *Tomas* — it is where his hands wander that I would wish to know.'

'And again I must ask, with the deepest respect due unto your royal person, whether or not you have grounds for such suspicion?'

Katherine stared him out, and gestured towards the Withdrawing Chamber with a slight jerk of her head. 'I have seen how he looks at my lady-in-waiting, Mistress Blount. Have you heard ought regarding her and the King?'

'Nothing, madam — I swear on my immortal soul,' Thomas protested.

'Talking of souls, is it true that those who marry within the forbidden degrees are condemned to be childless?'

Thomas thought carefully before he answered. 'If you refer to the Book of Leviticus, it is certainly therein written that those who lie with the wives of their brothers shall not have issue. But I am bound to add that the books of the Bible were not written by physicians, and that the failure to have issue is a burden borne only by those whose former marriages were consummated. I do not presume to enquire of Your Majesty whether or not...'

'I went to my marriage bed with Henry a pure maid!' Katherine yelled back at him, then turned fearfully towards the Withdrawing Chamber doorway in case she might have been overheard. She seemed to bring herself under control as she continued. 'Henry knows this full well.'

'If it is as you say, then you need fear nothing by way of God's retribution.'

'Then why do I only bear dead babies, *Tomas*?'

'I am no physician, Katherine. I tend only to souls.'

'And will you pray for *this* soul?'

'I do so nightly, Katherine. Yours *and* Henry's, that you may gift England with an heir to the throne that you both grace.'

'You may leave me now.'

'Your Majesty,' Thomas mumbled as he bowed low before her, before reaching the chamber door that an usher was waiting to open for him. Since the usher had been stationed *outside* the door, Thomas wondered whether or not their conversation had been overheard, a possibility that seemed to be confirmed when the usher gave him a lascivious grin.

IX

'You are late, Thomas,' Norfolk complained. 'Are the children disturbing your sleep?'

Thomas glared back at the Duke, reminding himself that he detested the man as much as he did his son, but for different reasons. If anyone at Court could outmanoeuvre Thomas in the matter of acquired intelligence — the tittle-tattle of the kitchens and backstairs — it was Thomas Howard Senior, the Duke of Norfolk, recently glowing in the halo of his military success and restored to his father's attainted title. And this particular piece of intelligence had probably come from within Thomas's own growing household.

His affair with Joan Larke had borne the inevitable fruit of the enthusiasm with which it had been conducted, and Thomas now had a five-year-old son named John, and a daughter Dorothy who had achieved her third birthday only days before this meeting of the Council. Not only did this make any priest of the Church of Rome vulnerable to the obvious jibes regarding the rigour with which he obeyed the vows he imposed on others, but it was particularly inconvenient for a Bishop who was also a member of the King's Council, seeking to impose moral imperatives on lesser men.

'His Majesty advises that he will not be attending Council today,' Thomas responded, ignoring the personal jibe, 'but he has asked me to advise the members that the matter of the betrothal of the Princess Mary is beyond any further discussion.'

'More's the pity,' Foxe muttered, glaring across the table at Thomas as he took his seat. 'We should be siding with Spain and the Empire, if we are to preserve the Pope from the French incursions into Italy.'

'If rumour be correct,' Archbishop Warham added in a tired voice full of resignation, 'we are doing that as well. Not only does Master Almoner possess a filed tongue, but also a forked one, it would seem.'

'Master Almoner is now My Lord Bishop of Lincoln,' Thomas growled back, hoping to provoke an argument with Warham that would divert attention from his latest advice to Henry, namely to keep open the back door to negotiations with the Emperor Maximilian, through whom Thomas was anxious to secure preferment from the Pope.

'His Majesty has certainly made some strange decisions of late,' Warham sneered with a sidelong glance at Norfolk, clearly intending to fall out badly with every other member of the Council. 'It must be the prospect of becoming a father at last.'

This last piece of vitriol verged on the treasonous, and it was as if the Archbishop and Chancellor was determined to be stripped of both offices at once, along with his head. Thomas committed this particular indiscretion to his copious memory, and comforted himself with the thought that during their recent audience, Katherine must, whether she knew it or not, have been in the early stages of pregnancy, which would account for the alarming nature of her confidences towards Thomas.

'If we may not debate the marriage with France,' Norfolk enquired, 'what *may* we take first on our agenda?'

'There is the matter of the ancient privileges of the burgesses of Canterbury,' Foxe threw in mischievously. 'His Majesty has asked that we deal with it, and since his Grace of Canterbury is with us today, and clearly in a mood to express his opinions, perhaps we might get that over with before his Grace falls asleep as usual.'

'They are claiming revenues that have belonged to Canterbury for as long as there have been records kept!' Warham protested.

'Records kept by the diocese itself,' Foxe reminded the Council. 'As the head of a diocese myself, I must express my uncertainty regarding their reliability.'

'Are you suggesting that the office of the most venerable see in the land keeps forged records?' Warham spat back. 'If so, then His Majesty shall have my resignation!'

'Don't tempt us, My Lord Archbishop.' Norfolk grinned at the assembled company, most of whom smirked at the table in response. Warham was so easy to provoke these days that it was almost a shame to indulge in it. Thomas could see what was coming, and did not wish his name mentioned when it did.

'As a diocesan bishop myself, and in deference to his Grace of Canterbury, are there any other records that might give credence to the matter one way or the other?'

'The suffragans claim to have their own records, which clearly reveal that the transfer of money to the diocese has only ever been informal, and was never part of the Cathedral charter granted by Henry II,' Norfolk replied.

'Informal?' Foxe prodded. 'Do you mean that the Archbishop has been taking bribes?'

That was sufficient. Warham angrily grabbed his papers and rose from his seat. 'I do not intend to remain in order to hear my holy office further insulted. I shall seek out His Majesty, in whichever whorehouse he may currently be located, and relieve myself of my burden of office.'

'And your head, if you continue in that manner,' Norfolk snorted as the Archbishop slammed the door noisily behind him.

'What do we recommend to the King?' Foxe enquired.

'That he allow the current arrangement to continue in the absence of any evidence of malpractice,' Thomas suggested. 'Also that he may need another Chancellor — and possibly another Primate of All England.'

'And which of those roles do you covet for yourself, Thomas?' Foxe asked provocatively.

'Both of them, no doubt,' Norfolk muttered.

Thomas had heard enough. 'At least I do not have upon my conscience the fact that I achieved high office by butchering ten thousand Scots.'

Norfolk smiled back triumphantly. 'My Lord Bishop of Lincoln should be able to speak with authority about butchery. It was his father's trade.'

The responding laughter burned in Thomas's ears as he wished them all, in his mind, the most painful death that God might devise. When the Council meeting ended, he hurried downriver to Bridewell, drank two flagons of Beaujolais, and was later carried to his chamber by two of his grooms, crying tears of self-pity.

A week later, Thomas sat outside the King's Presence Chamber deep in thought. He was now Bishop of Lincoln and was drawing the fat incomes from a variety of benefices. Thomas would soon be able to supervise the massive task of transferring all his acquired plate, ornaments, tapestries and jewels to the new palace at Hampton from the house in Bridewell that seemed too small to house, not only these, but also his rapidly growing household, including his mistress and two children.

By any standard of measurement, he was successful. But he was still the son of a butcher, and he would always be open to such taunts from his peers. Unless he could rise to such a position, either in the Church or at Court, that none dare challenge his lowly origins, it was a stigma he would always have to endure. The likes of Norfolk and his cronies, who had done nothing except be born, could only be put in their place by fear of the power wielded by men in a position to take their lives or their livelihoods from them. No-one dared insult the King, because of the power he held over life, death and wealthy status. It was time that Thomas put himself beyond the point at which men dared recall the dirty hose in an Ipswich puddle.

The business was routine, but important to Henry, and when Thomas was admitted to the presence, as Norfolk slipped past him in the open doorway on his way out with an arrogant sneer, he was fully prepared to explain to Henry.

'The Earl of Surrey will accompany the train to Dover with a company of mounted knights, and litters have been commissioned not only for the Princess Mary but also six of her Ladies, two of whom are, I am advised, nieces of Surrey's anyway. My Lord of Norfolk will meet the train at Dover, and will accompany the royal party to Calais, where he will hand over responsibility for passage to Abbeville to the Governor. Should you wish to accompany the progress as far as Dover, the Earl will of course defer to you at the head thereof, and will ride at your side, with half his command in the vanguard, and the remainder to the rear. It is to be hoped that this inclement Autumn weather abates before the end of the month.'

Henry smiled. 'You have such an eye for detail, Thomas, and as ever you have the matter managed down to the last piece of baggage. How well might you handle great affairs of State?'

'That is surely your great burden, Hal,' Thomas murmured, his eyes to the floor.

'A burden considerably lightened by your presence on my behalf in Council, where, or so I am advised by Foxe, you suffer insults because of your humble origins.'

'My father is a butcher, it is true,' Thomas reddened, 'but it is an honest trade, and my father is the finest in the county. Not a day passes, when I sit down to my dinner, that I do not thank God in his infinite mercy for the beasts of the field, and men with skills such as those of my father to convert those beasts into fine roasts.'

Henry chuckled. 'You must also thank God for your filed tongue, Thomas, and one that I would use for greater matters than simply deflecting the spleen of my somewhat arrogant Council. Your eye for detail, your constant thirst for tasks to be performed, and your skill in matters beyond the wit of mere soldiers have signalled you out as the obvious replacement for poor old Warham, who is nearing the point at which he will hang himself on his own tongue if I do not mercifully relieve him of those burdens that have made him an old man before his time.'

'Hal?' Thomas enquired, his heart beating at a rate perilous to health, and his rebellious stomach launching waves of acid into his throat.

'I wish you to become my Chancellor in due course, Thomas. In due course, but not yet. I have persuaded Warham to remain in that office for a little while longer, because I have a more urgent need for you on the Continent. However, you will not cross the Channel yet again simply in your current style. You have presumably received news of the death of Dr. Bainbridge while engaged in ambassadorial work for me at Rome?'

'God rest his soul,' Thomas muttered piously and hopefully.

'This obviously leaves open the see of York, Thomas, and I would recommend to the Pope that you be appointed to replace Bainbridge as Archbishop. I cannot place you in Canterbury while Warham lives, but once his days are ended we may once again combine Primate of All England with the office of Chancellor. For the time being, you must content yourself with York, and await the dead shoes of Warham. The Chancellorship shall be yours next year, regardless of what years Warham may have left to him.'

'As ever, Hal, your generosity leaves me speechless,' Thomas murmured.

Henry burst out laughing. 'The day you are without an appropriate word, Thomas, shall be the day the sun shines up my royal arse. And it is your skill with words that I would employ with the Emperor.'

Thomas looked doubtful. 'He may have me strung from the walls of Bruges, after your recent insult to him.'

'An insult that I would have you sweeten, Thomas. Go you to his Court and advise him that the check was intended only to Ferdinand of Spain, and that it was unfortunate that the dignity of the House of Habsburg also thereby appeared to have been slighted.'

'And if he does not accept your reassurance?'

'Then you may indeed be hanged as a decoration from the walls of his ducal residence. But that is the risk taken by all my emissaries, Thomas — surely you know this by now?'

'Indeed, Hal, and I do not shrink from the task, trusting as ever in God to be my guardian against the forces of injustice.

But it might be better were I to delay my journey until I may undertake it in the regalia of York. While Ferdinand may not scruple to hang a bishop, his nice conscience might stay his hand against an archbishop.'

Henry smiled. 'It shall be as you wish, but do not delay your installation.'

The last thing Thomas intended was to delay his ordination into this rich new post, and within days he took considerable personal delight in facing a grim faced William Warham as he invested him with the regalia of the second most important see in England. Thomas was now entitled to call himself 'Primate of England', with only Canterbury himself above him as 'Primate of *All* England'.

Maximilian smiled as Thomas bowed before him, one hand cautiously raised in order to retain the mitre on his head. 'It seems that each time we meet, you have been advanced in the Church. The first time was as a mere priest, then as a bishop, and now as Archbishop of York. When we meet again, shall you be Pope?'

'Please God that Giovanni has many years ahead of him, your Excellency. But should his Holiness have need of a cardinal, you would do me a great service by recommending me to such office, that I might further the work of defending Rome against the indignities of Louis' advance through the Italian states.'

'Your ambition, as ever, precedes you, My Lord Archbishop. Do you still enjoy our local wine? If so, and if it is not beneath the dignity of your new office to partake of the fruits of God's vineyards, shall we share a hogshead before you endeavour to explain to me how your King intends to make amends for the insult to my house and family by marrying off his sister to that old bastard of France?'

'Most certainly, your Excellency, but first I have a gift from my King as a token of both his esteem and his heartfelt grief that he may have offended you, when the insult was in truth only intended to Ferdinand of Spain. If I might be permitted?'

The Emperor nodded his approval, and Thomas looked behind him at the entrance to the Great Hall in which they were met, in which stood a tall young man dressed from head to foot in the livery of a priest of York, beside whom was a long barrow that had travelled all the way from Calais on a horse-drawn cart. Thomas waved his hand, and the young man solemnly walked down the hall pushing the barrow, then halted before the Imperial dais.

'You bring me vegetables?' Maximilian enquired, much amused. Then his face set in a look of amazement as the young man solemnly lifted the cloth from the trolley to reveal a massive suit of full armour, made from burnished gold and stamped throughout with the ancient symbols of the Imperial crown.

Thomas took advantage of the stunned silence. 'His Majesty King Henry is well aware of your love of armour, your Excellency, and hopes that you will accept this humble and loving gift as a small token of his regret that he should have appeared to cast a slight upon your royal house while intent merely on rubbing the nose of Ferdinand of Spain in the goat droppings in which it belongs.'

Thomas's mission was already accomplished. Relations between England and the Empire had been restored, Ferdinand remained insulted, and France would soon have a new Queen with Tudor blood in her bridal offerings. Thomas could now look forward to the coming year.

X

The New Year celebrations for 1515 were barely over when Henry found his patience with those closest to him stretched to breaking point on the rack of European diplomacy. As usual he sent for Thomas to guide him through what he must do, and fortunately for him his recently consecrated Archbishop of York was well prepared, as the result of several earlier audiences.

The first had been with the urgently commissioned French Ambassador Gilles de la Pommeraie, a personal friend of Francois of Angouleme, cousin of Louis XII. Gilles brought urgent news from the French Court of a momentous event that had previously only been rumour — King Louis was dead. The Lady Mary was now a widow, and if she was not currently carrying an heir to the late French king's throne, the question arose of who she should next be wed to. Pommeraie had been anxious to impress upon Thomas the importance of ensuring that Mary remarry within France.

The second audience had been with Queen Katherine. She had also heard the news from France, and she impressed upon Thomas her desire to see Mary matched with her nephew, Charles, soon to be King of Germany.

Thomas was attempting to formulate a line of advice that would satisfy both the Queen and the French Ambassador, while easing Henry's conscience and, at the same time, promoting his own ambition to wear a Cardinal's hat, when he almost collided with Thomas Howard, who emerged in front of him from the alcove in which he had been lurking.

'Thomas, I will not ask if you have heard the news, since it is all over the Palace, and I have already had a letter from my niece Anne, who is currently residing with my brother-in-law Thomas Boleyn, in Paris. She and her sister Mary have been banished from Queen Mary's service, and they are both in need of a place here at Court.'

It gave Thomas considerable satisfaction to be the one being asked for intercession with the King by the man who had dumped him in an Ipswich puddle in the years before each of them had risen in public life. He opted to prolong Thomas Howard's anxiety. 'I do not choose the Queen's Ladies, Thomas. Since your brother-in-law is now appointed Ambassador to France, you surely do not fear for their safety?'

'Of course not,' Surrey replied. 'Do not fence with me, my Lord Archbishop, since I am an expert dueller. My concern is that the Princess Mary should not be allowed her head in the matter of a choice of second husband.'

He was as subtle as a boar fighting off the royal hounds, and Thomas was enjoying himself immensely at the man's expense.

'It has been long known where her heart lies, regardless of what her head deems appropriate,' Thomas replied. 'If it were left to her, she would be the Duchess of Suffolk, which I imagine would not be to the liking of your father Norfolk, since it would take Charles Brandon even closer to the King's ear. Is it your wish that I urge the King against such an eventuality? Do you now *fear* the power that comes with being the King's brother-in-law?'

This was a particularly cruel jibe, but one that Thomas had no hesitation in delivering, given the many boyhood cruelties to which he had been subjected by Thomas Howard. Thomas's first wife, Anne of York and one of King Henry's several aunts, had died some years previously, and Howard's second wife, although the granddaughter of the powerful Percy of Northumberland, was in no position to guarantee him the King's ear.

'My concern is simply that the Princess Mary be brought safely back to England, where she may remarry under the wise guidance of her brother the King, and no doubt his closest counsellors, among whom you are numbered, according to my father.'

'It was, as I recall,' Thomas reminisced, 'you yourself who escorted her to Dover on her journey to France. Do you seek to be the person who escorts her in the reverse direction? With your two nieces in close attendance to impress upon her the chivalry and courage of her escort?'

'Just make sure it isn't Brandon,' Howard spat back as he turned to leave, 'else she may return in no condition to be further engaged as a royal chess piece.'

Thomas sought admission to the royal presence. Henry was biting his lip with anxiety as Thomas was admitted. He thrust a piece of vellum at Thomas as he poured himself another wine, and in his distracted state omitted, for once, to invite Thomas to join him. 'It seems that the Duke of Valois has already been in my sister's ear,' Henry complained. 'Read that, Thomas.'

The letter bore all the hallmarks of having been written in a blind panic by a frightened young girl, and left little to be imagined regarding her deepest desire.

I beseech your grace that you will keep all the promises that you promised me when I took my leave of you by the waterside. Sir, your grace knoweth well that I did marry for your pleasure at this time and now I trust you will suffer me to marry as me liketh for to do. Wherefore I beseech your grace for to be a good lord and brother unto me. Should you not, it is my intention to take upon my person the vestments of a bride of Christ in some nunnery where never no man shall know joy of me.

'Well, Thomas?' Henry asked, 'was ever a man so torn? I would that Mary marry into the House of Habsburg, as was my first intent until you persuaded me otherwise, and that would surely be of considerable value to the nation in its need to protect his Holiness from French aggression. It would also, as I am constantly reminded on those occasions when I keep the royal marriage bed, please Queen Katherine. And yet it is true that as a loving brother I made promise that Mary might make her second marriage with her own chosen partner, who I know to be my lifelong companion and good friend Charles Brandon. What am I to do, Thomas?'

Thomas had been weighing up the advantages and disadvantages — not for Mary, nor for the nation, but for himself. On the one hand, should he persuade Henry to hold firm and promise Mary's hand to Charles, the almost certain successor to the Holy Roman Empire, he would have gained a powerful ally in Rome in the matter of his ambition to don a cardinal's red hat. He would also be back in favour with Queen Katherine, who would naively believe that Thomas had been the one to persuade her husband to favour her nephew.

On the other hand, to advise Henry now that his first idea had been the better one, from which he had been dissuaded by Thomas, would do nothing to maintain the King's confidence in his counsel. There was also the need to maintain the good offices of Suffolk against the malice of the Norfolk faction towards the man they regarded as the upstart son of their local butcher. At least he could rub Surrey's nose in the excrement in which it belonged.

'It would be as well, Hal,' Thomas began, 'to avoid any suggestion that the Princess Mary has become a mere coin on the trading table of European politics. Less than an hour ago, Surrey referred to her, in my hearing, as "a royal chess piece". But at the same time, her physical safety should be assured, ere she become the hostage of Francis of Valois. She must surely be returned to England with all speed, that you may then perhaps persuade her where her duty to England must take her next.'

'And her dowry, Thomas? What is to become of that?'

'A matter of secondary importance, if I might make so bold. Nothing is more important than the safe return of your beautiful sister, the rose of all England, to the bosom of her family.'

'And who shall I send, Thomas? It was Surrey who took her to Dover barely three months ago; shall we send him to perform a like service on her return?'

This did not suit Thomas at all, particularly since it was the very thing that Thomas Howard wanted. There had to be a better way. 'Perhaps my lord of Suffolk, who has her welfare so close to his heart?'

Henry stared back at Thomas. 'The very man who is likely to melt *her* heart anew, and banish all thought of marrying a prince of Europe from her head?'

'Also the very man whose love for her will ensure her safe return from all obstacles that Francis might put in her way. He is one of the strongest, most valiant, men in the kingdom, and, as your sworn and lifelong friend, the most likely to carry out your instructions to the letter.'

Henry was finally persuaded, against his better judgment, and an astonished and jubilant Charles Brandon was advised that he was to lose no time in crossing the Channel to bring back to

England the woman of his dearest dreams. He was also told by Henry, in no uncertain terms, that he was to insist upon the return of so much of Mary's original dowry as he could wrest back from Francis, now hastily confirmed as the new King of France. Finally, he was left in no doubt that his life would not be worth living — and perhaps might no longer be lived at all — if he did not keep his hands off his precious charge.

Thomas had been present during this stern royal briefing, and he escorted Charles out into the antechamber, where he drew him to one side.

'My dear friend,' Thomas said, 'be in no doubt that I have all but placed my head on the block for you in this matter. Should ought go awry, Henry will hold me to account as well, no doubt, as yourself, and do not believe for one moment that he will spare either of us simply for love of his sister. Also, do not build up your hopes that you and she will be allowed to marry — I have much work yet to do in persuading His Majesty before that point will be reached. But you may depart in the comfort of knowing that today the French Ambassador advised me that King Francis is waiting to welcome you to his Court, from which it may be presumed that he has no objection to your venture.'

Suffolk grasped Thomas firmly by the shoulders, then embraced him warmly. 'My dear Thomas, when you promised me that day at Hampton that you would look to my interests with the Princess Mary, I had no idea that it would be so soon. I am eternally in your debt, and if there is ever anything I can do...'

'There is, Charles,' Thomas cut in. 'You can keep your hands off the Princess Mary and preserve *both* our heads from the block.'

Six weeks later, Thomas sat at his desk in his bedchamber with his head in his hands, groaning audibly, and shaking with disbelief. In front of him was the worst communication he had ever received. It was from Charles Brandon, and it seemed that they would both be heading for the axe. Thomas had clearly underestimated both Brandon's lust for Mary and the depth of his naivety, and they would both almost certainly pay with their lives — Brandon for what he had done, and Thomas for what he had placed him in a position to do, while giving King Henry the worst advice he had ever received.

King Francis had confided in Brandon that Mary had confessed her love for him, and that if Brandon would do him the honour of allowing Francis to organise a hasty wedding between the happy couple, not only would Brandon have his heart's desire, but a letter would be sent from the Court of France advising Henry of the French King's delight at this happy union. This letter was never sent, and they were married secretly in the chapel in Cluny a week later.

The letter that was provoking Thomas's groans had been written three days after their wedding, and it sought his intervention with Henry, if the two of them were ever to return to England safe in the knowledge that their heads were secure on their shoulders. Unaware of what had been taking place, both Henry and Thomas had been sending despatches urging Brandon to insist upon the return of the whole of Mary's dowry, and it was of little comfort to Thomas to be advised that all the plate, jewellery and coinage that had accompanied Mary on her outward journey would be making the return trip. Francis could well afford to part with it, since he had taken Henry's most valuable chess piece off the board, and somehow Thomas had to tell him.

He opted to do so privately, rather than humiliate himself in Council, and it was in a plain white alb that he walked slowly into the Audience Chamber and prostrated himself flat on his face before a startled Henry.

'What means this foolery, Thomas?' Henry demanded, not sure whether to laugh outright or send for a physician, since his Archbishop of York appeared to have become bereft of his wits.

'I place myself at your mercy, Hal, for you to do with me as you wish, rather than vent your wrath upon the two people who love you as dearly as they love each other, and since it was I who trustingly placed them where they might fall prey to the temptation of true love, it is I who must pay the penalty. I would ask only that you allow me to go to the scaffold in this simple vestment that symbolises my humility and shame.'

'Get up, you fool, and explain to me what it is that has so addled your brain,' Henry demanded. 'Who are these people of whom you speak?'

Without rising, even to his knees, Thomas spoke to the carpet. 'Suffolk and your loving sister Mary.'

In the deathly silence that followed, Thomas was obliged to look up in case the King had left the chamber. It was worse than that — Henry's face was crimson with rage, and he was experiencing difficulty in breathing. 'Say you that Brandon has had her?'

'It is worse than that, Hal — he has married her.'

'Dear Christ — no!' Henry thundered, as he hurled his wine goblet clean through the chamber window, and began thumping the arms of his chair like a child denied a favourite toy. Thomas took this opportunity to rise to his knees, and eventually Henry composed himself sufficiently to remember that kneeling before him was not only the man whose advice had led to this dynastic disaster, but also the very man who could best advise him how to deal with it.

'Off your knees, Thomas,' he commanded him. 'I seek your counsel, not your head.'

When Thomas appeared to be having difficulty raising his impressive bulk from the carpet, Henry waved a page from the side wall at which he had been standing awaiting further royal command. 'Assist my Almoner to his feet, and have a carpenter repair that window ere we all freeze to death. Now then, Thomas, you have no doubt already designed a strategy to take us round this formidable obstacle, other than the execution of my favourite sister and my childhood companion?'

'Indeed, Hal, and it may be that this unhappy and unwanted event may be turned to our advantage.'

Henry smiled conspiratorially. 'Already you promise to repay me for sparing your head. What have you in mind?'

'Well, Suffolk advises me that this state of affairs was only made possible by the deviousness of King Francis, whose Ambassador was but recently at my door seeking that the Princess Mary be betrothed to some minor French nobleman or other. It would seem that she refused any such offer, and that Francis sought to prevent her from being married into the Habsburgs by encouraging the heartsick Suffolk. This confirms that Francis sees a rival in Charles of Hapsburg, King of Spain, as well as King of Germany, and Holy Roman Emperor in all but name.'

'This much I could have worked out for myself, Thomas. What do you advise?'

'Overtures to Charles himself, Hal. While he may no longer hope for the hand of Princess Mary in marriage, he may look fondly on an approach by us for an alliance against Francis.

This way you will be insulting Francis, while at the same time making it clear to the whole of Europe that his devious schemes have brought him nothing but the enmity of England.'

'Do you propose that I appoint you as special envoy to Charles's court?'

'No, Hal. I propose that we entertain him royally here in London, with great pomp and splendour. We might even invite the French Ambassador.'

'After the recent fires here at Westminster, we would have to do so at Richmond, or perhaps Greenwich or Windsor. Yet I doubt that any of them could house a royal visit of such size. Is your new dwelling at Hampton completed?'

'No, but my London residence at York Place would be more than adequate, with any additional guests being housed at one of the royal palaces you name.'

'And you would organise it?'

'Down to the very last detail, Hal. It would be my pleasure, and would afford me one more opportunity to display my gratitude for the retention of my unworthy head.'

'Yet I fear that the Council will take this news ill. Norfolk in particular will be most aggrieved to learn that Suffolk has escaped with his head.'

'His head perhaps, but may we not reduce his wealth by way of punishment? He writes that he is returning not only with the Princess but also her dowry. That should of course be forfeit, and might I suggest that she be obliged to repay the outlays of her wedding, which amount to some twenty-four thousand pounds?'

Henry turned slightly pale. 'This would ruin the happy couple ere they had been wed a month. Is there no other way?'

'I do not suggest that they be obliged to pay the entire sum in one instalment, Hal. Perhaps over a period of six years, with an attainder upon default?'

'That would be kinder, certainly. But would it satisfy Norfolk and his faction?'

Thomas smiled. Here was an opportunity to play the ends against the middle, and the morning would not be entirely wasted. 'There are few occasions upon which Norfolk's son Surrey says anything worth listening to, yet he did but recently seek my assistance in a family matter. Two of the ladies who travelled to France with the Princess Mary are still there, it would seem, and are now seeking positions at the English Court. They are the ladies Mary and Anne Boleyn, Surrey's nieces, and — more to the point — Norfolk's granddaughters. Should you be inclined to prevail upon your dear Queen to include them among her ladies-in-waiting, it might be sufficient to silence Norfolk, and with him those of your Council who are foolish enough to listen to him. Katherine might well be disposed towards granting your request, given that you will shortly be showing so much honour to her nephew Charles.'

Henry's face broke into a broad smile. 'Thank God that you serve my interests rather than those of my enemies, Thomas. It shall be as you suggest.'

Thomas took the precaution of inviting the French Ambassador to take wine with him at York Place. He reminded him of the deviousness of his master before requesting, by way of penance, all the information he could supply regarding the Ladies Boleyn.

The Ambassador was eager to advise Thomas that, 'The Lady Anne resides with her father, and is so far advanced in

113

her studies, as well as her dancing, singing and lute playing, that she is accounted one of the finest prospects in Paris.'

'Do not contrive to have her married off to some French noble with more land than culture,' Thomas advised him, 'since she is required here at Court, to wait upon the Queen. And her older sister Mary?'

The Ambassador's face set in concentration as he sought the appropriate words.

'She is much more — how shall we say — *frivole*? than her sister. She is light-hearted, much given to laughter, gaiety, dancing and the like. She is received at Court, where she is chased by many fine young nobles.'

'And is she frequently *caught*, may I ask?'

'In truth, it is only rumour, and because of her undoubted beauty she is of course resented by many of the more senior ladies at Court, who spread unkind stories regarding her.'

'Please do not prevaricate, Gilles,' Thomas urged him as he refilled his guest's goblet.

'She has a reputation for her freedom with the men. Indeed, my master would be grateful for her removal from his Court.'

'But you assure me that this is just jealous slander by those ladies who envy her beauty?'

'Perhaps a little more than that, My Lord Archbishop. I know of at least two men at Court who have known her favours. I am sorry if this news does not please you, but you wished that I be honest with you.'

'Indeed I did, and I am most grateful to you for your candour,' Thomas replied, keeping the smile from his face at the prospect of the humiliation and embarrassment that he could cause for the Norfolk family by having her brought to London without delay, and slipped into the Queen's entourage.

XI

Barely a month later, Thomas and Henry met to discuss darker matters. King Francis had finally wrested the strategic city of Milan from the Confederacy of Swiss States that had held it for some time, and the balance of power in Europe had shifted dramatically. Milan was strategically important from the perspective of those who lived both north and south of it; to the Swiss it was a southern bastion against access to their Alpine passes, while to any conquering army from the north it was the gateway to the more southerly Italian city states, including Rome.

The Pope was now under serious threat, and Charles of Spain and Henry of England were the only two monarchs who could come to his aid. The Swiss Confederacy declared themselves strictly neutral after their massive defeat. Almost immediately afterwards, news came that Charles was facing a revolt against his rule in Spain by a conglomeration of Castilian cities known as the *comuneros*.

The King's Council stood firm against any official alliance with Charles, and Henry was watching this sudden rise of France with jealousy and apprehension. He was also frustrated by the apparent pacifism of Warham and Norfolk, and a little unnerved that for once Thomas could not sway the meeting. He summoned Thomas from York Place down to Westminster to discuss what they might do to promote their desire to ally with Charles of Spain without needing to consult the Council.

If Thomas could find a way through the impasse, he would not only confirm his primary status as the voice in Henry's ear, but he would also be well regarded by Queen Katherine, who was known to be well aware of Henry's dalliance with Bessie Blount, had dismissed her from her service in a fit of pique, and was quietly seeking revenge against those who had provided the facilities for the two of them to meet in secret. Thomas knew that he was vulnerable in this regard, and that it would best serve his interests to be able to reunite the angry Queen with her nephew.

'What are we to do, Thomas?' asked the perplexed Henry.

'I have in mind going on a pilgrimage, Hal.'

Henry frowned. 'You cannot desert me at this time, when there are so many urgent affairs of State that require your agile mind.'

'I have not yet said where my feet will take me.'

'Rome?'

'No, somewhere far more important to England at this time. Santiago de Compostela, to pay homage to the bones of St James the Apostle.'

Henry was still at a loss. 'How will praying to a pile of old bones help England at this time?'

'Because, Hal, if I choose to travel overland, I will need to pass through Castile.'

Suddenly Henry understood, and with a shout of joy he clapped Thomas on the shoulder, almost spilling his wine in the process. 'An excellent ruse, Thomas! No doubt on your journey through Castile you will be in a position to carry with you warmest greetings from a royal aunt?'

'That was my intention, Hal. And what message would you like me to bear from *you*?'

'Tell him that we wish him long life and good health, and that we would wish to be allied with him against the arrogant Valois boy who has the audacity to pretend to be a king, and who only succeeded in conquering Milan because there were no real soldiers there to prevent him.'

'And how soon shall this alliance be announced to the world?'

'As soon as the boneheads in Council can be made to see that it is in England's best interests to enter an early alliance with the man who will, in the fullness of time, also be King of Germany and Holy Roman Emperor.'

'They know this already, Hal, yet they remain hesitant.'

'They will not hesitate when you return with news of Charles's enthusiasm for such an alliance, and the Queen makes it known that such a possibility has gladdened her heart. Norfolk is still seeking positions at Court for his granddaughters, is he not?'

'He is indeed.'

'Then perhaps we might prevail upon the Queen to grant his wish in return for giving support to her nephew.'

Thomas nodded in agreement, mentally noting two things. The first was that Hal had referred to Katherine as 'the Queen', rather than 'Katherine' or 'my dear wife'. This suggested a cooling of relations between them that seemed to be confirmed by the fact that Hal saw the need to 'prevail upon her' to obtain his objective, whereas in the past she would lovingly have granted his every wish. It also signified that Thomas was now called upon to ingratiate himself with two separate people, whereas in the past the consent of one had brought with it the automatic consent of the other.

Two weeks later, Thomas was bowing the knee to the young King Charles of Spain. He was only a boy of fifteen, and his grasp on those territories to which he had succeeded at such a young age was tenuous. He had inherited his father's

Burgundian throne at the age of six and was still ruling under the regency of his aunt, Margaret of Austria. The Low Countries that came with the crown, and were Charles's traditional home, had just suffered a revolt by Fresian peasants which had yet to be suppressed, and they were also important to England for trade purposes. Finally, here in Castile, Charles was still seeking to put down the *comuneros* uprising. If ever a monarch with a shaky hand on several thrones at once needed a powerful ally, it was Charles.

'My grandfather Maximilian speaks very highly of your diplomatic skills,' Charles told Thomas in his heavily accented English as he signalled for him to rise. 'He also says you would be Pope.'

Thomas gave him the unctuous smile that seemed to reside permanently on his face these days as he rose somewhat heavily from his knees and took the chair indicated to the left of, and lower than, the royal dais. 'Your Majesty speaks excellent English, if I may make so bold.'

Charles smiled. 'I speak Spanish to God, Italian to women, French to men and German to my horse.'

Thomas assumed that he was expected to chuckle, so he did, before continuing in what he hoped was a suitably humble vein. 'And English?'

'I speak English to men of God who come to me with heartening news that my beloved aunt has persuaded her all-powerful husband to support me against the Valois threat to my various lands.'

'I certainly bring that hope, Your Majesty. But you must be advised that there are those in the King's Council who oppose such an alliance. My visit here is intended to reassure you that it is Henry's dearest wish that in the fullness of time our nations will be united, and that your dear aunt will be welcoming your presence in the country of her marriage.'

'And what of you, My Lord Archbishop? What is *your* dearest wish?'

'To see his Holiness the Pope no longer threatened by the heathen French who have granted sanctuary to those who preach heresies against our dear Mother Church.'

'Are those views shared by others in high positions within your Church?'

It was the perfect opening, and Thomas thanked God for this unique opportunity.

'There is only one above me in the English Church, and that is the Archbishop of Canterbury, who to my considerable regret and consternation still advises King Henry against armed intervention in Italy, where of course you have lands in Naples, Sicily and Sardinia that also require protection.'

'Is there some way in which I could assist you to rise above this man of Canterbury, in order to have a louder voice in the King's Council?'

It was like taking bread from a blind beggar. 'The only person who could override Canterbury would be a Papal Cardinal, but at present there are none such in England.'

Charles smiled triumphantly. 'I believe we understand each other at last, my Lord Archbishop. In return for bringing Henry and his soldiers to my side, you wish his Holiness to make you a Cardinal, yes? My grandfather was not mistaken about your ambition. Do you also wish to be the next Pope, perhaps?'

Thomas cursed his underestimation of this ugly young man's insight regarding matters of diplomacy, and kept his eyes on the floor. 'You understand that my wish to wear the Cardinal's hat is solely in order to further my King's ambition to assist you? You are, after all, his nephew by marriage.'

'Leave it with me, Archbishop Wolsey. The Pope sees me as his main hope of surviving the gradual encroachment of Francis of Valois into Italy, and eventually his capture of Rome. A word from me, and the gift of a red hat will be a small price to pay, particularly if I can advise his Holiness that alongside my armies will be the full military might of the greatest warrior king in Europe.'

Thomas lost no time in returning to Henry with the good news and was more than happy to keep the outcome of his 'pilgrimage' secret from others, as Henry requested. It was reassuring to be the only man in the realm entrusted with such a vital initiative, and tempting though it was to let Queen Katherine know that he had established cordial contact with the 'beloved' nephew she had never met, he kept his own counsel on the matter, not that Katherine seemed any longer to desire his company. She and her Ladies were permanently at Richmond, regardless of where the Court might be convened, whereas Henry seemed to prefer to live his life travelling between his own suite of rooms in Westminster and a special wing of York Place set aside for him, to which he could travel unchallenged for clandestine meetings with Bessie Blount.

However, any thoughts that Thomas might have entertained that Henry and Katherine were estranged were hastily suppressed by the news that the Queen was again with child, and would be likely to deliver in February of the following year. Given her history of miscarriages, stillbirths and infant mortality, there were few at Court who expected a live outcome, and the news was also to a certain extent diluted by tidings of another birth anticipated at the same time, to the Duke and Duchess of Suffolk.

Early in September, Thomas's endeavours in Spain bore their first fruit. Word came that Thomas had been appointed as Cardinal of St. Cecilia, and that his red hat of office was on its way from Rome to Dover, along with various Papal Bulls confirming his authority.

On 18th November, the skull-like features of Archbishop Warham shrank into a rictus grimace as he placed the red hat of Thomas's dreams officially on his head for the first time. Its feel upon his head was by then a familiar one, since he had spent many an hour before the glass in his private chambers, admiring himself from every angle. Thomas smiled graciously as the Blessing was pronounced above his head, then turned to join the procession that led him out of Westminster Abbey to be hailed by the crowd that had gathered outside to watch. Thomas pronounced a blessing of his own on the assembled multitude, and said a silent prayer of thanks to the God who had raised him so far in His service.

He was also shortly to rise in the service of another important power, this time the earthly one that he served. Warham was so disgusted with Thomas's rise within the Church that he advised Henry that he no longer wished to serve on a Council that had among its number 'the son of a butcher of animals who has become a shepherd of God's flock by his deviousness, his oily tongue and his slippery conscience.' Henry took the man at his word, and relieved him of the burden of the office of Chancellor that he had been administering of late with lacklustre and a growing inattention to detail.

On the afternoon of Christmas Eve 1515, Thomas sought audience with Henry. Henry did not, as usual, offer him a seat, and Thomas remembered enough Courtly protocol to stop himself from simply taking his customary seat in the window alcove of the Presence Chamber without invitation.

Henry smiled across at him as he filled two wine goblets and handed one to Thomas. 'I have not invited you to be seated because the adjoining seat is reserved for the Chancellor of England.'

Thomas bowed his head in deference. 'I do not expect his Grace of Canterbury to join us for this meeting.'

'Neither do I,' Henry smiled even more broadly, 'since he is no longer the Chancellor of England. I am now able to keep a long unfulfilled promise to you, Thomas. You may be seated only if you will accept the office.'

Thomas wasted no time in making full use of the new power that had been granted to him over those who still sneered behind his back at his humble origins. As Lord Chancellor of England and Keeper of the Great Seal, Archbishop of York, and Cardinal of the Church of Rome, he now had a power that all but rivalled the King himself, and the mutterings of the Howard faction grew both more audible and more bitter. A butcher's son now ruled their lives both spiritual and temporal, and the son of Robert Wulcy was not the sort who either forgot or forgave old slights.

To all outward appearances, however, the new Chancellor of England was the fount of all justice, the righter of legal wrongs, and the champion of the truth above the machinations and corruption of the wealthy. He presided four days a week over the already infamous Court of Star Chamber, as part of his more formal duties in the Court of Chancery, the 'court of conscience' that had been established to administer royal justice when the old common law proved inadequate. Out of this grew the 'Court of Requests', with which Thomas's name would always be associated as a man of God who was always ready to hear the petitions of all men, rich or poor, for justice in their cause.

The wide power that this handed to the incumbent would have blinded and corrupted men with purer souls than that of Thomas Wolsey, and he was not tardy in settling old scores, and lining his pockets with fees for early listings of matters that were bribes in all but name.

One of the first to regret having crossed him in his early years was the West Country magnate Sir Amyas Paulet. Star Chamber had the authority to haul even those of high nobility before it in order to answer to actual, or imagined, charges of disorder that threatened the peace and stability of the realm, and it was on one such warrant that Sir Amyas was summoned to Westminster. A triumphant Thomas ordered Sir Amyas into virtual house arrest inside his lodgings in the Middle Temple, of which he was now the Treasurer.

Queen Katherine, meanwhile, was escorted to her latest childbed in mid February 1516, in her favoured Greenwich Palace where, on the eighteenth of that month, she succeeded in delivering a healthy child. But she was a girl, christened Mary, and Katherine herself was now thirty-one years of age. Henry welcomed a nephew a month later, when his sister Mary, Duchess of Suffolk, gave birth to a boy who was named Henry, in honour of his bitterly disappointed uncle.

This disappointment was not hidden from Thomas during his many audiences with his protector, as they constantly monitored events across the Channel. Henry's affair with Bess Blount was now an open secret throughout the Court. Bess had long since been dismissed from Katherine's service, and Katherine spent her time praying for the male heir that would return her beloved Henry's attentions to her on a fulltime basis. At the same time, she was bitterly disappointed that the man she had trusted so innocently, and who was now enjoying Henry's total trust and confidence in his new role of Chancellor of All England, had acquired such royal patronage by making a suite of rooms available at York Place for Henry to meet almost daily with his pliant — and no doubt fertile — mistress.

For Thomas, while the rewards had been great, the stress and tension of being Henry's chief confidante were beginning to take their toll. In the Autumn of 1517, he met with Henry in his Audience Chamber at Westminster Palace.

'Is it possible, say you,' Henry enquired imperiously, 'that two people may endure a curse intended for only one?'

When Thomas feigned non-comprehension, Henry tutted in exasperation.

'Do not seek to evade my question with that well-practised air of ignorance, Thomas,' Hal responded curtly in a tone that Thomas had learned to be wary of. 'I refer to the Queen's failure to produce a male heir. God has clearly cursed her womb, but is it his intention to damn the entire nation in the process?'

'It grieves me so to hear you refer to Queen Katherine in that fashion. She sets an example to the entire Court with her piety and her grace...'

Henry's left fist came down on the arm of his chair, causing wine to spill from the goblet in his right hand. 'Enough, Thomas! Your loyalty to the Queen is well known, and in one regard it does you great credit. But she was bedded first by my brother Arthur, and for her unchastity she has been cursed with a womb empty of male children.'

There was no placating Henry when in one of these moods, and Thomas had gained the high favour that he currently enjoyed by being able to sniff the wind. It was time for a reassuring response tinged with diplomacy. 'It seems to me that the curse of which you speak — should it be such — is only intended for she who has sinned, but that since your hopes and aspirations are so closely bound with hers it is impossible for you not to be affected by it. If I might draw an analogy, those who stand too close in the front line of battle to a person for whom enemy arrows are intended are more likely to be felled than those tending sheep in a nearby field.'

'Say you, then, that were I to rid myself of her and marry elsewhere, I might have male issue?'

Thomas's stomach lurched a warning. Whatever his reply, even in confidence, it could blow up in his face. 'Hal, I say merely that if — and I must press upon you the "if" — God has chosen to curse Katherine, then surely she is in more need of the love and protection of a man such as yourself, who is so well regarded in God's eyes?'

'Do you think so, Thomas? Do you *really* think so?'

'I have not the slightest doubt, Hal. Never has England been blessed with such a period of sustained peace, in which men may turn their eyes up to God, rather than behind their backs for a dagger blow. Surely God will wish to preserve such lasting peace by granting you a male heir who may continue the Tudor line that so nobly preserves the prosperity of England.'

Unexpectedly, Henry burst out laughing and clapped a hand on Thomas's shoulder. 'Never was shit spoken so beguilingly, my dear friend. So what did you have to report to me on how our interests fare abroad?'

Since it was now safe to smile, Thomas did so. 'I have the ears of the Ambassadors of both Spain and France, and since each of them fears to be seen in the company of the other, I have been able to parley with them both without fear of being reported. Charles of Spain seeks our alliance to unleash his forces against Francis of Valois, while the French king seeks our assurance that we will do no such thing. England has become a wholesaler of peace, it would seem, and we might use this to our advantage with the Pope.'

'*Your* advantage with the Pope, Thomas,' Henry chuckled in reply. 'Were I his Holiness, I would fear for the continued presence of my mitre on my head with such a diplomat as yourself loose among the princes of Europe. So how say you that we make best use of this new position of influence?'

Thomas allowed himself a pause. 'Given our financial state at present, Hal, it would not be a propitious time to engage our army for either of the two young hounds who strain at the leash to be at each other's throats. And indeed, it would be against our best interests to side with either, thereby invoking the wrath of the other. Charles cannot, at this time, be assured of the Imperial crown upon the death of his grandfather Ferdinand, and yet we must ensure his continued friendship in order to preserve our trading interests in Flanders. Francis has the greater army, and is like to break down the walls of Rome itself ere long, thereby having Pope Leo at his mercy. We would therefore be best advised to retain his friendship, lest his mighty and triumphant forces be turned against us when, and if, he proves victorious in Italy.'

'And your suggested policy, Thomas?'

'A perpetual peace between all the nations of Europe. The Pope is known to be anxious to promote another Crusade, this time against the Turks who dominate access to the Holy Land.

If we are to attempt to broker a peace between these warmongering young hotheads across the Channel, it were best done in the name of the Holy Father. That way, we conceal our true motivation, and show no weakness or favour to either Francis or Charles until such time as we may conclude which of them is the stronger, and therefore the safer of the two with whom to seek an alliance.'

'I assume that as usual I may rely on you to ensure that no detail is overlooked, once the Council approves of your suggestion?'

Thomas smiled back as reassuringly as he could. 'There are, as you know, some who serve on your Council who favour ongoing war in Europe, ruinous though it may prove to the nation's coffers at a time when our subjects are sorely pressed to place beef on their tables. I refer of course to Norfolk and his faction. Would it not be better to deal privily with Charles and Francis in separate parleys, then seek the blessing of the Pope, then present Council with a ready-made scheme that they would not dare gainsay, should you speak out in favour of it?'

'Do it, Thomas, and do it on my authority, and with my blessing.'

XII

Three weeks later, one sullen November night as the freezing fog turned the torches at the York Place entrance into pale and shimmering yellow ghosts, three men heavily wrapped in cloaks were met at a side door by a liveried steward and hurriedly and deferentially led up a staircase to the Great Hall, where Thomas sat awaiting their arrival.

As the first of them threw off his heavy cloak and hurried towards him, Thomas threw his arms around the visitor. '*Bienvenido*, Charles. May I order some wine? Or some food?'

'Later, perhaps,' Charles replied. 'I assume that this meeting is with the knowledge and blessing of my uncle the King?'

'Indeed,' Thomas assured him, 'since I do nothing without his blessing.'

'And he wishes to send troops to my cause, the quicker to relieve his Holiness of the threat posed by the French dog?'

'He wishes his Holiness to be free of any threat from Francis, certainly,' Thomas assured him, 'but he wishes to do so in such a way as to save you money and men. Put shortly, he wishes to be the means by which you and Francis swear an oath of peace.'

'Never!' Charles spat defiantly.

'Consider it this way,' Thomas urged him, 'you wish his Holiness, and the Holy See in which he resides, to be forever free of the threat of invasion by France, and yet you still have uprisings of your own to fully suppress, do you not?'

'You are well informed, it would seem.' Charles conceded. Just then, one of the two men who had accompanied Charles pulled at his sleeve and drew him to a corner of the room,

128

where they conversed urgently but in whispers until Charles walked back over.

'I am advised that what you suggest would be in Spain's best interests at this time, but how can we be sure that the treacherous French eel will keep to his promise?'

'Because you will not be alone in incurring the blessing of his Holiness himself for walking down the path of peace. A double blessing for each of you should you pledge yourselves to the crusade against the Turks.'

'And my uncle Henry? He will also join with us?'

'Perhaps not on crusade, but certainly in any peace treaty.'

'Who else?'

'I thought perhaps also Burgundy, since you would wish to be assured that your own back is secure. Some of the German states may also be persuaded to join, although you will of course bring them under your own signature when the Imperial crown becomes yours.'

'*If* it becomes mine, and *only* if. They say that Francis has obtained much support within Germany for his claim. And of course he now dominates the Italian city states by fear.'

'All the more reason to urge him to the peace table,' Thomas oozed. 'And in return for your support in this, Henry would no doubt see his way clear to supporting your claim to the Imperial crown.'

'And you, Thomas? I have formed such an opinion of you that I doubt that all this work is being undertaken by you simply in the interests of King Henry. What do you hope to gain by it?'

'Rewards in Heaven?' Thomas smiled back conspiratorially. When Charles had no response, Thomas made his objective clearer. 'I can foresee a time at which, with my support — which means, of course, the support of England and its King

— you will be the Holy Roman Emperor, and Leo will have gone to his Heavenly reward. Rome will by then have been preserved from French aggression by means of the treaty I am in the process of putting together, and therefore who better to preside over the resulting Peace of God?'

Charles burst out laughing. 'My grandfather was right after all! You seek to be Pope, do you not? And you seek my support as Holy Roman Emperor?'

Thomas bowed in silent agreement, and Charles allowed himself more laughter before he requested that he be escorted to his chambers, where he might sleep off the rigors of what had been a very exhausting three days.

Thomas slept soundly in the belief that the first part of his plan — and in many ways the most difficult — had been achieved. It now required only the consent of Francis of France, and peace would break out across Europe, England would be saved the expense of battle and the need to choose where to commit its army, and the Pope would be obliged to Thomas in a very personal way. And Thomas had already seen the perfect road down which to walk towards an Anglo-French accord, while earning yet more gratitude from his royal patron.

This time the matter was best left to ambassadors and diplomats, and it was a perfect opportunity for the promising young lawyer Thomas Cromwell, who was forever importuning his employer within the Chancery for more demanding duties, to show his mettle. The main bargaining counter was an obvious one, and it should be attended to first.

In February of 1518, Francis had been blessed with a son. He would in due course require a bride from a royal house of Europe, and did not the English have an eligible candidate in the person of the two-year-old Princess Mary?

Thomas renewed his correspondence with the Bishop of Paris, who had long expressed a desire to see their respective nations joined together by marriage vows, and it came as no surprise when Francis reacted favourably to the suggestion. Almost without realising it, Francis was drawn into a peace treaty with England, which busy clerks in Chancery lost little time in committing to vellum for the signatures of the parties. It was a *fait accompli* before the Council ever became aware of it, and although Norfolk was highly indignant that a matter of such high estate had been negotiated by a butcher's offspring, Suffolk was delighted that Francis was at last to become such a friend to England as he had been to Suffolk in making it possible for him to marry the King's sister and get away with it.

It was all over bar the ceremony, and in this Thomas was as usual in his element. The French Admiral Bonnivet landed at Sandwich attended by the Bishop of Paris, and accompanied by a sizeable train that included over thirty high nobles, fifty archers, a troop of acrobats, musicians, tennis players and assorted lesser types that was met halfway, and escorted into London in a breath-taking cavalcade.

The Pope was represented by Cardinal Lorenzo Campeggio, his Legate for the occasion, who was able to whisper to Thomas, as they embraced in that chaste way perfected by men of the Church of Rome, that His Holiness had granted Thomas's request to be appointed *Legatus a Latere*. This was the equivalent of an appointment for life, and came with a power to convene every Catholic convocation in the realm, including Canterbury. Thomas had finally risen above Warham in the Church, although the old man was almost past caring anyway.

On October 3rd, 1518, a massive procession wound its way into St. Paul's to a High Mass conducted by Thomas in all his finery. Henry was attended by a thousand richly dressed nobles, and accompanied by the ambassadors who had, the previous day, signed the Treaty of London.

On 5th October, at Greenwich Palace, the two-year-old princess was promised in marriage to a French Dauphin who was across the Channel in his cradle. Consent to the match was given by Henry, for the bride presumptive, and the French Dowager Queen, on behalf of her grandson, while Papal Legates Thomas and Campeggio stood reverently to one side.

Queen Katherine retired to her chambers ahead of the magnificent banquet stage-managed by Thomas to celebrate his greatest diplomatic triumph, and as Henry finally sobered up, three weeks later, it was Thomas who was obliged to advise him that while he had been lying in Bessie Blount's arms in his private chamber in York Place, his wife had gone into premature labour and delivered yet another stillborn child.

Thomas stood to one side, embarrassed, as Henry sobbed quietly, the tears splashing onto his nightshirt as the Groom of the Chamber hastily prepared the morning quaff on a side table.

'Tell me once again that I am not cursed,' Henry mumbled as Thomas sought desperately for something to say. 'That effeminate popinjay Francis of France can sire sons, and yet I cannot. I am shamed across Europe, Thomas. The slimy lamprey even foreswore to attend the betrothal, as if England is not good enough to soil his feet on.'

'If he will not come to you, then might I suggest that you go to him?' Thomas countered as he sensed the royal rage regaining some momentum. 'Let me arrange a great tourney in the lands south of Calais, and let it be known that if Francis does not attend, he is no man.'

While Katherine had gone through the physical and mental agony of yet another stillbirth — and yet another daughter — it was the excited tittle-tattle of the travelling Court, now just south of Calais, that Bessie had just delivered a healthy boy who was to be named Henry in honour of his royal father.

Henry had sent for Thomas as soon as he had the news from Essex, and he was the first to confront Thomas with the knowledge that there was now a male royal bastard to be factored into the diplomatic equation.

'Congratulations, Hal,' Thomas offered automatically, as he began calculating how this might alter affairs of State.

'What say you now of the curse of God? It must surely be Katherine's curse alone, is that not now proven beyond doubt?' Henry urged him.

'So it would seem, Hal, but as I have had occasion to remind you in the past, God does not confide in me regarding these matters.'

'But was it not you yourself who advised that God's thunderbolt might be aimed solely at she who brought it down upon her head by her lustful pursuit of a crown?'

As always, there was danger whichever way he answered, and Thomas selected his most diplomatic tone as he nodded sagely. 'Certainly, to the sinner alone go the wages of sin. And regardless of what God may think of your weakness as a mere man, in being seduced by Spanish beauty and guile, you have proved to the world that the Tudor male line may continue, and that can only have been with God's blessing.'

'But even if I am forgiven, Thomas, what of England if the Queen is not? If it be God's will to deny her male issue, He is denying a peaceful and prosperous future to England. Do I not owe it to my people to cast aside she whom God has cursed, and plant my seed in one more worthy of the English crown?'

'Hal,' Thomas murmured, panic-stricken by the confidence he was being forced to share, 'while I can advise you as your friend, I cannot presume to give you counsel on such a weighty matter of State.'

'I wish for Bessie Blount to be well provided for, given the recent birth of our son. I also wish to rid myself of her now that she has become a burden and a possible source of gossip at Court. Make this happen, Thomas, preferably by finding her a husband among the many who lie around you at York Place or at Hampton.'

Thomas was sorely tempted to retort that Bessie Blount was already the subject of considerable gossip in Courtly circles, and that the Queen had no illusions on that score, so that Henry had no need to put her away at this late stage in their relationship. But the look on Henry's face warned him against any attempt to thwart the royal will, and he merely bowed his head in supplication as Henry continued.

'In return for being comfortably provided for in marriage, she is to be parted from her son, who is to be given the name Fitzroy and brought up in one of the royal palaces. The Queen will be furious, and it must be your honeyed tongue that conveys the tidings. Then I wish you to begin negotiations with the Pope to have Henry Fitzroy legitimised, that he may become my heir.'

Thomas stared in stunned amazement at a King who appeared to have taken leave of his senses. Thomas had no doubt that he could find a husband for the still very attractive and nubile Bessie, and he would, at worst, be prepared to brazen out the wrath of a Queen who seemed to no longer have much regard for him anyway, but the prospect of approaching Pope Leo X with a request for a Papal dispensation that would legitimise a royal bastard conceived in an act of blatant adultery that publicly insulted one of the most prominent and pious Catholic women in Christendom, and the aunt of the Holy Roman Emperor, was unthinkable.

Henry looked up aggressively when there was no reply from Thomas. 'Was it not for such services that I raised you from your humble station in life?' he thundered. 'May I remind you that by my hand you are Chancellor of England? Is there an office of State more elevated from which a king may be advised? Now, what must I do, for the future of England?'

'For the immediate future of England, Hal, you must approve these final plans for your initial meeting with King Francis. I had assumed that this was why I was being summoned, and I have the lists of those who will accompany you when you ride south.'

'Would it not be best for you to meet with him first, in order to sniff the wind?'

'Do we not have an Ambassador to advise us of the current humour of the man you will shortly be embracing in friendship as the father-in-law of the future Queen of France?'

'Boleyn? He has been in Paris these many months with his daughters, and his despatches have been both brief and infrequent. I would that you pave my way with your honeyed words.'

Thomas obliged, and with his usual pomp and dignity he passed within the walls of the French King's temporary palace at Ardres with his two ecclesiastical crosses held high in the air, horns blowing and pennants flying, to be met in the courtyard, as he dismounted, by Thomas Boleyn.

'Welcome, Your Grace,' Boleyn said as he bent to kiss the ring. Thomas reminded himself that he was dealing with a man married to a Howard, and adopted his haughtiest tone.

'Our royal master has sent me on a mission that should not have been necessary,' he advised Boleyn. 'But since your despatches are as rare as smiles from a plaster saint, he wishes to know how advanced are the preparations on the French side.'

'You may advise His Majesty that all is in hand for a triumphant procession, to be followed by the royal embrace on neutral territory.'

'Does King Francis wish to be advised of the precise order of their meeting?'

Boleyn gestured to his rear, where two liveried guards resplendent in tunics emblazoned with the *fleur de lis* emblem in embossed silver stood guarding the entrance door with crossed halberds. 'Please accompany me into the presence and deliver your honey.'

After being escorted down a succession of corridors, passing through several guarded doors, and being ushered with great ceremony into the Great Hall, Thomas was able to bow for the first time before the man who at present appeared to hold the balance of power across the whole of Europe.

'Archbishop Wolsey, I have heard much of you. Some of it good, some of it...'

'I bring loving greetings from my master Henry of England,' Thomas interrupted him in perfect French as he took in the long Valois face with the prominent nose, slightly hooded eyes and the suggestion of a wry smile.

Francis nodded in acknowledgement. 'You bring word as to how we shall meet three days hence?'

'Indeed, Your Majesty,' Thomas replied, breaking the seal on the vellum scroll he had been carrying. 'I had occasion to travel through the valley in which the two of you shall meet, and it would seem to be well positioned for such an auspicious greeting.'

'Ah yes, the *Val D'or*,' Francis mused aloud. 'It is well named, is it not? The "Golden Valley" in your tongue?'

'Indeed,' Thomas agreed, 'and I was much taken by the number of men armed with implements who appeared to be levelling the ground in its centre.'

'Symbolic, as well as practical,' Francis told him. 'It is fitting that neither of us shall stand upon higher ground than the other, although I am advised that your king is much taller than I, and indeed much greater in *all* his measurements.'

'He is blessed with a warrior's frame, certainly,' Thomas replied diplomatically. 'But as I approached this temporary palace, I passed through what I can only describe as a new city being constructed beside the village of Balinghem. There seemed to my untutored eye to be several pavilions in the course of construction, with many tents surrounding them.'

Francis chuckled and wagged a mock admonitory finger at Thomas. 'Fie, My Lord Archbishop. Your eye can hardly be described as untutored, given the construction that is taking place in your own camp outside Guines. My scouts tell me that your king has ordered the construction of a similar temporary town on his side. Apart from giving work to every carpenter and stonemason in Europe, it would seem that we are destined to compete with each other in pomp and finery.'

'Indeed, and beginning with your first meeting,' Thomas replied as he urged their business forward. 'This is the list of those who shall accompany my master to the edge of the rise on the northern side. He will then descend into the vale on horseback, accompanied solely by the young Marquess of Dorset, who will take his sword from him ere you embrace. You may perhaps wish to make similar arrangements.'

Francis chuckled once again. 'You may rest assured, My Lord Archbishop, that on the southern ridge you will be blessed with the sight of the finest nobles in France. I shall make the descent accompanied by the Duc de Bourbon, and to him will I entrust my blade while embracing your master. And now let me remind you of what you have been missing since your days in Calais.'

He snapped his fingers high in the air, and a liveried page strode forward with a large flagon of wine and two goblets. Once they were filled, each man raised his goblet and proposed the mutual toast to '*l'intente cordiale*'.

Thomas was standing on the northern ridge of the valley designated for the formal meeting, looking anxiously at the expressionless face of Henry as he gazed across at the massed plumes, pennants, coursers and shining armour of the French contingent. His attention was distracted by the blowing of heraldic trumpets, and the scurrying through the English party of men-at-arms bearing the order that everyone bar the King was to remain rigidly still, with weapons sheathed, on pain of death, while the King descended slowly on horseback down the slope into the valley, which looked to all intents and purposes like a ploughed field following the levelling that had taken place during the course of the past few days.

The two monarchs sidled their massive war horses alongside each other, and reached out in a firm embrace. Then they dismounted, and each unbuckled his sword and handed it to his noble equerry before they embraced more bodily, and gave every appearance of being pleased to meet at long last. Thomas heaved a sigh of relief, and once the order had been passed down the line that the English were free to move again he climbed back onto his mount and headed back the few miles to the English camp, in order to reassure himself that all was in place for what promised to be the diplomatic extravagance of the decade.

The sight that met his eyes was unrivalled anywhere in the known world, and most closely resembled a massive Crusader camp established with all the wealth that resided in the world. In what had once been two and a half acres of dull, flat land of no great agricultural value had been created a veritable city of marquees and lesser tents. In its centre was a grand pavilion constructed partly of stone for many courses, above which had been erected wooden frames on which had been stretched hundreds of yards of 'cloth of gold', a heavy but luxurious fabric woven with silver and gold thread. Above that rose a further thirty feet of artfully crafted wooden frames that had been painted to resemble the stones of a great cathedral. Across the top of the entire edifice had been stretched specially oiled cloth painted a leaden hue in order to resemble roof slates, into which glass panels had been expertly inserted in order that those within might feel themselves to be in the open air.

This virtual palace was arranged in four blocks, each over three hundred feet in length, in the centre of which was an impressive courtyard. In all, the English palace occupied an area of twelve thousand square yards, and before it were three fountains that spouted red wine, fresh water or spiced claret. There was a 'chapel' that resembled a cathedral with its ornate hangings and saintly statues, but which had a gallery to one side that was well appointed enough to host a banquet of its very own. Even the lesser ranks below the royal party — the pick of England's noble houses, together with representatives of every county in the realm, and not overlooking the Church, which had sent its leading bishops and many lesser clergymen

— were sumptuously accommodated in almost three thousand tents that were the pride of the London needleworkers who had been richly rewarded for producing their best work in the shortest time.

Then it was on to the nearby tiltyard, where on 9th June, the day after the formal meeting ceremony, King Francis rode in with a heavily armed but select escort to view the ground upon which the nations' champions would clash and clatter in three days time. Both monarchs proudly entered their names in the list, followed by many nobles on either side. Having reassured himself that the bluff fighting men on either side were unlikely to come to premature blows due to their inability to understand each other's tongues, Thomas retired to his allocated chambers.

The following day was the first encounter between the two nations in the temporary tiltyard, and everyone was ordered out to watch the brutal exchange between the warriors and monarchs. Queen Katherine was there with her Ladies, and Thomas noted how close she seemed to be with her sister-in-law Mary of Suffolk. Charles Brandon was being assisted into his armour as Thomas walked across to the English 'safe' area, where men, horses, grooms and heralds were all but colliding with each other as they sought to prepare for a day of chivalric aggression.

'Have you come to bless my fortunes in the tourney, dear friend?' Charles asked Thomas with a nervous grin.

'God has clearly blessed you already, with your warlike frame and eternally youthful vigour,' Thomas replied. 'I came merely to enquire why your wife and sister-in-law are conversing with such animation. Is there some issue I can resolve between them?'

'Ever the supportive friend,' Brandon winced as the groom took in another notch on the strap of his breastplate. 'They are merely competing for the services of Mary Boleyn.'

'As many men at the French Court have recently done, from my information,' Thomas muttered. 'You would be wise to keep your wife's new lady-in-waiting at home, rather than expose her to the nobles at Court.'

'Truly?' Brandon enquired with a raised eyebrow. 'Perhaps I should advise Mary to let her serve Queen Katherine, as she is insisting. Yet Mary is so fond of her that it would be a sad loss.'

Thomas thought for a moment, then decided to take the plunge. 'Charles, you and I are dear friends, so I feel that I may safely confide in you. His Majesty will shortly be marrying off Bess Blount, and unless his affections for Queen Katherine have been fully restored, his wandering eye will fall upon Mistress Boleyn if she is prominent in your household when he visits. You would not wish to incur Katherine's ire, as I have done, by being the means by which he was able to consort with Mistress Blount.'

'And yet it would seem,' Brandon replied as he was lowered onto his quarter horse ahead of riding out into the *pas d'armes* opening parade, 'that one may, like yourself, earn much advancement and favour in Henry's service by bringing about such meetings. We shall lose no time in inviting him down to Westhorpe once we are home. And now, blessing or not, I must join the line. As ever, Thomas, I am in your debt.'

He cantered off, and Thomas had to swiftly dodge the mud flung up from the horse's hooves. In leaping back, he was almost mown down by another mounted knight on his way into the main ring, and he reminded himself that this was no place for a man of God. Besides which, he had a letter to write to Rome, and a daunting interview to request with the Queen.

The tourney lasted in all for three days, and Henry and Francis lost no time in tilting at each other, with mixed results. Henry succeeded in breaking more lances than Francis in the many charges down the field, but it somehow seemed that Francis was always more loudly cheered from his side than Henry was from the English ranks.

Henry attempted to outdo Francis in the matter of accoutrements, and on the final day even succeeded in draping his horse with cloth of gold and pearls. The Earl of Devonshire did what Henry had no doubt wished to do, when he unseated Francis and broke his nose. On this somewhat sour note, the contests came to an end, and it was left to Thomas, in his luxurious chapel, to grant a general indulgence to all who had participated.

'I feel that Francis bested me in the tourneys,' Henry confessed later to Thomas, a thoughtful look on his face, 'so I have in mind challenging him to a wrestling match. I have rarely found a man who could best me at wrestling, and by this means I might rescue some of my reputation as a man of warlike action.'

Thomas refrained from stating the obvious fact, known to every Courtier, that it was not a wise move to beat Henry at anything, so that his frequent successes were not necessarily a true reflection of his actual ability. 'There is still a day left ere we must depart, Hal,' Thomas said encouragingly. 'Do you wish me to be the bearer of the invitation to Francis?'

'Who else, Thomas? And also make the arrangements for a suitable ring to be erected on the tiltyard field for which we have no further use.'

Thomas lost no time in riding south with the invitation, and just before noon the following day, before the entire assembled English and French Courts, the two kings, suitably stripped down to their shirts, doublets and hose, walked warily round each other until the Earl Marshall of England dropped a white cloth to the muddy ground, and the two monarchs came together in a grappling motion that sent them round in circles like two rutting stags with their antlers locked.

Henry obviously had the height and weight advantage over the man three years his junior, but Francis was more supple and wily, and more than once managed to avoid being thrown by neatly stepping sideways. His agility began to annoy Henry, particularly after the French ensemble began laughing, hooting and baying their appreciation of their King's athletic prowess.

As Henry grew more red in the face he also grew less cautious, and as he attempted to pull Francis towards him in what was intended as a bear hug, Francis slipped his leg behind him and broke the hold as Henry fell over backwards into the mud. Earl Marshall Norfolk had no option but to declare Francis the winner, to the delighted shouts and renewed hoots of the French in the crowd.

Henry picked himself up, bowed formally to Francis and walked off the field towards the rope barriers. As he did so, he caught sight of an apprehensive looking Thomas standing behind the Duke of Suffolk. Henry stormed over to Thomas and glared down at him from his superior height, mud still dribbling off his doublet.

'You've given me better advice than that, Thomas. You made me look a fool, as did Francis. The Queen shall get her wish. Invite Carlos of Spain to visit England without delay.'

XIII

Thomas sent for his trusted senior envoy Thomas Cromwell, who knew Europe, and particularly France and Italy, well, following his years as a mercenary soldier, and who, like his patron, had risen from humble origins, in his case a blacksmith's shop in Putney.

Cromwell was instructed to sail on the next tide to Spain, there to persuade the Emperor Charles that the warm sun of English friendship was once again shining in his direction, and that King Henry wished to meet with him in private at Canterbury Cathedral. He was to land at Portsmouth, from where he would be discreetly escorted through the southern counties of England by the still relieved and grateful Duke of Suffolk, royal brother-in-law and hardened soldier, to the chosen meeting place.

Archbishop Warham was sent on pilgrimage to Rome while the Archbishop of York conducted services at Canterbury in his absence, and employed every available minute of his spare time converting the somewhat austere ecclesiastical residence into a palace fit for a visiting monarch who was anxious to keep his precise identity secret. His eventual arrival, on a frosty night in February 1520, was not a matter that Henry could keep from Charles's aunt, Katherine, and she was already in residence with a select number of her Ladies as Charles's arrival was announced by Suffolk.

While Thomas was preparing for bed he received an unofficial visit from Henry, who seemed enervated beyond the prospect of retiring for the night. 'Who is the Queen's new lady-in-waiting, Thomas? The one with the blue gown and the entrancing white neck and brown eyes?'

'That will be Norfolk's granddaughter, Mary Boleyn. She is comely, is she not?'

'Most certainly she is, Thomas, most certainly she is. Is she wed, or betrothed?'

'No, Hal, but if I may respectfully anticipate your next question, neither is she a maid.'

'And of what concern should that be to me?' Henry demanded.

'It is to be regretted,' Thomas replied in his most outraged tone, 'that she has so disgraced the family name of Howard by the freedom with which she distributed her favours throughout the Court of France — including, or so it rumoured, even to Francis himself. It is unfortunate that My Lady of Suffolk was so indebted to her for her ministrations following the unfortunate death of Louis that she was prevailed upon, by her delicate conscience, to repay the debt by urging your dear Queen to take her into her service.'

'She's a whore, say you?'

Thomas allowed his embarrassed gaze to fall to the floor. 'It is not for a man of God such as myself to employ such a word to describe one of Her Majesty's Ladies, but...'

'Thomas,' Henry interrupted, 'it is too late at night for your diplomatic games. Answer me truly — is it spoken abroad that she is a whore?'

'Yes, Hal, much though it grieves me to —'

'Yes, yes, spare me the holy oil, Thomas,' Henry demanded. 'See to it that she is wed without delay.'

'Hal?'

'Wed, Thomas. Married. Eased into the bed of some limp-cocked noble of the realm who will toast his good fortune while leaving her unsatisfied. God knows we have plenty of those lurking around the Court, if my information be correct.'

'I would not know, of course,' Thomas assured him, while mentally running a list of potential candidates through his mind.

'Then find out, and see to it,' Henry insisted. 'On other more important matters, I would have you speak first with Charles on the morrow, to sound out his deepest thoughts regarding affairs in Europe. I wish to send Francis a message that wrestling me to the ground in Guines may have cost him his ambitions in Italy. We must be allied again with Charles, either against Francis directly, or at least bound by such treaties of non-aggression against each other that Francis will think twice before attacking either of us. Ensure that Charles is left in no doubt of our desire ere I meet with him formally.'

'Certainly, Hal, although I think that you will find Charles to be just as anxious as are you to rub Francis's nose in the shit.'

The next morning Thomas was up bright and early, hearing both of his Masses at the hands of Canterbury's Dean before the pale winter sun had even shown its face. He was helping himself to his second goblet of wine, and toying with a piece of cheese and a slice of fresh bread, when Charles made his appearance.

'Thomas, what have you in store for me today?'

'What would you wish, Your Majesty?'

'Let us not play those games again. You wish to be Pope, and I wish Henry's alliance against the French bastard. What could be simpler? We can agree that before we leave this breakfast board, and then I can remount my horse and depart for Portsmouth.'

'It is not I who must agree, but His Majesty,' Thomas pointed out tactfully, earning himself another hoot of laughter from Charles.

'Even in Spain it is known that the safest way into Henry's ear is through the mouth of Thomas Wolsey. One of our Ambassadors reports that if you want to know what Henry will do, you ask the man in the red hat what *he* wishes to do. It is even rumoured that he does so for a price, and, if we understand each other, the price of England's support against Francois is the best seat in Rome for its current Archbishop of York.'

Thomas made a great display of sighing. 'You must understand, Carlos, that the King is his own man. True it is that I am most fortunate in that, on occasions, he seems to value my counsel, but I can only act as an ambassador for his wishes. There can be no guarantee that what we discuss over breakfast he will agree to over dinner.'

Charles smiled slowly before replying. 'And there can, as you well know, be no guarantee that the College of Cardinals — of which of course you are now one — will prefer you over another claimant to the Papal throne. Thus is life made more difficult for us both. But please make known my wishes to he who you claim to have no influence over.'

It was agreed in principle before the sun was at its full height over Canterbury's ancient towers, but Charles was persuaded to remain for one more night, in order to begin his return journey to Portsmouth fresh and fully rested.

As Henry and Thomas stood in the West Bell Tower, watching the small group of horsemen wending their way through the streets to the gate that gave access to the Ashford road, Henry took his opportunity. 'Have you yet given thought to a husband for Mistress Boleyn?'

Thomas had spent half the previous night giving thought to the matter, but his solution needed to seem as if it came from Henry himself. Thomas had an uneasy suspicion that Henry already had carnal designs on the fresh new recruit to the Queen's retinue, and if Thomas was to avoid even more of Katherine's ire, he must minimise the opportunities to put that desire into action. If he could marry Mary Boleyn off to one of Henry's own Gentlemen of the Privy Chamber, then there would be less opportunity for the King to bed her in any of the royal palaces. This would, of course, once more turn York Palace, as it was now generally known, into a well-appointed brothel, as it had been when Bessie Blount had been in the height of favour, and once again Thomas would not be able to claim to be in total ignorance of how, and by whom, his guest quarters were occupied.

'I had thought that for someone from such a noble family as the Howards, only someone of equally noble blood would suffice as a spouse. However, as is quite appropriate, you have most of them in your intimate service in the Privy Chamber.'

Henry thought for a moment. 'Harry Norreys is but recently married, and as for Francis Bryan, it was you yourself who urged me to expel him from my service in the Privy Chamber due to his wild debauches. Nick Carew is affianced to Bryan's sister, God help him, and while Will Crompton is between wives, he has important duties close to my interests.'

'I was thinking of Will Carey, Hal.'

It would be a wise choice, if Henry agreed. Carey was related to the powerful Percys of Northumberland, and Henry Percy Senior was a close friend of Thomas's, and had proved invaluable in the capture of Tournai a few years previously. The young Harry Percy was a page in Thomas's household, most frequently based at York Palace, and best positioned to keep Thomas aware if the King sought to use the official residence of the Archbishop of York as a trysting place with Mary Boleyn.

Henry nodded slowly in agreement. 'A wise choice, Thomas. He is my third cousin through the Beaufort connection, and would be a suitable husband for one of Her Majesty's Ladies. See to it that he is left in no doubt where his duties lie towards his King, although given the Lady Mary's obvious beauty he is hardly likely to regard that as an onerous imposition. And while we are on matters of wedlock, have you yet chosen someone who might wish to end the carnal drought of Mistress Blount?'

Thomas almost laughed out loud, but checked himself in time. If there was one woman in Christendom least likely to be lacking in carnal exercise, it was Bessie Blount, even if she *had* but lately risen from her childbed after launching a royal bastard into the world. But Henry had obviously finished with her, and there would no doubt be a generous payoff, both to her and the man chosen to take soiled royal goods to be his lawful wedded wife.

'I had in mind Gilbert Talboys,' Thomas said reassuringly. 'He is greatly indebted to me, given that I rescued his father from the madhouse, and much taken by the lady herself. She has a smile that would enchant any man.'

'She also has thighs that move with the speed of barn doors flapping in a spring gale,' Henry chuckled, 'but there is no need to acquaint him with that until he discovers it for himself.'

'Leave it with me, Hal. But now we must consider how best to announce to the world that England and Spain are once again sharing a bed.'

Back in London, those arrangements were swiftly made, and news was sent across the Channel to Calais that it would be hosting a most significant conference down the road at Gravelines in July. The resulting Treaty of Bruges, drafted in haste but with great care by Thomas Cromwell, pledged both England and Spain against any treaties with, or military assistance to, France during the next two years, and as a further insult to King Francis the betrothal of the now six-year-old Princess Mary to the Dauphin was repudiated, and Charles of Spain undertook to wed her in due course. If Queen Katherine had any private objection, she chose not to express it publicly, and a sumptuous banquet was held behind the forbidding walls of the English fortress of Calais to celebrate this great reunion of England and Spain.

There was less rejoicing when the tricky Charles took advantage of England's promise not to come to France's aid in order to relaunch his own attack on Francis's troops in Italy. He had also begun to lean heavily on the tired old Pope Leo X to lend him both military forces and the blessing of God for any aggressions towards his old enemy Francis, on the ground that the French king was giving sanctuary to Martin Luther and his Lollard supporters, who were openly challenging the supremacy of the Church of Rome in the Christian world. Since one of the terms of the Treaty of Bruges committed English troops to the aid of anyone who attacked Spain, all that Charles now had to do was provoke Francis into such an attack, and all prospect of peace in Europe would sink without trace.

Francis was well aware of this, and sought to hide his hand in the actions of others he funded and equipped to make border incursions into Spain, and Spain's ally Bourbon. His deception was revealed when the commanders of the invading armies were sternly repelled by an indignant Charles, who called upon Henry of England to honour the Treaty. Henry needed no excuse to exact revenge against Francis and assuage his wounded pride, and in July 1522, Henry Brandon, Duke of Suffolk, clattered into Brittany and Picardy at the head of twenty thousand troops and began laying the countryside to waste in anticipation of being joined by Imperial troops under Charles's command in a combined attack on Paris. When Charles diverted his troops south to Italy instead, Suffolk retreated behind the walls of Calais, and yet another English initiative to regain its lost lands in France had come to nought.

Henry was livid with rage, and barely spoke to Queen Katherine for an entire month. Even then it was only to remind her of what a treacherous dog her nephew was, and this opinion was shared by the man who Charles had double-crossed the most, Thomas Wolsey. His hopes of becoming Pope through the quiet influence of the Holy Roman Emperor were shattered when Pope Leo X died less than a year after the treaty to which Thomas had acted as midwife, and Charles urged the Conclave to elect his former tutor Adrian of Utrecht as Pope Adrian VI. Thomas pretended to anyone who asked that he cared more for serving Henry than he did for serving God in the highest office available within the Church of Rome, but he privately cursed the man who had outwitted him and dragged England by the nose into a war that it could ill afford, while demonstrating to Thomas's enemies that he was not infallible when it came to international diplomacy.

Whether or not Henry shared those doubts, he was still in dire need of counsel suited to his own ambitions to dominate Europe, so Thomas continued to be occupied almost daily in forming a silent audience to Henry's ravings against his Imperial nephew, and prospective son-in-law.

When not so occupied, Thomas was busy making his own domestic rearrangements. The ease with which Bessie Blount had been palmed off onto Gilbert Talboys encouraged a thought that had been fermenting under his own cassock for some time, namely that it was fitting that he ease Joan Larke out of his household, along with their two children. He had avoided any more overt scandal by leaving her and the children at Bridewell when he transferred to York Place upon acquiring the mitre and cross of York. Then one day, in Chancery, he found himself judging a property dispute from Cheshire involving a modestly wealthy widower called George Legh, and in a private conference with the litigant he agreed to judge in his favour if the gentleman would be prepared to wed Joan.

Thomas also had occasion to appoint a new gentleman usher for his staggeringly massive household, stretched across Bridewell, York Palace and Hampton Court. It came about almost by accident, one day in the Exchequer Court when he was examining some Pipe Rolls, and had occasion to comment on the need for greater regulation of his own personal household. In his company at that moment was the 'Clerk of the Pipes', Thomas Cavendish, of whom Thomas had formed a high opinion, and who advised him that his agile-minded, but bored, son George was languishing at home in Padbrook Hall, in Thomas's native Suffolk, looking for something worthwhile to occupy his time and attention. A short interview later, and Thomas had a loyal servant who would always be at his side.

Pope Hadrian did not reach a third year in office, and upon his death in 1524 the faithless Charles persuaded the Cardinals, in Thomas Wolsey's absence, to appoint Clement VII. Thomas once again let it be known that he welcomed the new incumbent with more joy than he would have received the office himself, and set about proving that he might have been the better choice by sweeping out some of the more fouled monastic stables within his own English regions of responsibility. However, as always, he did so at considerable benefit to himself.

Thomas lost no time in emphasising his piety to the new Pope by bringing to his attention the laxity in the daily routines of almost thirty holy houses under his administration, which the Pope authorised him to close down. It is unlikely that he also authorised Thomas to pocket their wealth, but he would probably have approved the purposes to which it was put.

There was, however, no hiding the fact that Thomas had lost a great deal though Charles's treachery, and his preference would thereafter be for an alliance with France. Charles had, however, benefitted considerable from abandoning the English forces on the eve of what would have been a triumph two hundred years in the making. He had marched south at the head of the greater part of his army, and challenged Francis everywhere he could find him within the Italian city states. He eventually ran him down on the outskirts of Pavia, and following a four hour battle that decimated the French force, Francis himself became hostage to Charles, who had finally gained the dominance over Europe that he had long craved, while at the same time humiliating his almost lifelong rival.

The news was not received in London with the joy that it might have been. For one thing, it had been Henry's policy, on Thomas's urging, to juggle between the two powerful monarchs like a fairground entertainer with apples, in the hope of preserving a manufactured peace that would not require any expenditure on English forces. But of far more concern to the two intensely vain men in charge of England's foreign policy was Charles's public repudiation of his betrothal to the

Princess Mary. This was not a studied personal insult, but recognition of the fact that Charles's victory had come at a huge financial cost, and he had his eyes on the huge dowry that came with the hand of Isabella of Portugal, regardless of what he might think of the physical attraction of the rest of her.

Pride, both personal and national, dictated that England now throw in its equivocating hand with Francis, and early in 1527 Thomas Cromwell was once again set to work, under his patron's supervision, putting the final touches to a peace treaty between England and France that became known as 'The Treaty of Hampton Court'. Public overtures were made to Charles to release the person of King Francis himself, while private invitations were sent from Charles, via his ambassador, to Thomas, suggesting that he urge upon Henry the wisdom of joining Charles in a final joint conquest of France, whose lands would be carved up between England and Spain.

Tempting though this prospect was, Thomas argued strongly against it, both with Henry and with the Council. For one thing he had no reason for trusting in any more of Charles's promises, and for another the English Treasury had been seriously denuded by the last expedition sent out under Suffolk, which had been forced to retreat when Spanish troops were not forthcoming. There was an unfortunate history of English forces waiting in the field for Spanish support that never came, and Thomas was privately concerned that Charles would stand back and let the English do all the hard and dangerous work, then claim the spoils for himself.

It was doubly unfortunate for Thomas that the leadership of the pro-war faction within Council was now in the hands of the Third Duke of Norfolk, Thomas Howard, his old enemy from the Ipswich days. The Old Duke had died the previous year, and his son, previously the Earl of Surrey, had succeeded him with Henry's blessing. The King relied on seasoned warriors like Norfolk and Suffolk, and it was unfortunate that the two most powerful nobles in the nation disliked each other, probably out of mutual jealousy, although neither of them would admit it.

Suffolk was still profoundly grateful to Thomas for interceding for him when he married the royal sister Mary without Henry's permission, but he looked askance at the Archbishop's constant preference for international negotiation rather than simple old-fashioned war. He knew that his ongoing popularity with Henry depended on his ability to bring, and command, thousands of men under his war banner, and it was in his interests to maintain the perception of military threat from overseas, or at the very least the tempting prospect of territorial gains on the continent, and he was reluctantly obliged to side with the more openly bellicose, and verbally aggressive, Norfolk, when he thumped the table during the first Council meeting after the capture of King Francis, and took the opportunity to blame it all on the butcher's son whose rise to national eminence he bitterly resented.

'Thanks to this meddling priest, who were best left to tend his father's pigs, we have been betrayed by Spain, and are now being invited by Charles to invade France, at considerable cost to ourselves, in order to assist *him* in the securing of the spoils!'

'It is the best opportunity we will ever be given to take back those lands across the Channel which are rightfully ours,' Suffolk argued.

'And the cost?' Norfolk thundered. 'Wolsey cost us the best part of the Treasury by being duped by Charles of Spain into assisting him in France. And with what result? Parliament will not grant us more taxes, to be sure, and we own no more land in France than we did when we started on this foolhardy exercise. Were I not convinced that the Chancellor of England is an errant fool who was guided simply by his own incompetence, I would recommend that he be tried for treason!'

'Enough, Norfolk!' Henry demanded. 'Wolsey has ever enjoyed my confidence, in this as in many other matters of which you remain unaware. Our business today is to decide whether or not to invade France as invited by Spain. Thomas, you have thus far maintained your silence — what say you?'

Thomas was in a difficult bind. The last thing he wanted was to be forced to admit that he had indeed been hoodwinked by Charles of Spain, and that he had grave doubts regarding the honesty of the man's intentions were England to cross the Channel once more in alliance with him. He was also anxious to renew an alliance with France, in order to revenge himself on Charles, but the man with whom he would wish to sign a new treaty of everlasting friendship was currently languishing under house arrest on the borders of his own country — or what was left of it — and Spain. However, Norfolk's angry reference to finance, from his position of authority as Lord Treasurer of England, had shown him the way through the impasse.

'As Norfolk reminds us, we are not best placed financially to equip another expedition into the lands beyond Calais,' Thomas explained.

'Thanks to your mismanagement!' Norfolk yelled.

Thomas took a deep breath and glared at Norfolk across the table. 'You are no longer a credible sight playing the schoolyard bully, Norfolk, and the precise reasons for our current situation are complex, as His Majesty is well aware. The purpose of today's meeting of Council is to consider our future options, not to assign blame for past misfortunes.'

'And why should we listen to *your* advice, when it was the cause of our misfortunes in the first place?' Norfolk snapped back.

Suffolk placed a restraining arm on his, and made his second contribution to the discussion. 'We have not yet heard his advice, Norfolk — at least let the man speak. Thomas, what say you?'

'I say,' Thomas replied with all the dignity at his command, 'that we make diplomatic overtures for the release of Francis, and then make great show of receiving him here at Court. He will be grateful for our intercession, and flattered that a nation as powerful as England still wishes to be associated with his cause. He will then be all the more disposed to sign a treaty most favourable to England. We will still be accounted a force in Europe, at no cost to ourselves.'

There was sullen agreement around the table, and Thomas was instructed to commence the negotiations he had just recommended. He was then asked how he proposed to replenish the Treasury after the massive demands made upon it by the recent debacles in alliance with Charles. He assured the meeting that he had plans afoot for *that* too, then announced that if there was no more business for the day, he was required to judge matters in Chancery that had been delayed until he was available.

Thomas hurried home, eager to advise his latest visitor that matters were progressing satisfactorily. He cast his outer robe off into George Cavendish's waiting hands, and was assured that the influential guest was still there, and being 'entertained', by Thomas's newly appointed Secretary, Stephen Gardiner, one of the most lugubrious clergymen Thomas had ever encountered.

Jean-Joachim de Passano, despite his Italian name, was a French diplomat in the service of the Dowager Queen Louise of Savoy, mother of King Francis, and he had arrived two days previously to entreat Thomas to do his utmost to persuade King Henry of England to bring pressure to bear on Charles of Spain to release Francis from his custody following his ignominious defeat at Pavia. Apart from affording Thomas an early opportunity for revenge on the Holy Roman Emperor who had thrown his weight behind a rival candidate for the Papacy, this initiative both slotted nicely into Thomas's overall policy of seeking negotiation in Europe rather than costly wars, and had also provided him with the opportunity to divert Council away from the seeming disaster of their original treaty with Charles, which was now just so much waste paper.

Joachim rose swiftly to his feet with a broad smile, which Thomas returned. 'Joachim, *mon ami*, let us drink a toast to this great venture that I have today launched on behalf of both our masters.'

Joachim almost laughed with relief as he enquired, 'Your Council, it has said yes?'

'It took little persuasion on my part, so highly is Francis regarded by King Henry, and his current difficulty occurring so soon after their recent joyful meeting in Normandy.'

'And when will you leave for Granada?' Joachim asked hopefully.

Thomas frowned. 'I cannot simply pass all my many duties to others and leave the country at their mercy, Joachim. It may well be that the next stage in the proceedings will be entrusted to one of my senior envoys, perhaps Thomas Cromwell, my trusted deputy in all such matters.' He placed an arm around Joachim's shoulder and steered him towards the roaring fire. 'Come, my friend, let us take our ease before supper, and celebrate the prospect of England once more coming to the aid of its nearest neighbour.'

If Thomas and Joachim were of one mind, Henry was less convinced. He was falling more and more under the influence of the Norfolk faction, which had now been supplemented by Thomas Boleyn. While this latter worthy could claim to have recent diplomatic experience in Paris, that was France, and Thomas had difficulty in persuading Henry that he was best advised by those who had recent experience of Charles and Spain.

After several frustrating sessions in which Henry seemed to have been primed to resist any suggestion of opening negotiations on behalf of the imprisoned Francis, Thomas began to suspect that the true reason lay elsewhere, and this suspicion was confirmed over supper a week after Joachim had left, offering to return with the Queen Dowager herself if this would move matters forward.

As Thomas was gazing into the distance, thinking deeply, one of his pages, Harry Percy, wandered through the Great Hall on his way to the servant's scullery. He was the son of the mighty Percy of Northumberland, a seasoned warrior, the hero of Henry's campaign in Flanders, and guardian of the northern borders against any marauding Scots. Young Percy had been sent to Thomas's establishment to learn all there was to learn about Courtly life and affairs of State, and being a page in the household of a man as powerful as the Lord Chancellor of England was a considerable rung on the ladder of public life.

Harry bowed slightly on his way through. Thomas raised a hand to delay him, and pointed to the chair on his left. 'Stay and take a little wine with me, Harry, for I have need of your counsel.'

'*You* have need of *my* counsel?' Harry enquired, disbelievingly.

'In some matters,' Thomas conceded. 'I am aware that when we travel to Court, in order that I may advise His Majesty, you take yourself off to consort with the Queen and her Ladies. I am also apprehensive that the Queen may be falling too much under the influence of Boleyn and his cronies, who wish to wage war on France while it is weakened by the imprisonment of King Francis by Charles of Spain, who is of course Katherine's nephew. Have you heard any conversation of this sort during your dalliance with her Ladies?'

Harry suddenly coloured deeply, and was anxious to explain himself. 'In truth, much of my time is taken up in admiring the music of Master Smeaton, who is frequently also in attendance. But this matter of which you speak — is that why John Joachim has recently been biding with us? Brings he entreaties from the French Regent?'

'None of your business,' Thomas reminded him curtly, 'and do not seek to evade my question. Is the Boleyn influence growing over the Queen?'

'Not that of Sir Thomas, so far as I have observed,' Harry assured him. 'But, as you will be aware, there is *another* Boleyn who influences the King himself.'

Thomas was well aware that, as he had gloomily predicted, Henry had taken Mary Boleyn as his mistress shortly after her marriage to William Carey, and he was regularly carousing with her here in this very building. Once more the stately London residence of the Archbishop of York had become a royal whorehouse, and Thomas dreaded those occasions when he was obliged to wither under the acid stare of Queen Katherine, who was of the belief that Thomas was conniving at it in order to increase his influence over Henry.

Thomas tutted quietly and selected a piece of chicken breast, in the hope that it would not turn to bile in his stomach, as so much rich food seemed to do these days. The cook had stern instructions to stay her hand when it came to spices, else she would be seeking a new position.

'Is there no sign of the King tiring of his latest dalliance?'

'As yet, no,' Harry replied. 'But if there be any subtle influence over the Queen from the Boleyns, it may well come from the sister, who seems altogether more silent and guarded than the twittering Mary.'

'Mary has managed to make a Queen's Lady out of her sister Anne?'

'In truth, sir, she did not require a sister to make a lady of her. She is most learned, most douce of temperament, and the least prattling of those who sit around the Queen. She has a quiet beauty, a restrained manner and the most entrancing of—'

'Yes, thank you, Harry,' Thomas interrupted him with a wave of the hand. 'When I have in mind appointing maids of honour to the Archbishop of York, I shall of course consult you,' he added sarcastically, then grinned in case he had rebuked the blushing youth too far.

'May I now go in search of my supper, sir?' Harry enquired. '

'Yes, thank you, Harry,' Thomas replied with another wave of the hand. 'You have been most helpful, and mind that you report to me if you note any further change in the Queen's manner towards the matter of which we spoke.'

As it transpired, Thomas did not have to wait long in order to test the water in that regard. At the end of a brief session with Henry, discussing certain matters of taxation, and being strongly warned by the King not to make any plans that would necessitate the calling of a Parliament that was already on the point of rebellion, Thomas was advised that Katherine wished to see him.

'For what reason, Hal?'

'How would I know?' Henry replied. 'She never speaks to me, except through my Groom of the Chamber, enquiring gently when it will be my pleasure to resume the royal marriage bed. As if *that* offered any pleasure these days!'

With trepidation, Thomas heard his arrival being announced over the gentle lute playing of Mark Smeaton, a languid, slim youth with a mop of dark hair spilling out from under his feathered bonnet as he sat in a corner coaxing a lyrical waltz from the strings. The Queen looked up over her needlepoint, and gestured with a downward cast of her eyes for Thomas to advance further into the chamber and take a seat.

As he did so, his eyes lit upon Harry Percy, seated in another corner and playing a game of chess against a young lady who would otherwise have seemed unremarkable, but for her penetrating dark eyes, which contrasted markedly with the white of her neck. Thomas had learned to play chess during his days at Oxford, and had become quite skilled; however, he had never known two opponents conduct the game with the giggles and furtive looks from under the eyebrows that were being exchanged between his page and the new arrival who must be Mary Boleyn's sister, Anne.

'My Lord Archbishop,' Katherine said coldly with the curtest of nods, 'pray tell me why it is so important to my husband that you place obstacles in the way of my nephew in his greatest moment of triumph.'

'Madame?'

'Do not "*madame*" me, My Lord Archbishop. Since we are no longer "*Tomas*" and "Katherine", you may address me as "Your Majesty".'

'Then I repeat, Your Majesty, why should you believe my motive to be solely that of thwarting the Emperor Carlos? My desire, as ever, is to best preserve England from a war it cannot afford to lose.'

'And cannot afford to *finance*, if my information be correct,' Katherine replied disdainfully. 'And the reason for that may be found in your extravagance in sending Suffolk into France with so many men, only to return with no victory to show for it.'

'There *would* have been victory, Your Majesty, had your nephew honoured his treaty obligation to come to our banner north of Paris,' Thomas countered, mentally noting that someone — almost certainly Norfolk or Boleyn — had been in her ear regarding the current state of the Exchequer.

'And is this why you persecute Carlos when even now he is basking in the glory of his victory over the French idiot?'

'What Carlos is presently engaged in, according to my latest information,' Thomas retorted, slightly red in the face, 'is a warlike progress through Italy that threatens the very Pope himself, in his citadel in Rome.'

'Carlos is a good Catholic,' Katherine assured him, 'and would do nothing to harm the Pope. But if you are so anxious on that score, and so close to his Holiness withal, why are you not there in person, defending him?'

'Because, Your Majesty,' Thomas explained patiently, 'it were better that the balance of power in Europe be maintained *between* Carlos and Francis.'

'Better for your ambition, you mean?'

'No, Your Majesty — better for England, of which you are Queen.'

Any reply that Katherine had intended became enveloped in a disdainful snort, as her eyes snapped sideways towards Mary Boleyn, whose gaze dropped to her needlepoint with the speed of a portcullis with severed chains. Katherine glared back at Thomas. 'You may leave us, My Lord Archbishop.'

Thomas needed no further invitation, and bowed his way backwards out of the presence, as protocol demanded. As he looked up, he caught a malicious smirk on the face of Mark Smeaton.

On the short wherry trip to the Exchequer, where he had urgent business, Thomas reflected on the sorry pass into which matters had been allowed to drift. Charles of Spain was positioned so as to take the remainder of Italy that was not already under his military control, Francis was languishing in some Spanish prison, England had once again played the part of the jilted bride at the altar, the nation was in financial ruin, he was out of favour with the Queen, and Henry seemed to be reluctant to follow his next advice.

Once in his Chancellor's chamber, he lost no time in sending for Thomas Cromwell, and seeking his best advice on how to replenish the Treasury without further taxing the people.

Cromwell smiled reassuringly. 'We could always seek a donation, Master.'

Thomas began to laugh, then realised that he was the only one doing so. He stared back at Cromwell in disbelief. 'Are you serious, man? There would hardly be a man in England with his wits firmly inside his head who would voluntarily hand over a groat in the King's cause at present.'

'Did I say aught about it being voluntary?' Cromwell replied. 'You, as Chancellor, are the gatekeeper to the royal prerogative, are you not? And under that prerogative, His Majesty can command all manner of support from his people in time of great national emergency?'

'And what emergency would *that* be,' Thomas demanded sceptically, 'bearing in mind that there is currently no threat to the nation, since Charles is in Italy, and Francis is his prisoner?'

'The emergency that *was*,' Cromwell explained. 'It was necessary to send troops under my lord of Suffolk to protect England during the recent wars, and that required the outlay of much money. Money which we are now obliged to recompense ourselves with, against the *next* such emergency.'

'Thomas,' Wolsey explained patiently, 'I am currently seeking to persuade Henry to petition for the release of Francis from bondage in Spain. He is currently as much of a threat to England — now or in the immediate future — as I am of besting Norfolk in the tourney.'

'And how many, apart from the members of Council, are aware of that?' Cromwell argued.

As Thomas sought hard for an answer, the smile on Cromwell's face grew broader, and he raised his eyebrows mockingly as he watched his patron struggling to reply. Instead, Thomas posed another question. 'How say you that we package this unpleasant surprise?'

'We call it a "friendly" or "loving" grant,' Cromwell suggested, 'and we make it clear that it is a once-only levy, not to be repeated annually, but is merely intended to ensure that peace continues to reign within our shores.'

'And the amount?' Thomas asked.

'A matter for you, sir,' Cromwell replied deferentially, 'but since it is just for the one occasion, one-fifth would seem appropriate.'

'Too high,' Thomas protested, 'but we must ensure that the Church is called upon to pay more than the laity, to avoid accusations that I was guarding my own bailiwick. Make it one-sixth and one-third.'

'One third?' Cromwell repeated, horror-stricken.

'Only for the Church,' Thomas reassured him. 'One sixth for everyone else. Including the nobility who have grown fat off the prosperity that so many years without invasion have granted them. As for its name, call it an "Amicable Grant for the Preservation of the Realm from Foreign Invasion", or something similar. See to it. Tomorrow, if not today.'

XIV

Thomas was too overjoyed to be as suspicious as he ought to have been when Council's opposition to his proposal to assist in securing the release of Francis of France suddenly melted. Thomas was instructed to invite Joachim and Louise of Savoy over to England, but to arrange for their arrival to be kept as secret as possible, and for any actual treaty signing to take place in a secure place outside London.

The obvious place, to Thomas, at least, was his country house in Hertfordshire known as 'The More'. It had come to Thomas as part of his 'possession' of St Albans Abbey, and was large enough to host a treaty conference in the peace and anonymity of the countryside just north of London that could be reached easily by horse in half a day. The house was largely of the red brick favoured by Thomas for his reconstruction of Hampton Court, and it boasted a massive 'long gallery' over two hundred and fifty feet in length, in which were assembled, in late August of that year, not only a coterie of diplomats proudly headed by Jean-Joachim on a return visit, but also the Regent of France during the exile of King Francis — his very able mother Louise of Savoy. She was particularly entranced to be allocated, as her lady-in-waiting, the serious-minded, restrained, ever accommodating and fluent French speaking Anne Boleyn, accompanied by her father Thomas, the former Ambassador to Paris with whom Louise was very familiar, and who she trusted implicitly.

Henry himself was present for the evening social events in the week or so during which the serious business was conducted by day, leaving the gallant King to escort the Lady

Anne onto the dance floor as the Court musicians specially imported from Westminster blew and plucked their way through several evenings of high merriment, made the more possible by the absence of the Queen, who studiedly snubbed any opportunity to mix socially with the woman she regarded as the mother of Charles's sworn enemy.

The lively brain of Thomas Cromwell was fully engaged framing into treaty language the good-natured mutual exchange of promises that flowed with the banquet wine. These were surreptitiously noted down at the time of their making by Stephen Gardiner, in his capacity at Thomas's Secretary, and in the certain knowledge that he at least would remain sufficiently sober for the task.

The eventual treaty terms were, on balance, favourable to England, since Louise's only concern was to acquire England's intercession with Charles for the release of Francis. This was promised, in return for France's undertaking never to allow a return to Scotland of the skulking Duke of Albany, who had been acting as Regent for the young James V, son of Margaret Tudor, Henry's sister, by her marriage to the late James IV. Margaret herself had taken, as her second husband, the Earl of Angus, and the resulting dispute over custody of the heir apparent had led to a renewal of the 'Auld Alliance' between Scotland and France that had the potential to completely outflank England on both its northern and southern borders.

There were other concessions on both sides, including the long-awaited return of the remainder of Mary Brandon's dowry from the brief period during which she had been the Queen of France, but there was little remaining doubt that England was now committed to negotiating with Charles for the release of Francis, and it only required the approval of Council for

Thomas or his deputy to cross the Channel to begin the process.

Thomas had expected at least a token resistance from the Norfolk faction, but thought little of it when it was simply nodded through, Norfolk himself suggesting that Thomas should ensure that he took a sufficient retinue with him to ensure both his safety and the dignity of England. When asked where his ultimate destination would be, Thomas answered, 'Wherever I may find Charles and nip his beard with the sharpness of my argument that he does his image in Europe no favours by acting as jailer to a brother monarch.'

'Will you visit Rome while you are in Italy?' Henry asked Thomas as they strolled from the meeting in muted conversation.

'I had in mind sending Gardiner to parley with his Holiness,' Thomas told him. 'You remember Stephen from our time at The More? The boring clergyman with the face of a tormented badger, and a line in conversation that would send a stone statue running for sanctuary?'

Henry chuckled. 'I would have you speak to the Pope yourself, Thomas, in order to persuade him of the continuing risk to my soul of lying with my brother's wife. I have ceased to do that, of course, as no doubt your spies have reported back to you, but I would be free to marry elsewhere, in order that the realm may be secured by the birth of a legitimate male heir. God forbid that it falls to the Princess Mary, who never seems to raise her thoughts above her psalter.'

'I had not forgotten, Hal,' Thomas reassured him, 'and you may rest assured that all my future discourse with Clement shall be with a view to impressing upon him the peril in which England stands.'

When Thomas finally left for the Continent, it was with a retinue that, for him, was modest. A pair of men bearing his two crosses, George Cavendish as his personal attendant, two English cooks to preserve his increasingly delicate stomach against foreign dishes, a confessor, several grooms and an assortment of pages. Harry Percy was not among them, as Thomas had charged him with the important duty of listening carefully to the tittle-tattle of the Queen's chambers, and committing all to memory. Finally, and against his instinct, Thomas opted to set off with Stephen Gardiner by his side, rather than Thomas Cromwell, who would be required to remain in England to monitor the success of what he had ultimately labelled the 'Amicable Grant.'

The first interview on the list would have to be with Charles of Spain, Thomas reasoned. He was, in any case, in no hurry to visit Rome, in case his Cardinal Legate status reminded Pope Clement that he was in need of secular guidance as well as the spiritual grace that came with being surrounded by priests in his Vatican bubble. The latest intelligence that Thomas gathered was that Charles was in Tuscany, planning to march south.

Three weeks later, on the outskirts of Arezzo, Thomas's relatively humble progress was halted by a column of soldiers wearing the livery of Bourbon and speaking in a rough German tongue that not even Thomas could interpret. He waved his hands in the air, and shouted in Spanish that he had urgent business with the Holy Roman Emperor, and was escorted inside the ancient town walls, where he was instructed to dismount from his horse and await further commands. He did so grumpily, complaining to Stephen Gardiner that the Emperor's hospitality seemed somewhat lacking of late.

'Have you come with an apology, that you do not advise your King to invade France at my request?' Charles demanded as Thomas was offered a seat.

'No more than I seek your apology for setting your former tutor onto the Papal throne, where he remained less than two years before you then promoted the Medici,' Thomas growled.

'As I explained to you in London,' Charles advised Thomas triumphantly, 'these things can never be guaranteed. And now you come with further tidings of the will of King Henry — what have you persuaded him to do this time?'

'He seeks the release of King Francis from your captivity.'

'Does he have the ransom available? You clearly did not bring it with you, since your saddlebags have been searched, and yielded nought of any value other than changes of garments and prayer books.'

'King Henry does not propose to pay any ransom, my lord, but urges you, as a man of compassion and a fellow monarch, to show the hand of mercy to one defeated in battle.'

Charles gazed at Thomas in curiosity. 'I am a little nonplussed that your King did not take the opportunity to take back those lands in France that have long been claimed by England. Has he not the finance to wage further war?'

'His war chest was certainly heavily depleted by the cost of having twenty thousand men under the Duke of Suffolk staring at the north gate of Paris while you came on your Italian holiday.'

Charles burst out laughing. 'Tell your King that I shall release Francis when he makes it worth my while to do so, and not when the King of England sends an ageing priest to urge me to do it. You and your party may rest here ere you return home with that message.'

'We plan to travel on to Rome, Your Excellency. I have business with his Holiness.'

'So do I, My Lord Archbishop. So do I,' Charles replied with an enigmatic smile.

Five days later, Thomas knelt before the Pope, kissed the Papal ring and was raised to his feet by the pontiff, who offered him a seat next to him in the *Stanza di Eliodoro*. As Thomas gazed in admiration at the recently completed fresco, he was aware of workmen moving in and out of the chamber, carrying small items of furniture, and the occasional staturine, out through the magnificent double doors. Pope Clement saw him looking and shook his head sadly.

'We are moving to a place of greater safety, my son. In these times, one cannot be too careful, and the contents of the Vatican are valuable beyond reckoning.'

'Safety from whom, Holiness?'

'Who else? Charles of Spain, whose title of Holy Roman Emperor does not persuade me that he has no plans to empty Rome, as he emptied Milan and Pavia. As for me, my life will be expendable enough, since Charles has it within his remit to appoint my successor ere my blood has cooled in my catafalque.'

Thomas was genuinely horrified. 'My master the King shall learn of your plight, Holiness. The will of God cannot be held ransom to the ambitions of a mere monarch!'

'A mere monarch like your King Henry?' Clement answered with a wry smile. 'He is much the same as all the others whose power comes from the strength of their army and the size of their war chests. Why would he assist me, if it suit his purpose to be allied with the Empire?'

'He does not so desire, *Magister*, and in fact I have but lately come from Charles, who refuses to have anything further to do with Henry of England. But there *is* a matter on which Henry would seek your indulgence — literally — and it may be that in return therefor he might be persuaded to declare war on Charles, should he threaten either your person or your holy office.'

'This matter has been raised with me previously, has it not? He wishes to be absolved from his marriage to the *Infanta* of Aragon?'

'Indeed he does, your Holiness. There seems little prospect of any male issue, and in the absence of same his realm is in the same peril as that which would seem to currently assail you.'

Clement shook his head sadly. 'I cannot assist in the matter, Thomas, for two reasons. The first is, as we were just discussing, I am under threat from the Queen's own nephew, who would hardly be likely to spare the Holy See, or my own unworthy person, were I to be seen to give my blessing to the ejection of his aunt from the throne of England. The second is more spiritual; the marriage of Henry and Katherine took place with Papal dispensation from my predecessor. Were I now to revoke that dispensation, it could only be on the ground that it was wrong in the first place, thereby admitting Papal fallibility. Would *you* take that step in my place?'

'We cannot be sure of the true meaning of Leviticus on the matter,' Thomas argued, to which Clement gave an ironic snort.

'Nor can I be sure of the true meaning of the Emperor as he points his army south, and until that meaning is clear, *and* I receive from you a better case than I have so far received for the dissolution of a union blessed by Rome, you must return empty-handed. And now I must prepare myself for the evening Mass that the people of Rome seem to find so comforting in these troubled times. You may, of course, take advantage of our fine *hospitium* during your stay, and your entourage will find many fine inns in the surrounding streets. So until tomorrow, *pax vobiscum, mio figlio.*'

The ringed hand was placed over Thomas's disappointed head in the act of the departing blessing, and he rose from his knees and bowed out of the chamber deep in thought. As he passed into the warm afternoon sun of the *cortile*, Gardiner was waiting for him, an anxious look on his serious face, and a scroll in his hand, which he thrust towards Thomas as he scuttled towards him.

'This arrived by fast horse from Master Cromwell not ten minutes since. The seal remains unbroken, as you can see.'

His heart pulsing harder with dread, Thomas broke the seal and read what for Thomas Cromwell was a very short communication indeed.

Master,

I urge you to return to England at your earliest. The nation is in uproar, and the King is blaming you.

XV

As the humble procession wound its way down from the crest of Southwark Hill, the entire city, with it spires and towers, was laid out before them in all its clutter, and another wave of stomach acid hit Thomas's throat. There had been something else, too, since he had left the vessel at Dover — a burning pain just below his breastbone, as if something inside him had been left out too long in the sun.

They had stopped for refreshment at a farm in Kent, and something had urged Thomas to take a pitcher of milk fresh from the cowshed, and for a while it had eased the torture. But now, as he saw the city becoming more detailed with every yard that they trotted north, and he reminded himself that his first priority must be to seek a royal audience, the pain resumed and Thomas prayed to God to take it away.

As they approached the southern end of London Bridge, they became aware of a large group of armed men in the royal livery, with the Tudor Rose prominently displayed on their tunic fronts. Two of the soldiers appeared to exchange a few words, and one of them urged his horse gently forward in order to meet them. He raised his hand to his helm in a respectful salute as he addressed Thomas.

'My Lord Chancellor?' he enquired.

'I am he,' Thomas replied apprehensively.

'Captain Ames, of the Gentlemen Yeomanry. My orders are that you and your party are to be escorted to the Tower.'

Thomas's heart lurched, and more acid hit his throat. 'Will His Majesty not grant me audience before imprisoning me?'

Captain Ames smiled reassuringly. 'You are not consigned to the Tower as a prisoner, My Lord, but for your own safety.'

'Why should a senior man of God require military protection?' Stephen Gardiner enquired from Thomas's left.

The soldier grinned. 'You have obviously been out of the city for some time. The merchants are in rebellion, and the mob has seized various of the shops and warehouses along the north bank of the river. I am to ensure that you pass over London Bridge and into the Tower via Thames Street without injury or insult to your person. Those orders come directly from the King, or so I was told.'

'How did you know that we would be returning early from our mission across the Channel?' Thomas enquired.

'Of that I have no idea,' the Captain admitted, 'but we have been positioned here for several days, awaiting your arrival. Yesterday we were visited by Master Cromwell, who was most solicitous that we treat you with all kindness. He remained with us for much of the day, then had to return to his duties at the Exchequer.'

'Very well, Captain, you must of course carry out your orders. To the Tower it is.'

Thomas was recognised before they even reached the northern stanchion of London Bridge on their progress over the oily waters of the river. Shouts went up, and obscenities were hurled at him. By the time they turned solemnly right into Thames Street that was not all that was being hurled at him. The front rank of Yeomen horsemen used their mounts to force a way through the ever thickening crowd, but by the time that they reached the Western Postern of the ancient Tower they were all but surrounded, and several foot soldiers were required to leave their posts at the gate in order to threaten the yelling mob with their halberds.

Thomas dismounted shakily, and was hurried into the White Tower. Once inside he was relieved of his travelling cape and ushered into a large downstairs room that he remembered from the days immediately after the death of the old King. Seated in its centre, with only a few royal grooms standing around him, was the present King, dark of countenance and clearly agitated at being delayed from other business. He glared at Thomas as he jerked his head in a sign that he was to take the seat next to him, and he was, by custom, the first to speak. 'Well, Thomas?'

'Well what, Your Majesty? What means this unruly rabble outside?'

'They are calling for your head, as Lord Chancellor. As well as mine, in their wilder moments. Your new tax has excited much disquiet among the city merchants and those who gain their livelihoods by them. It has also been necessary to send Norfolk north-east, in order to offer the peasants of your home country the choice between resuming their lawful trades or being hanged for treason.'

'I meant only the best, Your Majesty,' Thomas assured him meekly, aware of the haughty sneers of the Grooms of the Chamber who stood around Henry, all of them high-born and therefore most highly peeved by the 'Amicable Grant' that in their case was less than amicable.

'Well, your best has resulted in a tumult, Lord Chancellor, and there is only one strategy that I can fathom in order to put it at an end. I shall revoke the tax, and blame it entirely on you.'

'Only fitting,' Thomas mumbled, his eyes firmly on the carpet.

While his head was down, Henry turned to the grooms in attendance. 'Leave us,' he commanded.

As they melted backwards through the internal door, Thomas became aware of Henry holding a goblet of wine out towards him. Thomas shook his head. 'I have a burning malady in my gut, and fear to make it worse.'

'As you wish,' Henry replied in a more friendly tone. 'Now take a look around you, Thomas. Is this chamber not familiar?'

'Indeed, I thought it so as I entered, but more recently my mind has been taken up with other matters.'

Henry chuckled. 'You must forgive me for my stern manner just then, but it was important that word be spread abroad that I am displeased with you, and how better to broadcast it to the nation than to let it be known by those fawning popinjays?'

'Hal?'

'You may recall,' Henry continued with a distant look in his eyes, 'that it was in this very chamber some twenty years or so ago now that we sat discussing what was to be done. I was a frightened boy, fearful that the mob would tear me limb from limb, and it was you who rescued me from that fate, and gave me wise counsel that secured my throne. Today that same mob — or, more likely, their offspring — are baying for your head on a spike, and I have returned the favour which I have long owed you. But it comes at a double price. First, as I have already informed you, I intend to repeal your ill-conceived tax and to cast the entire blame on you. However, once the hated imposition is removed, it will hopefully only be your reputation that will suffer.'

'You are most gracious as ever, Hal, and I can only repeat my heartfelt sorrow that my well-meaning actions have led to this sorry pass. If there is aught else...'

'There is, Thomas, as I have already presaged. It concerns Percy's son, who is a page in your household, as I am advised.'

'He is indeed, Hal. Has he caused you some displeasure? If so, he shall be dismissed from my service forthwith.'

'He *has* caused me displeasure, Thomas, but not in the usual way. He has, it would seem, engaged in an understanding of some sort with the Lady Anne Boleyn, one of the Queen's Ladies.'

'I know of her, Hal — she is the second daughter of your Treasurer Thomas Boleyn, I believe?'

'And the niece of Norfolk, to boot. It seems that young Percy has of late been in regular attendance on the Queen and her Ladies, and has so far captured the affections of the lady in question that she has eyes for none other.'

'And there is someone you would rather that she favour?'

'There is indeed, Thomas, there is indeed. I wish you to instruct Harry Percy that his visits to the Queen's apartments must cease forthwith, and that he must make no other efforts to contact the Lady Anne. Or else.'

'It shall be as you wish, Hal. Northumberland himself is a good friend of mine, as you will be aware, and it will be as naught to prevail upon him to take the lad back north to his estates.'

'Excellent, Thomas, excellent. And now, if you wish not wine to seal this happy understanding between us, is there anything else I can summon up from the somewhat meagre kitchen of this sombre place?'

'Perhaps a pitcher of fresh milk?' Thomas said, to hoots of laughter from his royal saviour.

It was almost a week before Thomas deemed it safe to leave the security of the Tower and return to York Palace. The rest of his party had gone ahead of him on the first day, and everyone in his household, and further abroad, was aware of the shaky ground upon which he walked, although not of the more friendly conversation that had followed the formal dressing down from the King.

One of the first to seek him out after his return was Thomas Cromwell, and he began by offering his resignation.

'On what ground, Cromwell?'

'It was my folly that led to the royal displeasure.'

'It was the refusal of the people to pay your excellently conceived levy that led to the royal displeasure, Cromwell. And *you* did not introduce the cursed tax — *I* did.'

'But it was my idea, Master.'

'And an excellent one, as ever. The King has not chosen to dismiss me simply because those upon whom the tax was imposed refused to pay it. Neither, therefore, do I seek *your* dismissal.'

'You are most generous, Master,' Cromwell mumbled, his head bowed.

'And you are most loyal, and gifted withal with a fine head for matters of State. Not only that, but you have a wife and three children who depend upon you for their bread. I would not take that bread from their mouths simply because those over whom you have no control choose not to support the King during these straightened times.'

'If there is anything I can do to repay your generosity...' Cromwell stuttered, reminding Thomas of an almost identical offer he had made to Henry a week since, about which he had thus far done nothing.

'There is, Cromwell. Seek out Harry Percy, and have him attend me. Then send word to the Earl of Northumberland that I wish him to journey down here to escort his son back north. Then return to your family.'

Harry Percy made his way into the Great Hall and bowed gently, unaware of the great storm that was about to rage around him. Thomas did not, as was his custom, offer him a seat, but sat staring at him as he stood there, a picture of youthful naivety.

'What did you think you were at, Harry?' Thomas enquired by way of an opening gambit.

'My Lord?'

'It would seem,' Thomas continued, 'that while I was with the King, conducting great matters of State, you were idling away your time in the Queen's apartments.'

'Indeed I was, sir, as you are well aware, since on occasions you saw me there. The company is most agreeable, the music is excellent, and the diversions most entertaining. Should I not have taken such opportunity to acquaint myself with the protocols of Court life? Was that not why my father sent me to London?'

'Certainly for that,' Thomas conceded, 'but not in order that you might fritter away your noble title and line on some foolish girl.'

'You speak of whom, My Lord?'

'Do not dissemble with me, boy!' Thomas shouted. 'I am reliably — *very* reliably, I might add — advised that you have allowed your affections to become attached to a niece of Norfolk — and I do not mean the one who tangles the bedcovers in this very place thrice a week.'

'You speak of her sister Anne?'

'Who else? Tell me, Harry, how far has it got with this spawn of Boleyn?'

'I pray you, sir, not to speak of her in those terms. She is the sweetest, most chaste, most becoming, most gracious...'

'And most anxious to wed one of the foremost titles in the land, no doubt. What did you think you were about, you foolish coxcomb? You will, in due course, inherit one of the greatest estates in the realm, one that will command a bride from the very topmost level of English society. And although her uncle Norfolk may, in his conceit, claim to have acquired one of those by the sheer effort of being born, Boleyn, when he is not in his counting house, is but one of the King's emissaries, destined to travel Europe with the royal command in his saddlebags.'

'As are you, sir,' Harry replied unwisely.

'Silence, boy!' Thomas thundered. 'I ask again, how far has it gone?'

'In truth, sir, we have pledged our love, but no more than that. A furtive kiss once, in the corridor behind the Queen's Bedchamber, and that but fleeting. But I have pledged my heart to her, and she has assured me that there will never be another call on her affections.'

'You have not laid a hand upon her?' Thomas demanded.

Harry looked shocked. 'Sir, you insult us both by that suggestion. Our love is of the highest, the most courtly, the most chaste...'

'And the most inconvenient to the King, who wishes her for someone else.'

'Himself?'

'Have a care, Harry, for words such as that, if deemed treasonous, even *I* cannot rescue you from. All I know is that His Majesty wishes you to dissociate from this girl immediately, and have no further concourse with her. Not even of the chaste variety that you claim to have.'

'But sir, how may I bring myself to attend upon the Queen, with all her Ladies in attendance, when both the Lady Anne and I will be shielding broken hearts from the world?'

'That question is easily answered, Harry. I have sent for your father, and by the end of the week I expect him here in Westminster to accompany you back to your estates in the north.'

Harry's jaw sagged, and tears began to well in his eyes. 'I beg you, sir, not to have me removed from the very soul of my heart's desire! I am naturally most contrite, should I have occasioned some displeasure in the King, but whoever it is that he has in mind for the lady, he will never love her as truly as I. Nor, I may take the conceit to assert, will she now settle for any hand in marriage other than mine. I pray you, sir, reconsider this act of cruelty that will tear two hearts apart!'

'You may leave me now, and prepare your bags for their northern travel,' Thomas replied coldly, shaking his head at the folly of youth.

XVI

It was early March 1526, and news had just reached Thomas and the rest of the Henry's Council of the signing of the Treaty of Madrid, under which King Francis was to be released in return for two of his sons being held hostage for his good behaviour towards Spain, to which he surrendered all further claims in Italy. He also handed over Flanders, Artois and Burgundy, and agreed to take the hand of Charles's sister Eleanor in marriage.

All in all, a somewhat humiliating surrender by Francis, who had sent word to England that he wished to sign a treaty of perpetual peace. The Council were now principally met to discuss what this should contain, and who should negotiate it, but Henry was late again. Rumour had it that he had been closely closeted with Thomas Boleyn, now styled Viscount Rochford, allegedly in return for his loyal service as Treasurer of the Household. Thirty minutes after the meeting had been due to commence, Henry strolled in, his arm around Boleyn's shoulder.

'Gentlemen,' Henry announced, 'since our business today concerns the requested treaty with France, I have invited Rochford here to attend, given his many years of experience as our Ambassador to Paris. Then later he and I shall be riding to the hunt in Kent.'

Thomas was convinced in his own mind that the diplomatic duties with France were about to be allocated to Rochford, a suspicion deepened when he caught Norfolk's grin of triumph across the Council table. But, to his immense surprise and relief, Henry turned to him and asked if he would make yet another journey across the Channel on England's behalf, and leave Francis in no doubt that England was his friend.

'May we also tell him that Charles is so much our continuing enemy that we will join with Francis and his Holiness the Pope in league against him?' Thomas enquired. When eyebrows began to shoot up around the table, Thomas explained. 'I recently received an envoy from Pope Clement, seeking our support against Charles, who advances daily nearer and nearer to Rome. He would have us sign a treaty to oppose any threat upon the Holy See, and I am led to believe that similar proposals have been sent to Francis. Do I have the authority of Council to intimate our provisional agreement to such a proposal?'

'You and I will discuss this privily,' Henry interjected sharply, and it fell silent until Norfolk could no longer resist the opportunity to make further trouble for Thomas.

'I am bound to observe that thanks to the Chancellor Wolsey here, we have not the finance to enter into any alliance against Charles that would require an army.'

'That is the fault of Charles himself,' Suffolk fired back in Thomas's defence. 'Had he come to our banner outside Paris, *we* would have been the ones with our feet on Francis's throat, and we would now be in possession of those French estates through which Thomas will need to travel in order to meet with Francis.'

'That is now history,' Henry interposed, 'and our thoughts must be turned to the future. Particularly the *immediate* future, and Rochford and I have an appointment with the Master of the Hunt in Kent. Thomas, walk a little with me outside. In the meantime, this meeting of the Council is at an end.'

'Thank you for your renewed confidence in me, Hal,' Thomas murmured as Henry steered him into a far corner of the outer chamber, following a hand gesture to Boleyn that he should hold back.'

'It is not *renewed* confidence, Thomas, since it was never lost. Call it, instead, ongoing confidence. But this matter of the Pope's of which you spoke — will you have an opportunity to visit Rome, in order to pledge him our support?'

'I do not think so, although of course I could always make the time, if you deem it that important.' Thomas replied with a raised eyebrow to invite further confidences.

Henry looked furtively behind him before adding, 'I would have you tell him that he shall have England's support in return for his co-operation in the matter of an annulment of my marriage to Katherine. I wish to wed elsewhere, and that while my loins still generate offspring, preferably male.'

'I will certainly raise the matter with the French king,' Thomas assured him, 'and through him we may acquire the Pope's indulgence in your matter.'

'See that you do, Thomas. I will not take kindly to another failure like the last one.'

'It is a bad humour brought on by your incessant labours in the royal service,' the physician assured Thomas when he reluctantly sought relief for his recent complaints. 'I can of course bleed you to rid you of that humour, but you must also rest, and foreswear rich foods. And you do not require the services of a physician to tell you that you carry too much in the way of bodily flesh.'

'Am I well enough to travel?' Thomas enquired.

The physician gave him a disapproving look. 'Did I not just advise you that you must rest? If you choose to travel within the next month, you may seek the services of another physician, since I will not hazard a guess as to the likely outcome, given your current state of health.'

'And the occasional vomiting?'

'Simply your body seeking to rid itself of the bad humour. It is a good sign.'

Thomas was not the sort of man to be held back from prestigious work in the King's service by a mere stomach malady, and two days later his massive entourage held up the traffic on London Bridge by a full twenty minutes as it wove its way south, via Dover and across the Channel, to Calais, and from there down into Picardy, where they were met by a large escort of armed French soldiers, in case Charles of Spain had retained any of his German mercenary contingents on the Alsace border between their two nations.

Everywhere Thomas went, he was hailed like visiting royalty. The mayors of every town of any size, and the abbots of every monastic house of any importance, insisted on halting his progress while a laudatory ovation was read out, usually in Latin, for Thomas to graciously answer in Latin of his own.

He finally met up with Francis and his mother Louise in Amiens, where they spent two weeks in mutual protestations of love and affection, accompanied by feasts the like of which would have caused apoplexy to Thomas's physician. Then it was on to the Castle of Compiegne, where the real business of the treaty was hammered out between Thomas and the Chancellor of France.

XVII

Thomas stepped cautiously off the wherry onto the landing steps of Richmond Palace, prior to making his way slowly through the gardens. Ahead of him were his menservants, Roger and Giles Wakely, not in their usual clerical robes, but each armed with a sword and a heavy staff. They were there as a precaution, since one could not be too careful these days.

A note had been delivered by a page and handed to Thomas Cromwell with instructions that it be passed on, seal unbroken, to the Chancellor in person. Thomas had opened it, and although he could not identify the hand, it was clearly that of an educated and clear-headed individual, perhaps a woman, given the somewhat elaborate lettering. It simply read.

Please attend at Richmond Palace at noon tomorrow. Approach by way of the river walk.

Thomas began to walk through the ornate garden, remembering a day now long past when he had encountered Thomas Howard and his royal wife on one of these very avenues between the yew hedges. Ahead of him the Wakely brothers scoured the approaches, occasionally employing a wooden staff to prod through a hedge for a possible assassin. As they turned onto the first of the rose walks, they stopped and stared ahead, as if unsure whether or not to proceed. Roger inclined his head in a sign for Thomas to join them and look for himself. He did so, and there at the end of the Walk was the Queen, with several of her Ladies.

Katherine said something to her Ladies, who fell back and allowed the Queen to continue towards Thomas unaccompanied. The Wakely brothers lowered their weapons out of respect, and bowed deeply as she came within earshot. Katherine appeared to be amused as she looked directly at Thomas.

'Well met, Your Grace. Walk with me a pace, although without your handsome bodyguards, who might perhaps prefer to escort my Ladies back to the river terrace.'

As a chorus of feminine giggles confirmed that they had obeyed the royal command, Katherine turned a sterner eye towards Thomas. 'Have things reached such a pass between us that you need an armed escort to walk with me in a palace garden?' she enquired petulantly.

Thomas smiled faintly before replying, 'I had no idea who had sent the note, and I no longer recognise your writing, which I may say has improved somewhat since those days when you were mastering our quaint language. It was you who sent the note, was it not?'

'It is true that I had it sent, but the actual hand was that of Lady Norreys. I did not wish it attributed to me, should it be intercepted; I also wished our meeting to appear accidental.'

'And why would that be, Your Majesty?'

'Today we are "*Tomas*" and "Katherine".'

'My question remains,' Thomas insisted.

Katherine looked furtively behind her, then took Thomas's arm and steered him further down the path. 'I wish you to tell me why my husband has sent William Knight to Rome.'

Thomas was temporarily taken aback by the news. For once, his network of agents throughout the Court had failed him, and he was now being informed that the King's Secretary, the somewhat ageing Archdeacon of Huntingdon, and Henry's frequent choice of ambassador to the Holy Roman Emperor Charles since Thomas had come down firmly in favour of the alliance with France, had been sent on a diplomatic mission to the Pope.

He was perhaps an obvious choice, given that Pope Clement was now the virtual prisoner of his own Emperor. The previous year, to Charles's considerable embarrassment, some of the wilder German elements of his mercenary troops in Italy, being staunch followers of the heretic Luther, and owed arrears of pay, had stormed Rome and sacked it, medieval style. Clement had been wise enough to remove most of his most precious possessions in advance, as Thomas had witnessed personally, and had managed to escape to his fortress castle of Castel Sant'Angelo on the bank of the Tiber. Although Charles had publicly condemned what his troops had done, the fact remained that Pope Clement was effectively his prisoner, and would be even less inclined to grant an annulment of Henry's marriage to Charles's aunt.

Thomas was not so much concerned that Knight had been sent to Rome instead of him as the fact that he had not been consulted, and did not know why — although he could guess.

Katherine tutted in that way of hers. 'Come, *Tomas*, this is Katherine you are talking with. Do not pretend that Henry does not consult you before taking *any* action.'

'Regrettably, he seems to have done so on this occasion, Katherine.'

'Admit it, *Tomas* — he has been sent to secure a divorce in order that Henry may marry that Boleyn baggage.'

'She is already married, is she not?'

'You should know, *Tomas*, since it was you who arranged it. She is also about to give birth to her second child — please God that it is not another royal bastard. I was not referring to

Mary Boleyn anyway, since her bargaining piece became old currency many years ago. I speak of her sister, and my treacherous attendant, the Lady Anne.'

'And what of her, say you?' Thomas enquired disingenuously, earning himself a disdainful snort from Katherine.

'I was clearly wrong to hope that our old friendship might be prevailed upon to enable you to confide in the former girl to whom you showed such kindness when she was all alone in a Court that was foreign to her. I will ask you straight one more time, then leave you to admire the many fine blooms in this palace garden. Does Henry wish to put me aside and marry the Lady Anne?'

'As you have just had cause to learn,' Thomas replied diplomatically, 'His Majesty does not consult me in all things, least of all matters of the heart.'

'But matters of God?' Katherine persisted. 'I recall that we have had this conversation on a previous occasion some years ago now, but cannot the Bible be employed to argue that a marriage between a man and his sister's widow is a sin before God, and no marriage at all?'

'That depends, madame.'

'You may dissemble to "madame" if you choose, *Tomas*, but tell "Katherine" truly — if I went to Henry's bed a maid, would that make the marriage a true one in God's sight?'

'You must understand, Katherine, that there are differences of opinion even among learned clergymen as to how portions of the Bible are to be interpreted...'

'Good day, My Lord Archbishop,' Katherine hissed as she turned smartly on her heel and walked swiftly back up the Rose Walk calling for her Ladies.

It was not to be anticipated that this conversation had gone unreported, and the following morning Thomas looked up from his Chancery ledgers for the cause of the loud disturbance in the outer chamber. He barely had time to rise to his feet to investigate before the door was flung open, and Henry stormed in, slamming the door behind him. He glared at Thomas, who lumbered to his feet as quickly as he was able, bowed politely and awaited the storm.

'Why were you meeting with the Queen, Wolsey?' Henry demanded, red in the face. Thomas noted the ominous sign, and wondered which of the Queen's Ladies had reported the encounter. They had clearly been wise to make their meeting seem accidental.

'It was a chance encounter, Hal,' Thomas assured him.

'And why were you at Richmond in the first place?' Henry demanded suspiciously, 'and with your two tall henchmen searching through the shrubbery with weapons?'

Thomas had prepared for this question in advance. 'There was a report — perhaps best described as a false rumour, as it transpired — that a man had been espied with a box which he left concealed in the shrubbery, and which it was believed might contain monies concealed from the Treasurer of the Household. As Chancellor, it was clearly my duty —'

'Whatever the reason for your presence,' Henry cut him off, clearly unconvinced, 'what passed between you and the Queen?'

'Merely pleasantries, Hal, since we rarely see each other these days.'

'There is good reason for that,' Henry reminded him brusquely. 'As you are well aware, there is considerable doubt regarding the legitimacy of our marriage, and it is therefore better that we live separately. The Queen has not taken well to this decision on my part, and for the main avoids attending at Court.'

'On the matter of the marriage,' Thomas enquired gently, 'is there any news from the Archdeacon of Huntingdon?'

'Only that Charles blocks his access to Clement. He has been reduced to sending messages via the Swiss Guard, and the only replies have been to the effect that he is considering the matter.'

'It is indeed a grave matter,' Thomas agreed.

Henry looked him directly in the eye. 'How would it be were you to convene a court of all the bishops here in London, to decide the matter for yourself, Thomas? Surely, if the weight of the Church in this country was behind our request, the Pope would need to consider it very carefully, would he not?'

'I'm sure he considers it carefully even now, Hal,' Thomas sought to reassure him, 'but he is in a very difficult position, and not just on the question itself. He is of course dependent upon the good will of the Queen's own nephew to retain his head on his shoulders.'

'Bullshit, Thomas. Dissembling, mealy-mouthed bullshit. If Charles is nothing else, he is a staunch Catholic. How many Catholics could you find prepared to execute a Pope?'

Thomas bowed his head in silent agreement with the wisdom of that, but Henry was clearly in the mood to expand the matter further.

'Have we yet the finance available to launch an army into Italy? If I could free the Pope from his current "difficulty", as you choose to call it, would he not then be better disposed to my cause?'

'He might well be, Hal, but that would not change what is written in the Bible.'

'*Fuck* the Bible!' Henry thundered, causing Thomas to involuntarily cross himself. He looked up at Henry, fearful that he was to witness yet another of his wild rages, but the King seemed to appreciate the gravity of his outburst, and begged Thomas for both his pardon and his absolution. Thomas was also hoping that he had forgotten the issue of the availability of finance for an armed incursion into Italy, since the Treasury was as bankrupt as ever. Perhaps he should offer Henry *some* hope.

'I would deem it both an honour and an act of friendship to call a Church Convocation, which I may do without Canterbury's leave, given my Legatine status,' he offered. This seemed to mollify Henry somewhat, as his breathing rate returned to normal and he nodded his agreement.

'However, Thomas, in addition to the matter of the annulment of my marriage to Katherine, which of course I seek only to avoid further sinning before God, I would also seek a dispensation from his Holiness to marry again, and perhaps to a lady whose sister I have previously engaged carnally. Without such a dispensation, such a marriage would also offend God, would it not?'

Thomas was tempted to reply that it would offend Katherine even more, but managed to bide his tongue, and with some relief he saw Henry depart, somehow heartened by the knowledge that Thomas was to consult with his fellow prelates with a view to making overtures to Rome. For all the use *that* was likely to be, Thomas reminded himself gloomily.

The convocation duly met at York Place a month later, and there was little difficulty in arriving at a unanimous opinion that the Papal dispensation that had authorised the marriage of Henry and Katherine would have been invalid had it been the case that Katherine and Prince Arthur had consummated their union in the few weeks before the sweating sickness claimed the young prince's life.

The more difficult question was whether or not the same would be true if that union had not been consummated, but it was put to one side for lack of evidence one way or the other, and because opinion was divided. For some, Leviticus only condemned such a second union on the basis of the sexual activity that would, in the ordinary way of things, have occurred within the first. However, there was a minority opinion that the ban on a marriage to one who had first been married to one's sibling arose from the mere fact of the pronouncement of marriage by a clergyman ordained by God, regardless of whether or not 'carnal connection' had followed.

There was, however, little doubt that if Henry wished to marry Anne, he would need a Papal dispensation because of his prior 'knowledge' of her sister Mary. Word was sent to Pope Clement that these were the combined opinions of the Legatine Conclave of England, and that King Henry would be greatly indebted to his Holiness if he could pronounce in those terms. Clement was not, however, prepared to make such a decision personally, for two reasons. The first was that he shrank from any suggestion that his predecessor in office had been in error, and the second was the close proximity of the armed forces of the Emperor Charles, many of whom had already demonstrated their lack of ongoing respect for the Church of Rome as the result of the many abuses within it revealed in the writings of Martin Luther.

Henry was smiling as Thomas was ushered into the presence, and he waved a scroll in the air. 'You have seen this, Thomas?'

It was Thomas's turn to smile. 'Indeed I have, Hal, since it was sent first to me, and it was I who broke the seal before passing it directly to you.'

'The Pope has made us the judge in our own cause, has he not?' Henry announced triumphantly.

'Not quite, if I might urge caution on that score, Hal. He has appointed Cardinal Campeggio to sit with me in a final trial of the case, and he has undertaken that he will be bounden by it.'

'And you are in favour of an annulment, or so you have assured me these several years?'

'Thus far, I am inclined, with the majority of the senior members of the Church here in England, to believe that your cause is a just one.'

'I have heard that you take bribes in your Court of Chancery, Thomas. No, do not look so shocked, since I think naught of it at this time. But I may well incline to a different view if you cannot be persuaded to find in favour of your King, and the one who placed you where you now are. Some might call that a bribe, Thomas — I call it "a recognition of where your duties lie", and perhaps "the doorway to your continued enjoyment of those offices". Are we clear on that point?'

'We could not be clearer, Hal, and I hope not to disappoint you. But it is not just I who will be sitting in judgment, and I may not be able to persuade Campeggio to my point of view.'

'This man Campeggio, did we not appoint him Bishop of Bath when he was the Pope's Ambassador here in London?'

'You did indeed, Hal.'

'And was he not therefore one of those in your recent Conclave who found in my favour?'

'Unfortunately not, since he was not in the country at that time. Indeed, he has never presided over a single Mass in his diocese, since he remains in Italy while paying others to perform his offices.'

'As do you, by all accounts,' Henry chuckled. 'But surely, he owes his income from Bath to us, does he not?'

'He does of course, but he also owes much to Clement in recent years, most recently of course his appointment as Legate. From such offices are Popes chosen.'

'Although not in your case, Thomas,' Henry reminded him. 'Had it been so, then I would long since have been free to marry again and sire legitimate heirs. Were the Church here in England one and the same with the Church of Rome we would not be conducting this conversation.'

'Probably not,' Thomas conceded. 'On the matter of Campeggio's impending visit, I have taken the liberty of having the bishop's London house, which is generally known as Bath House, opened, fumigated and refurnished at the nation's expense, in order that he may think himself well accommodated and highly regarded during his stay.'

'Of course, Thomas. Just see to it that he is also well apprised of the ruling we are expecting from him.'

XVIII

There were months of frustrated waiting for the long-anticipated arrival, which was considerably delayed by Campeggio's latest attack of gout, and his insistence that he would not cross the Channel in anything other than a flat calm sea. Once installed in Bath House, he then demanded several weeks in which to consider the precise terms of his commission, while instructing that suitable premises be located and fitted out for what was to be a unique court hearing in England. Those premises were eventually identified and equipped in Blackfriars, to which Henry and Katherine were summoned like common litigants in a secular cause. They were also instructed to move from their respective palaces at Westminster and Richmond to premises in Bridewell closer to the place of trial.

On 18th June 1529, all was ready for the grand opening of the trial of the century, and it was attended by a host such as had never been seen before in a courtroom. Thomas and Campeggio sat on a high dais above the entire proceedings, and immediate across from them sat Henry under a Cloth of State canopy, while several feet below him sat Katherine. The various legal officers involved in the case sat vertically below the Legates, requiring that they rise from their benches and walk into the centre of the narrow courtroom before turning to address the judges.

And there was no shortage of them. The arguments for the King were entrusted to Doctors Sampson and Bell, both of whom were later rewarded with bishoprics, while Katherine was to be represented by Doctors Fisher and Standish. The proceedings began formally enough, with the call for silence and the formal reading of the Pope's commission to enquire into the validity of the royal marriage.

On an instruction from the Bench, the crier called out, somewhat unnecessarily, 'King Harry of England, come into the court, that your matter may be adjudged.' Henry acknowledged his presence, and then the call was made for Katherine. Instead of formally confirming that she was already present, she rose from her seat, walked to the centre of the courtroom, turned back, knelt immediately in front of Henry and delivered the longest speech in English that she had ever been known to utter.

With a face racked with pain and disbelief, she called out in a firm loud voice, 'Sir, I beseech you for all the love that has been between us, and for the love of God, let me have justice and right, take of me some pity and compassion, for I am a poor woman and a stranger born out of your dominion. I have here no assured friends, and much less impartial counsel. I flee to you as the head of justice in this realm.

'Wherein have I offended you, or what occasion of displeasure have I deserved against your will and pleasure, now that you intend, as I perceive, to put me from you? I take God and all the world to witness that I have been to you a true, humble and obedient wife. I loved all those who you loved, only for your sake, whether I had cause to or no, and whether they were my friends or my enemies.'

At this point she looked pointedly back up at Thomas, who almost cringed under the honesty of her stare, before she continued.

'This twenty years or more I have been your true wife, and by me you had diverse children, although it has pleased God to call them out of this world, which was no fault of mine. And when you had me first, I take God to be my judge that I was a true maid without the touch of man. And whether that be true or not, I put it to your conscience.'

A very embarrassed Henry hissed, and made signs with his hand for Katherine to rise from her knees and resume her seat, but there was no stopping her.

'If there be any just cause by the law that you can allege against me, either of dishonesty or any other impediment to banish and put me from you, I am well content to depart to my great shame and dishonour. And if there be none, then here, I most lowly beseech you, let me remain in my former estate, and receive justice at your princely hands.'

'I imagine that many a husband would like to hear such from his wife,' Campeggio muttered in Thomas's ear, but he was too busy to reply, taking in, as he was, the compelling justice of one of the finest defence cases he had ever heard pleaded.

Katherine was moving towards the closing thrust of her impassioned but cleverly structured argument. 'You may condemn me for lack of sufficient answer, since I have no impartial counsel, but such as are assigned to me, with whose wisdom and learning I am not acquainted. You must consider that these men cannot be impartial counsellors for my part, since they are your subjects and taken out of your own council beforehand, and dare not, for fear of your displeasure, disobey your will and intent, being once made aware thereof. Therefore I most humbly require you, in the way of charity and for the love of God, who is the just judge, to spare me the extremity of this new court, until I may be advised what way and order my friends in Spain will encourage me to take. And if you will not extend to me so much impartial favour, your pleasure then be fulfilled, and to God I commit my cause.'

She rose sedately to her feet with the assistance of one of her Ladies who had tears streaming down her face, but instead of returning to her allocated seat, Katherine gave a low curtsey towards Henry and walked, her head held high, towards the door of the courtroom. There was a deathly hush, only broken when Henry called upon the crier to call Katherine back into court, which he did — twice.

Katherine stopped briefly as she approached the doorway, turned round and instructed those who had gathered around her. 'On, on! It makes no difference whether I remain or not, for this is no impartial court for me, therefore I will not tarry.' And with that she swept out of the courtroom and disappeared from sight.

Henry showed every sign of having been deeply moved by what he had just heard, but with some difficulty he composed himself, rose unsteadily to his feet, and addressed Thomas and Campeggio.

'Although the Queen has departed the court, I will, in her absence, declare unto you, and also to all the lords here presently assembled, that she has been, to me, as true, obedient and conformable a wife as I could in my fancy wish or desire. She has all the virtuous qualities that ought to be in a woman of her dignity, or in any other of baser estate. She is assuredly a noble woman born, for if they were her only qualities they would well attest to her nobility.'

'I imagine that many a wife would like to hear such from her husband,' Thomas told Campeggio, before deciding that the time had come to clear his own name. He raised his hand for attention, and looked down at Henry. 'Your Majesty,' he requested, 'I most humbly beseech you to declare before this assembled company whether or not I have been the chief mover in this matter, as I am suspected of being by many gathered here today.'

Henry smiled across reassuringly. 'My Lord Cardinal, I can well excuse you of that accusation. In truth, you have, if anything, been against me in the matter. And so that no-one here assembled remains in doubt, let me apprise you of the special cause that has moved me to have this court convened. My conscience was first pricked by the French King's Ambassador, the Bishop of Bayonne, while we were negotiating the terms of a marriage treaty between my beloved daughter, the Princess Mary, and the King's second son, the Duc d'Orleans. He sought a delay in the negotiations, in order that he might advise Francis whether or not the Princess Mary was legitimate, given the marriage that had formerly taken place between the Queen Katherine and my older brother, the late Prince Arthur.

'This played strongly upon my mind, and then I took to reflecting on the fact that I might have incurred God's wrath by taking Katherine to wife, as evidenced by the fact that He has not sent me any male issue that have survived. And such a curse upon me must also be a curse upon England, which is the dearest consideration to my heart.

'I therefore thought it meet that I convene this hearing, for the sake of the realm of which I am the head and the protector, in order to test the law that governs the situation in which I find myself. I did not do so out of any carnal desire for another, or for any dislike of the noble lady whose impassioned plea you heard just now, who I would be fair content to remain wedded to for life. I first sought the learned counsel of each of the bishops and other holy men present here today, including you, my Lord of Canterbury. Is that not so?'

Archbishop Warham rose wearily onto his aged feet and nodded, before proclaiming, 'That is truth, if it so please Your Highness. And we have all placed our seals upon our consent to have this matter tried here today.'

'Not I,' came a voice from the front row of prelates.

In the ominous silence that followed, the Bishop of Rochester rose to briefly announce, 'You have not my consent to these proceedings.'

A terse argument then ensued regarding whether one of the many seals on the foot of the Convocation document was that of the Bishop of Rochester, and the faces of many of the other assembled clergymen suggested that they too wished that they had the courage to retract what Thomas had bullied them into. Henry brought it to an end by reminding the recalcitrant Bishop that he was only one among many, and that the absence of his seal did not invalidate the proceedings that were underfoot.

There was then a heated debate regarding whether or not those proceedings might continue in the absence of one of the parties. Thomas looked sideways at Campeggio, and saw the sweat rolling down from under his cardinal's cap; realising that he himself was in danger of heaving his meagre breakfast back up if he did not find some relief from the intense and suffocating atmosphere of an overcrowded courtroom on a hot summer's day, he suggested that proceedings be adjourned for the day, to which Campeggio readily agreed.

The following day the courtroom was closed to all but those directly involved. Queen Katherine had sent word that she did not intend to be present to dignify the proceedings with the appearance of a fair trial, and so Campeggio invited the advocates on both sides to outline their arguments.

Henry's main theme was the one he had already foreshadowed, namely that his marriage to Katherine was invalid, and should be annulled, because of her prior marriage to Arthur. There was some delicate enquiry as to whether or not Katherine had been correct in her assertion before God that she had been a virgin on her wedding night to Henry, and everyone on Henry's side of the argument insisted that since this was a matter that could not be established one way or the other, it must be assumed that she was not. This meant that it must be assumed that the marriage to Arthur had been consummated, in the absence of any proof of the truth of Katherine's assertion to the contrary.

At this point the Bishop of Rochester, as if he feared no retribution from Henry, rose and repeated his conviction. 'The only truth we need consider is the truth that the King and Queen were married in the sight of God, and as the Good Book says, "Whomsoever has been joined together in the sight of God, let no man put asunder." We blaspheme against God's holy ordinance by even considering this matter. If a marriage before God, conducted by one of His ordained ministers, can be declared invalid, then what value the ceremonies of marriage conducted in every church in the realm on every day of the week? We make adulterers of our fellow countrymen, and bastards of their children.'

'A pretty argument,' Thomas countered, 'but it does not fit the case. How can the marriage of Henry and Katherine have been condoned by God, if it broke His holy commandment as found in the Book of Leviticus? You cannot render holy what is unholy simply by waving a ringed hand across the heads of the sinners.'

'I was under the impression that my Lord Cardinal was one of the judges, and not the appointed proctor of the King,'

Rochester reposted sourly, and Campeggio placed a restraining arm on Thomas's sleeve, muttering 'He has a point, my friend', whereupon Thomas fell silent.

The ecclesiastical arguments for and against droned on for several more days, and to the impartial observer, if one could have been found, the merits seemed equally balanced. At the end of the second week, Campeggio suggested to Thomas that they might adjourn the proceedings for several days, to allow the parties to prepare their closing addresses, and Thomas was more than happy to concur, although his inner sense was that matters were not progressing towards a clear ruling in Henry's favour.

As he was leaving the Blackfriars building and descending the steps towards the river, intent on going home to York Palace, he heard his name being called. He turned, and there stood Thomas Howard, Duke of Norfolk, with an armed retinue.

'Have you come to push me into another puddle?' Thomas enquired wearily.

Norfolk grinned back viciously. 'Not this time, but if the matter goes against the King, my sympathy for my niece will be somewhat eased by my delight in seeing the massive puddle into which you will have pushed yourself. Good day to you, Thomas.'

XIX

Thomas was awoken from a fitful slumber by George Cavendish shaking him gently by the shoulder. 'Master, Sir Thomas Boleyn seeks to speak with you urgently.'

'What hour is it?' Thomas asked sleepily.

'It wants five of the morning, Master, but Sir Thomas insists that, regardless of the hour, he must speak with you, since he brings instructions from the King that cannot be delayed.'

'Very well, George. Allow me to acquire more garments, and to visit my closed stool, then have him admitted.'

Ten minutes later, an agitated Thomas Boleyn sat on the edge of Thomas's bed, watching George assisting him into his boots, and listening to the gentle cursing of a senior man of God. 'It is not I who wishes this, but His Majesty, you understand?'

'Whichever,' Thomas replied grumpily, 'it is no more likely to meet with success than our venture in the court.'

'Nevertheless, it is the King's command, and I have played my part by bringing you his instruction. I must now depart for Hever.'

'Pray give my regards to she who is at the root of all this upheaval,' Thomas muttered sarcastically.

Boleyn smiled thinly. 'She is currently at Richmond, although daily she expects to be dismissed from the Queen's service. She sends her best wishes that your enterprise may thrive.'

'No doubt she does, My Lord, but I will pray daily that she does not meet the same fate as the tragic lady upon whom I shall be calling within the hour. But the blame for this lies not just with her, for she is the hand puppet of others such as yourself and Norfolk. Between you, you have caused the greatest disorder in the nation, for which you will be held accountable one day. Depend upon it, you will reap little reward, either in this world or in Heaven, for the mischief which you have wrought upon the realm. Should I fall from the King's favour through all this, mark my words that the next spent corpse to land upon me in the same hole will be yours.'

'I have delivered my message, My Lord Archbishop, as this worthy gentleman here can testify, and so now I take my leave,' Boleyn replied coldly as he bowed and left.

Thomas travelled uneasily to Bath Place shortly after Boleyn's departure, having declined all attempts by Gorge Cavendish to get him to eat or drink something. Thomas was aware that anything he consumed would come straight back up, and the renewed burning just below his breastbone, which had kept him awake intermittently through the night, warned him that anything that progressed beyond his throat would not be welcome.

At Bath Place he collected Campeggio, and assured him that he was neither sleepwalking nor deranged, but that if Thomas Boleyn was to be believed, it was the King's command that they travel to the Bridewell in an attempt to persuade Queen Katherine to abandon her cause and concede that her marriage to Henry had been a sin before God.

They were shown into the Audience Chamber at her lodgings, and a protesting Lady Norreys went gently into the bedchamber to awake her royal mistress. Katherine emerged in her nightgown, with a robe demurely wrapped around it, wiping the sleep from her eyes and attempting to straighten her tousled hair.

'What is so urgent, My Lords? I have not yet heard Mass.'

'Neither have I,' Thomas replied ruefully, 'and I would venture a wager that neither has Campeggio here. But we come on the King's urging.'

'With an apology for the wicked way in which he has humiliated me before all the nobles of the realm? Since you come not with a company of armed men, I perceive that I am not to be conveyed forthwith to the Tower for my treason in defending my honour against vile slanders. Nor do I intend to end my own life by falling on a bodkin — so what is it that His Majesty requires of me *this* time?'

Campeggio glanced sideways at Thomas, who cleared his throat in embarrassment, and explained, 'It is Henry's wish that you declare your defence in the matter, that it may proceed to judgment; we may also give you, privately, our opinion regarding the justice of your cause.'

Katherine's face set obstinately as she looked from one to the other. 'I think that, insofar as I am capable, I made my case very plain, my Lords. It is simply this, that since I went to my marriage bed a maid, untouched in particular by the late Prince Arthur, there can be no question of any sin before God. I lost my maidenhead to His Majesty, and to none other, and my body has thereafter remained solely for his ease and comfort, and — if I may say so without causing a blush on the countenances of two men of God — for my pleasure, out of which have been born several children. It is not for me to fathom the will of God, as to why all but one of those infants was taken from us. But it owed naught to the Book of Leviticus, of that I can assure you.'

'But madam,' Thomas pointed out, 'if your defence be based on such ground, wherein lies the proof?'

Katherine glared at him angrily. 'Other than the oath of one who fears God? Or should I have kept the bloodstained sheets?'

'We are bound to advise you,' Campeggio ventured, 'that absent of such proof, and should His Majesty swear to the contrary, your case lies uneasily.'

'But not my conscience, My Lord Cardinal,' Katherine replied starchily. 'And should His Majesty choose to peril his soul by swearing falsely, then likely we shall not be reunited in Heaven.'

'But you must see our dilemma,' Campeggio argued.

Katherine pierced him with a stony stare before replying, 'Do not waste your breath, and delay my hearing of Mass, by attempting to explain to me that it will be your decision to give Henry what he wants. To that I am resigned, and I would ask only that I be allowed to withdraw from the public gaze, both to hide my embarrassment and to further commend my soul to God.'

'You would accept banishment to a nunnery perhaps?' Thomas enquired optimistically, provoking a torrent of obscenities in Spanish that even caused the multi-lingual Campeggio to blush. Then Katherine waved her hand in a dismissive gesture, and both men bowed, as if to leave the presence.

'Not you, *Tomas*,' Katherine ordered him. 'But your fellow conspirator may withdraw, as may all my ladies except Mary Norreys. *Now*!'

As the remainder bowed gratefully from the royal displeasure, Thomas remained uncomfortably in the centre of the Audience Chamber, swallowing down yet another instalment of bile. Katherine saw his obvious discomfort, and waved him into a chair as she took the one next to his, and indicated that Lady Norreys might also be seated behind her. Then she looked more kindly across at Thomas.

'I asked that Lady Norreys remain in order that there might be a witness to what I have to say — also that it might not be misreported, sad to relate. My Lord Archbishop, wearing your Lord Chancellor's hat, and not that ridiculous red bonnet that makes you look like a self-satisfied rooster, what think you privately of what I had to say in your court?'

'Katherine,' Thomas replied softly, 'it was in truth one of the most moving defences I have ever listened to. Had I not been one of your judges, it would have caused my eyes to water.'

'But would that water have fertilised your conscience, my old friend?' Katherine asked with all the sympathy she could muster, 'or is it the case that you will pursue Henry's will to your own downfall?'

'Meaning?'

Katherine reached out and touched his hot hand with her own cool fingers as she looked him firmly in the eye, with an expression that reminded him of that of his physician warning him off rich foods. 'When I was a child in Lisbon, the sailors on the wharves had a saying. It was "Kill the rat and starve the flea". Do you comprehend its meaning?'

'I believe so,' Thomas replied sadly, 'and I fear that it is apt to my situation.'

'You understand that I speak only by way of analogy? I do not compare my dear husband to a rat — it is the evil course on which he has been directed by others that is the rat in my imagery. But you, *Tomas*, are the flea that feeds off that rat. Henry is determined to be rid of me, that he may marry his latest harlot, and should he fail in that his rage will be terrible. Those who fail him will surely feel that wrath, and when you can no longer supply him with what he needs, your cause will also be lost. You are aware, no doubt, that you have enemies at Court?'

'Only too well,' Thomas replied ruefully. 'But methinks that they also are feeding off the same cause.'

'Indeed they are, *Tomas*, but they *are* the cause, and they will prevail. I retain no doubt that Henry will put me aside, one way or the other, and that he will bed the Boleyn girl — the second of them, that is. She may well become the Queen of England in her turn, but all my desire and energy is now directed to the fate of my beloved daughter, the Princess Mary. I would sooner cut off my right hand than have her declared illegitimate, and it is for her, and her alone, that I maintain what to you must seem like a futile and stubborn resistance to Henry's desires. For myself, I would gladly become a holy sister, but I must — as ever I have done — think of others. Yourself included.'

'Katherine?'

'You must do what you must to ensure that Henry gets his wish, else you will be ruined, *Tomas*. I wished to speak with you thus, in private, to assure you in advance of my forgiveness for what you are about to do, without abandoning my defence in other ears. You once loved me, *Tomas*, and I still have a fond memory in my heart of the kindness that you showed me when first I became Queen. And so I warn you of what will happen if your efforts do not bear fruit for Henry, and to assure you that I bear you no ill will if they do. Now you may leave me to hear my Mass.'

Thomas rejoined Campeggio in the front entrance, and explained away the redness around his eyes as a lifelong affliction.

Just over a week later, Thomas and Campeggio announced that they had reached a decision. The courtroom was crowded to overflowing as Henry took his place in a special gallery that had been hastily constructed to one side, where he might clearly hear the judgment being handed down without the need to join the sweaty and eager crowd beneath him. There was considerable frustration when Campeggio insisted on reading out the judgment in Latin, a tongue unfamiliar to some of those assembled, and capable of misinterpretation even by those who professed skill in the language.

After he had finished, there were anguished calls for a translation, and when Campeggio nodded his consent, Thomas cleared his throat and began. 'The Cardinal Legate Campeggio declares that he is unable to give a ruling in the cause without first seeking the guidance of his Holiness the Pope.'

He was almost drowned out by howls of protest and disappointment. He waited until the worst of it had subsided, then raised his voice to be heard further.

'He adds that the eyes of the world are upon the outcome of this matter, given the exalted status of the parties and the conflict in evidence. We have both sat here for several weeks as emissaries of his Holiness, and it is to him that we must refer this most difficult of matters. We are not here to please either party, regardless of how mighty they might be in the estimation of others. We are here, rather, to see the will of God upheld, and we would not perjure our souls this close to death by making any false judgment in the matter. This court therefore stands adjourned for the time being, until we receive the counsel of he who granted us our commission in the matter.'

'Shame!' 'A waste of time and money!' 'Back to where we began!' came voices of protest, as Henry was seen to depart swiftly from his gallery. He was out of both sight and earshot when one voice louder, and more angry, than the rest, cut through the hubbub of confusion and frustration. 'It was never merry in England whilst we had Cardinals among us!'

It suddenly fell silent, and the crowd parted to reveal the irate, red face of Charles Brandon, Duke of Suffolk. Campeggio opened his mouth to speak, but Thomas placed a restraining hand on his arm and spoke for both of them.

'My Lord of Suffolk,' he reminded him, 'you above all have cause to be grateful to at least one Cardinal. Upon your return from France with your new bride, without the intercession of *this* Cardinal, lowly though he may be in your estimation, your head would no longer rest upon your shoulders. Without a head, you would have possessed no tongue with which to slander us in public in this wise, when we have done no more than perform the will of his Holiness the Pope, at the request of Henry the King. The same King who spared your head from the block.

'Tell me, my lord, if you were sent as an emissary of King Henry to some foreign court, and were there placed in a quandary as to where lay His Majesty's best interests, would you not deem it fit to refer the matter back to him for his final judgment? Why, then, do you defame us, who only perform our duty to the one who has appointed us on *this* mission? Fie, my lord — speak you more peacefully to those who seek only to pursue a cause first raised by he to whom you owe your head.'

Suffolk opened his mouth, as if framing a retort, but instead closed it again and hastened out of court with his head down.

Matters were even further delayed when the Pope let it be known that he would postpone any final decision until his own courts were in session, which was months away. Henry opted to send his secretary, Dr Stephens, to Rome with a polite request to get on with it, and then stunned everyone by demanding that Queen Katherine remove herself from Court. She did so, and spent several months in various convents in and around London, separated from her daughter Mary, but not before she had formally dismissed Anne Boleyn from her service so that she had no legitimate reason to remain at Court. Henry responded by commencing a royal progress with the Lady Anne in tow, and by early October they were resident at Grafton Manor, in Northamptonshire, which Henry had purchased only three years previously.

It was to this somewhat inadequate residence that Thomas and Campeggio were summoned, after Dr Stephens had returned with the depressing news that his Holiness intended to take such time as such a grave matter merited, and Campeggio was seeking leave to depart England in order to return to Rome. Thomas had no doubt that he would do so with further instructions from Henry, and that the Papal Legate would be graciously received and royally entertained at Grafton. This belief was confirmed when Campeggio and he were welcomed in the courtyard of the ancient pile with all due ceremony, and Campeggio was escorted to the chambers that Henry had ordered to be prepared for him. However, Thomas was considerably taken aback when the Groom of the Stool, Harry Norreys, explained to him with a red face that such was the cramped accommodation within the somewhat crumbling edifice that Henry was in the process of restoring that no rooms had been allocated to Thomas. However, Harry Norreys graciously offered Thomas his own, and Thomas accepted, not wishing to be publicly excluded from whatever inner circle was foregathered there.

Thomas was even more put out when he entered the Great Hall for supper, and noted that both the other Thomases, Boleyn and Howard, were already there ahead of him, and were no doubt accommodated in better chambers that his. Boleyn smiled like a serpent about to strike as he welcomed Thomas over to the board and gestured for him to take a seat.

Norfolk looked up from a leg of pork that he was hacking lumps off, and growled, 'I am surprised that you dared show your face in here.'

'We were summoned by the King,' Thomas assured him. 'Campeggio will no doubt join us shortly, but is apparently being shown around the grounds ere sunset. He seeks leave to return to Rome, and not before time, since it would seem that Dr Stephens was sent packing by his Holiness.'

'He may not be the only servant of God sent packing,' Norfolk sneered as he swigged from a goblet to wash down the meat, then nodded towards the remains of the roast suckling. 'Help yourself, Thomas. As your experienced eyes will tell you, it is an excellent side. Perhaps you will be allowed to go back to your true trade, now that it would seem that you prosper not as a purveyor of His Majesty's will. We have been taking wagers on whether or not you will be allowed to retain your head.'

'If you wagered with your heart rather than *your* head, I need hardly ask where your money has been hazarded,' Thomas responded, just as Henry entered with Campeggio. Everyone began to rise, but he gestured them back into their seats.

'I have but lately taken supper in my chambers with the Lady Anne, but I will take some of that wine, if you have left any.'

A page hastened to fill a goblet and hand it to the King, who raised it in the air.

'A toast to the Cardinal Legate Campeggio, who laboured long and hard to find a legal solution where one cannot apparently be found. But it is no matter, since it would seem that Queen Katherine has deigned to raise her ample arse from the throne. So where do *you* intend to go, Wolsey, to hide from my displeasure?'

Thomas quickly surmised that Henry was very drunk, and would need very tactful handling. 'To wherever Your Majesty deems it appropriate, as ever. I thought perhaps my benefice of Winchester.'

'Why not York, where you have never yet set foot?' Norfolk suggested. 'Winchester may not be far enough away, I suspect.'

Henry laughed loudly, and Thomas wanted the carpet to open up beneath him. Henry belched and swayed slightly, as he grimaced back at Thomas. 'It will certainly not be Rome, at any hazard,' he joked, and everyone around him laughed politely. Then he turned to Campeggio. 'My apologies, my Lord Cardinal, but as you will have gathered, we are not well pleased with our Archbishop of York here. However, our displeasure does not extend to you, even though it was not possible for you to arrive alone at a judgment that would have pleased us beyond measure. We shall hope that you have better fortune upon your return to Rome. When do you plan to leave us?'

'I had perhaps thought the day following tomorrow,' Campeggio replied in his slightly strained English. 'Thomas has very kindly offered for me to lodge one night at his house at The More as I journey south.'

'You might be well advised to take up that offer while he still has those premises at his disposal,' Henry replied with a sidelong glare at Thomas. 'However, I must not keep the Lady Anne waiting any longer. I came down merely in order to ensure that you make our honoured guest welcome, gentlemen. As for our *dishonoured* guest, you may make of him what you will.'

With that he turned slightly unsteadily on his heel and lurched out, leaving Norfolk with a huge grin across his gloating countenance, Boleyn with a worried frown, and Thomas with an intense desire to vomit out of sheer terror, even though he had not eaten for two days. He spent a further two hours sitting uncomfortably at board while others around him gorged on roasts, nibbling at small pieces of fish and praying that they would stay down. Then he excused himself on the ground of his tiredness after his journey, and fell to his knees before the portable cross in his chamber, praying for deliverance from an evil that was not of his making or design.

XX

The next morning Thomas was taking the air in the ornamental garden to the rear of the house when he heard a footfall behind him, and turned to see Henry approaching. He bowed deeply, and mentally prepared himself for more of the royal sarcasm. Instead, Henry took his arm and raised him upright with a smile of contrition.

'Forgive me, my dear friend, but I was very drunk. I was under the influence of a fine Burgundy, a beautiful lady and her vengeful uncle.'

'It is I who must apologise, Hal,' Thomas admitted, 'for my failure to deliver what you most wanted.'

'What I most want is lodged upstairs, Thomas, as you are well aware. It bears hard upon me, to have her so close, yet not close enough. But it was not your fault that the matter was left to his Holiness, as I keep explaining to those who prevail upon me to blame it all on you.'

'Norfolk was ever ill disposed towards me,' Thomas replied bitterly, 'ever since I bested him at school. You are fortunate indeed that Norfolk fights your battles on the field, while I fight them in chambers. Were it the other way around, you would be most badly served.'

'Yet it is no longer simply Norfolk,' Henry explained. 'For some reason, the Lady Anne loves you not, and whatever she wants, her doting father will obtain for her.'

'That is easily explained, Hal,' Thomas said. 'You may recall that I had occasion to banish Harry Percy from my service, and request that his father remove him north, safely away from his infatuation with the lady. She, it would seem, in her girlish

218

innocence, took badly against me for that, yet if she did but realise it I thereby left her free for a far better prospect.'

'Was she *really* enamoured of Percy, Thomas?'

'As a man of God, I cannot judge maidenly infatuation, Hal, but I have since heard that she cursed me up hill and down dale. There is little wonder now that she seeks to revenge herself upon me, when I am so vulnerable. And of course Norfolk is her uncle, and I fear that he plays upon her mind in order to best me at every turn.'

'I must speak frankly with you, Thomas, since I owe you so much in my life thus far. I am urged by Anne, and by Norfolk, to have you impeached for treason. They say you are in league with England's enemies.'

Thomas laughed out loud, then froze when he saw Henry draw a parchment from his doublet, and he recognised his broken seal on it. Henry handed it across with the hurt expression of someone who has been betrayed. 'This was found in Campeggio's bag when it was being searched on his arrival. By now he is no doubt noting its loss, but please tell me true, Thomas — is this your hand?'

Thomas could not look him in the face, try though he might, and despite the fact that his life might depend on convincing Henry that he meant no treason by it. 'Yes, Hal. It is my hand.'

'You were seeking audience with Charles of Spain, our sworn enemy, and the Queen's nephew, at a time when we so dearly need the friendship of France and a lack of impediment to an annulment? Please explain why that could not be seen as treason?'

'Only by someone who wishes me ill, and has not the faith in me that I hope I have earned from you over the years.'

'Then pray tell me, what were you about?'

'I sought to prevail upon him to influence the Pope, so as to speed the process of the annulment, hopefully in its favour.'

'Truly, Thomas?'

'Truly, on my immortal soul. Why else would I seek audience with a man who has twice humiliated me in the face of Christendom?'

'That is why I ask the question, Thomas. You once sought to be Pope, did you not?'

'That was several years ago now,' Thomas protested. 'It was while we were still negotiating with him against Francis. And it was he who offered to influence the election, if I could sway you to his will.'

'So you were prepared to be bribed in the execution of your duties toward me?'

'No, Hal! It was offered to me only *after* the agreement had been brokered. This I swear!'

Henry looked disappointed, and turned to walk back to the house. Then on a whim he turned to address Thomas again. 'Have a care, my old friend. Inside yon house are those who would encompass your downfall, and by your past actions you have exposed yourself to accusations. It is only because of our long-standing friendship, and because I owe you so much from those days in which I was uncertain of my new role, that I am prepared to accept your word on this occasion. But please do not stretch that friendship any further, Thomas — it makes it very difficult to resist the urgings of those I now hold dear that you should be stripped of your offices, and perhaps worse.'

'The Lady Anne?'

'She certainly, but only on the urgings of Norfolk and her father, I suspect. But regardless of who may lie behind it, Thomas — have a care.'

'I will, Hal — and thank you.'

The following night, Thomas was roused from a deep slumber by George Cavendish knocking on his chamber door.

'What is it, George? Are we on fire?'

'Not yet, master, but Norfolk and Suffolk demand to see you.'

'At this hour? Are they drunk?'

'Not so far as I could deduce, master.'

'We must remedy that, George. Serve them wine, and tell them that I shall be out presently.'

Ten minutes later, Thomas entered the main hall down the stairs from his bedchamber, dressed in his Cardinal's robes.

Norfolk lowered his wine goblet and sneered. 'We are not here to hear Mass, butcher's boy! Hand over your seal of office!'

'I beg your pardon?' Thomas enquired with nervous dignity.

Norfolk was clearly not in the mood to be trifled with. 'If you would take that stupid fucking red bonnet from round your ears, you might hear me more clearly. The King demands that you hand over the Chancellor's seal.'

'And you have his hand on that? Some written token of your authority?'

'We come direct from the King,' Suffolk told him more calmly, 'and we are commanded to bring back the Chancellor's seal.'

'Charles,' Thomas replied with more confidence than he felt, 'were I to hand over my great seal of office — the seal of the nation of England that I have proudly served these twenty years — I would be accounted one guilty of high treason, which is no doubt Norfolk's intent. Bring me your written authority, else I shall hand over nothing.'

'You will be accounted treasonous ere long anyway,' Norfolk snapped, 'so save us the time and effort of returning with the

King's command under his own hand, and just give us the fucking thing!'

'I will when I receive the King's written authority to do so.'

Norfolk flung his goblet at the wall and turned on his heel. Suffolk followed meekly behind him, and as they reached the doorway, Norfolk turned. 'I forgot to mention that Henry also requires that you vacate this palace forthwith, and take yourself off to your house at Esher, which goes with your Bishopric of Winchester. The same no doubt goes for Hampton, which the King was mightily displeased to learn had been built with monies that belonged to him.'

'Another of your lies, Norfolk?' Thomas defied him.

Norfolk's countenance was approaching purple. 'This at least is no lie. We shall return upon the morrow — see to it that you are in all ways ready to flit. And next time, serve us better wine than that nun's piss!'

The next day Thomas's Treasurer of the Household, William Gascoigne, had almost disappeared inside the mountain of hangings, linen, plate, statuary and books in the centre of the main hall of York Palace that Thomas had ordered out from every cupboard and other storage place in the entire building. William was standing there, armed with a vellum scroll and a quill that he kept dipping into an ink pot as he stood in its midst with a frown, endeavouring to list it all as pages and grooms kept adding to the pile.

'If this sale is open to the general public, I am in need of more plate,' came a jocular voice behind him, and Thomas turned and walked forward to embrace Thomas Cromwell.

'It is no sale, Thomas, but an accounting to the King, who by the gleeful hand of Norfolk commands me to make this ecclesiastical house his property, along with all that is in it. I expect Norfolk to return shortly with the official document, and I wish it to be obvious when he does so that I am well ahead of him in my anxiety to do the King's bidding.'

'It is rumoured throughout the city that you have been ordered to the Tower,' Cromwell advised him gloomily.

Thomas smiled weakly. 'If so, then it is via Esher, since I am commanded to take up my residence in the London dwelling that comes with my Bishopric of Winchester. Will you attend me there?'

'Too close to Putney for my tastes,' Cromwell replied with a look of disgust.

'Forgive me, Cromwell,' Thomas replied, 'for I had forgotten that you, like me, were base-born. But at least I was raised in a market town in the countryside, and not a blacksmith's forge.'

'It was also an alehouse,' Cromwell reminisced, 'whose landlord kicked and beat me after enjoying too much of his own hospitality. Enough of him, ere I puke to his memory. Do you wish me, as my first duty of the day, to check the inventory that seems to be overwhelming poor William over there?'

'Do you still wish to serve one who has fallen from Henry's grace?' Thomas enquired, a tear forming in the corner of his eye.

'And why would I not? You raised me thus far, although it may only have been to rid yourself of Gardiner's gloomy company. Now that he is safely consigned to the task of terrorising his parishioners in the West Country, who else but your new Secretary is best fitted to ensure that His Majesty is not defrauded of a single piss-pot?'

There was a loud disturbance in the doorway as Norfolk blustered in with a triumphant smirk, waving a small vellum. 'Here you are, "Doubting Thomas". The King's hand on your removal from this whorehouse of your making. Take this paper, read it, then shove it up your fat arse. Good day to you also, Cromwell. Are you here for the pickings?'

'No, I am here about my duties.'

'Why does a fallen priest require a man of your abilities, Cromwell? When you have come to your senses, and realise where your true future may be found, we could have work for you in Westminster.'

'For the time being I am content with my current duties,' Cromwell replied coolly, 'which on this occasion require that I ensure that His Majesty receives all that to which he is entitled. He is no stranger to this house, or so I am advised. Perhaps that was *before* it became a whorehouse.'

Norfolk merely smirked. 'I see that you share your master's desire for a very public execution. Shall I advise King Henry that Tower Green must be prepared to dispatch not just the dog but the flea that resides on it?'

'Here you are, Norfolk,' Thomas said by way of intervention before matters got any worse. He solemnly removed the chain with the Great Seal from around his neck and held it out for Norfolk to take. 'Tell His Majesty that not a single item remains unaccounted for, since the dog is an honest one, and his flea is most adept at compiling inventories.'

Norfolk withdrew with a malicious chuckle, and Thomas shook his head at his impetuous Secretary. 'Cromwell, you must guard that impish wit of yours, if you are to survive without me. And survive without me you must, if Norfolk and his cronies get their dearest desire. Now tell me, to whom will the Chancellor's seal be handed?'

'There is as yet no formal notice, but Palace rumour has it that it will go to Thomas More. If so, he and Henry will soon be at odds, if the King allows the Lady Anne to sway him to her Lollard sympathies. I own that I too share them, but if it were left to More we would be saying Mass every hour, and every household would be blessed with a likeness of the Pope in every room.'

'A strange choice indeed, for a King who currently has no love for Rome,' Thomas agreed. 'More was most aggrieved when I closed those monastic houses that had turned into whorehouses, and he is unlikely to think too highly of you, after the assistance you rendered to me in that regard. Have a care, Cromwell.'

'This from a man who is rumoured to have one foot on Tower Hill already!' Cromwell joked. 'But when I have finished with this inventory, do you wish me to put aside old memories and accompany you up-river?'

'If you would be so good that would be greatly appreciated. You might also see to the safe transfer of all my household, or at least such of them as wish to move to Esher. I fear that the house will not accommodate them all, and as for its fittings and accoutrements, I apprehend that they will be less than adequate.'

'I feel sure that, like me, they will follow wherever you lead, Master. There was a time I swore that before I ever set foot within five leagues of Putney I would pull out my own eyes, but here I go. And if I can do that, what of those for whom it has not such terrible memories?'

'You are the most constant of companions, Cromwell. Come, let us make our way down to the private steps where, hopefully, I still have a wherry and a bargeman.'

Ten minutes later, Thomas hesitated on the topmost step, the barge awaiting him a few feet down, and gazed out into the stream. 'Are my eyes betraying me, or is the river much busier today than it is wont to be at this hour?'

'Your eyes do not betray you, Master,' Cromwell replied sadly, 'but your former admirers and flatterers do. Since daybreak there have been vessels waffeting up and down this stretch, hoping for the sight of you being escorted to the Tower.'

'Is that a mark of my unpopularity?'

'No, Master, it is a mark of the King's inconstancy. Here, let me take your arm.'

'Thus far but no further,' Thomas instructed him gently as he sat in the vessel and signalled for the boatman not to push away from the steps. 'I would not be the cause of your returning grief at the sight of the unhappy scenes of your childhood, and no more would I have you pluck out your own eyes. You have served me truly, and I ask only that you send me word by messenger of how you go, and how I am spoken of at Court. Can you grant me that undertaking?'

'Gladly, Master. I intend to seek a seat in the Parliament, where I shall ever make it my business to ensure that your reputation is treated with the reverence it deserves. If I might make one brief request, ere I step back ashore. Would you bless me and my family?'

'With all my heart, Cromwell. Bend your head, that I need not attempt to stand in this swaying vessel that is so beset by the waves caused by all these other craft that contain gawpers at my downfall who shall shortly be disappointed.'

Cromwell bowed his head and received the blessing, then, with tears rolling down his face he stepped ashore, and Thomas gave the order to cast off.

George Cavendish had taken the long way round, via London Bridge, along with the horses and Thomas's mule. Thomas mounted with assistance from Giles Wakely, and they began the last stage of the journey, up the gentle slope between garden butts. At the top of the slope were a tangled collection of houses, a church and several commercial premises. Long before they reached the top, a rider could be seen coming hard down the road from Richmond, and Thomas raised his hand to halt the humble procession.

'Is that someone come to escort me into the Tower?' he enquired nervously.

'I think not,' George Cavendish replied as he shielded his eyes against the noonday sun. 'else they would have taken you when we first took to the water. Rather it is some emissary from the Palace.'

He was proved right when the rider drew closer, and Thomas recognised Sir Henry Norreys, who dismounted when he reached them, and bowed gently to Thomas as he held something out in his hand.

'From His Majesty,' he announced. 'He commends himself to Your Grace, and asks that you be of good cheer, for you are as much in his favour as ever you were, and he sends this token thereof.'

Thomas reached out and took the gold ring, set with a rich ruby. Tears began to well in his eyes as he recognised the jewel, which was the special token that he and Henry exchanged whenever they sought to confirm that the message was a genuine one, and of some importance. Through his welling tears he heard the rest of Norreys's message.

'His Majesty bid me assure you that even though you probably regard yourself as unkindly done by, his actions do not arise from his displeasure, but are simply at the urgings of others of whom you are aware, and who are not kindly disposed towards you. He bid me tell you that you will be recompensed for the loss of your goods at twice their value, and that you will want for nothing, even though your abode shall be more humble for a brief while, until the storm against you subsides. Therefore take heart, show patience, and be of good cheer.'

Through his tears, Thomas knelt on the ground and removed his velvet under-cap to remain bareheaded as he mumbled a prayer. Then he looked back up at Norreys and begged his forgiveness, adding, 'A sudden joy overcame me that was no respecter of time or place, and I thought it my bounden duty to render thanks to God for this joyful news from he whom I most revere in this earthly life.'

Norreys knelt down beside him and placed a consoling arm across his shoulder. 'Forgive my forward behaviour, My Lord Cardinal, but it saddens me to see you treated in this fashion, after all the comfort you have given to His Majesty, and to Queen Katherine, these many years.'

'How goes Katherine, say you?' Thomas enquired.

Norreys sighed. 'They say she will not eat, and has sworn to die of starvation until she be reunited with the Lady Mary, who is kept close confined at Richmond, though word is that she is shortly to be sent north.'

'It is sad, is it not?' Thomas responded.

Norreys's face clouded over as he sought an appropriate response. 'For myself as a man, I would have to concur, Your Grace. But as a Courtier I keep such opinions to myself. And now if you would forgive me, I must return to the Palace ere the sun begins to sink. These lanes are not safe after dark.'

Thomas fiddled inside his robes, and when he removed his hand it contained a small gold chain with a cross attached. He handed it to Norreys, with instructions that it be passed on to Henry. 'It is said to contain a sliver of the true cross, and I have worn it next to my skin these many years past. In better times I would not have parted with it for any price, or to any

228

man, but today it would seem most apt that I pass it on to my dear friend Hal. Tell him that it is my dearest possession, next to the memories I keep in my heart of happier days in his company. And so, pray take your leave, good Sir Harry, and mind to mention me kindly to your sovereign.'

XXI

Thomas Wolsey looked up joyfully from his sparsely loaded board, and his eyes widened in delight as he hurried across from the table to embrace Cromwell. 'Well met, my dear Cromwell. As you see, I make a scant early supper, but you are welcome to share it, if you enjoy fish. It is all that my rebellious stomach will accept these days, and then not always. But why are you here? Surely my letters are adequate, and I know that you wished not to revisit Putney.'

'I came by way of Hampton,' Cromwell told him, 'where I was fortunate in that your bargeman still plies his trade privately. From thence across river, where I was able to hire a sorry nag that is currently enjoying the hospitality of your stables. But had I been required to ride right through the ghost of my father, I could not foreswear this visit.'

'Be seated, Cromwell, and partake of some wine, ere you tell me what is so urgent. Am I for the Tower?'

'Not yet,' Cromwell assured him as he accepted the cup handed to him by a page, the state of whose livery suggested that the laundry facilities at Esher were non-existent, 'but I come to warn you, in two ways. The first is that all our correspondence is almost certainly intercepted by those in Norfolk's pay, so that we must be circumspect in what we write. The second is that you are down for attainder for praemunire.'

Thomas's eyebrows rose over his trencher, then he thought deeply. 'It is indeed the case that I introduced many foreign powers into the country, but it was always at Henry's bidding, or with his consent. If I am guilty of praemunire, then so is he, if it is possible for a monarch to be so indicted.'

'Not in law,' Cromwell replied. 'But in equity?'

Thomas nodded sagely. 'You speak more wisely than you imagine. The common law cannot find me guilty, but of course praemunire is a Chancery matter, as I should know. I shall be hoist with my own petard, but what of Henry?'

'Be damned to Henry!'

Thomas looked across at him apologetically. 'Try not to choke on a fishbone, my dear Cromwell, but I shall confess my guilt without need of any trial.'

'To save Henry the King?' Cromwell asked in sheer disbelief. 'It is he who placed you where you now are, surrounded by your enemies, and stripped of all office.'

'Not all office,' Thomas reminded him. 'Certainly of those offices that I had at the King's hand, but certain of my offices in the Church came from the hands of various Popes, and it is from these that, in the main, I still enjoy food and shelter. I have already lost York Place, of course, and were I to protest to his Holiness this would do Henry's current matter no favours. So I am content to lose that, along with Hampton. But this house in Esher, plus various other establishments that belong to the Church, cannot be taken from me except with the consent of his Holiness. Certainly not by Norfolk, or even by Henry. And so I will bow my head to the praemunire.'

'But you are innocent!' Cromwell objected.

'So is Henry, but my only defence would be through him. I cannot expose him to that.'

'You would forfeit so much, simply to save His Majesty from embarrassment?' Cromwell enquired incredulously.

'And why not? I am simply rendering unto Caesar that which is Caesar's. I may be adjudged guilty in the court of common prejudice, but I remain true to my own conscience. I will climb upon Henry's cross in his stead, and on his behalf.'

'I shall spare no effort in acquainting His Majesty of your nobility, humility and grace in this matter.'

'It will avail nothing, Cromwell, since others are intent on my total ruin. For all it is worth, you might as well so inform Norfolk.'

'Why is he so against you, Master?'

Thomas smiled. 'It was ever so, even when we were boys. I think he resents my learning. Had I managed to persuade his Holiness in favour of his niece, he might have looked more kindly upon me. But my failure in that regard merely re-sharpened his angry blade.'

Cromwell was still indignant at the perceived injustice. 'When your attainder is announced before the Parliament, I shall make it my business to ensure that all men know of your true allegiance to the King, and to the nation that you served so well for so many years.'

'Have a care that you do not stir up Norfolk and his hounds against you, Cromwell,' Thomas warned him.

Cromwell smiled. 'Rather will I play him at his own game. He wishes me to come further under his influence by virtue of accepting some office within his grant. So will I do, but only in order to be closer acquainted with his intentions towards you, of which I may warn you in advance. My father taught me one thing, apart from how to avoid kicks to the privy parts. He had a saying that "A dog that will fetch will carry." By this means will I work for your interest.'

'Dear, loyal Cromwell. How goes your family in Cheapside?'

'Middling well, thank you Master, although there is much sweating sickness in the surrounding streets, and I fear daily that they will succumb. Remember them in your prayers, Your Grace, and that shall be reward enough for me.'

'Your other rewards will come in Heaven, Cromwell, since what you are setting out to do must surely attract God's blessing.'

Four days later, Norfolk arrived, demanding Thomas's presence in the Hall halfway through his second Mass. There was a malicious glint in his eye as he handed over a vellum. 'By the King's hand, before you try to be tricky again. You are to remove yourself from here and move to Richmond.'

'I am restored to Court?' Thomas asked breathlessly.

'No,' Norfolk replied with a cold grin. 'Rather the gatehouse, which even then is too grand for someone of your breeding and current standing with the King. Have your entire household assembled out here without delay, that I may advise them also.'

'May I not be permitted to do that myself, in kinder tones than you are likely to employ?'

'They would not thank you for it, given that I intend to offer the best of them a more secure future than they may currently look forward to.'

'But how can this be?' Thomas enquired, genuinely mystified, 'since this is the official residence of the Bishop of Winchester, which I still am, and which position was confirmed by the Pope himself?'

'After it was *granted* by the King,' Norfolk reminded him. 'Everything that Henry granted is to be taken from you, after your very wise confession to praemunire. Had you sought to defend yourself, you would have been found guilty and executed.'

'What of my see of York?'

'My instructions from Henry extend only to this house, more's the pity,' Norfolk growled back. 'Now, will you summon your household, or must I?'

Once everyone was gathered fearfully in the Hall, Thomas explained to them, tearfully, that he could no longer retain any of them in his service other than George Cavendish, if he would consent to reduced wages, and a few kitchen staff who had nowhere to go, and would otherwise be rendered destitute. The tears eventually overcame him, and Norfolk took over, promising them that the King, in his generosity and mercy, had undertaken to find employment for them all, although this would take some time, and they were to travel with Wolsey to Richmond Lodge, and there await further instructions from the Palace further up the drive. And with that he departed, declining Thomas's offer to take wine and drink to His Majesty's continued health.

Late that evening, George Cavendish found Thomas on his knees before the altar in his private bedchamber, praying for the strength to bear the disgrace and humiliation that was being heaped upon him. He refused all offer of food and drink, instructing George that what little was left in the larder was to be conserved for the retainers who still remained in his service.

When Thomas had still not eaten for three days, a terrified George Cavendish penned a hasty note to Thomas Cromwell at his London house.

The note found Thomas Cromwell knee deep in paperwork necessitated by the King's confiscation of Thomas's livings of Winchester and St Albans. Henry had ensured that Thomas retained a modest pension from the incomes, and had assigned the remainder of the revenues to various minor nobles. These nobles were now seeking confirmation from Thomas himself that the assignments were legitimate, and the clearest way of achieving that, in the common law trained mind of Cromwell, was to grant them deeds of assignation that were signed by Thomas, then countersigned by the royal hand. This gave Cromwell many excuses to be in the King's company, where he could keep him advised of Thomas's welfare. When Cromwell received George Cavendish's urgent missive, he sought an immediate audience with Henry, who he found in company with the Lady Anne in his privy chamber.

Cromwell bowed, and wasted no time. 'Sire, my master Thomas Wolsey is like to die within the week.'

'Leaving us to clean up his mess,' Anne observed coldly. Henry looked back at her pleadingly. 'He is my friend, and once my closest confidante, my sweet. He has done much for England, and it is only meet that England should now do something for him. What is the nature of his malady, Master Cromwell? Is it the sweating sickness that has beset much of the city?'

'No, Your Majesty. The sweating sickness has not yet reached Richmond, where, as you will be aware, my master is currently lodged. According to his gentleman usher, whose note I have here, he has taken to his bed and refuses to eat or drink.'

'Is his sickness one of the spirit, or is there some bodily cause?' Henry asked, concern written across his face.

Cromwell shook his head. 'I know not, since I have not seen him for some time. The documents that he signs go to him by messenger, and then by return here to Westminster. I have not laid eyes on him since his translation to Richmond.'

Henry thought for a moment, then looked back up. 'Go you and seek out my physician Doctor Buttes, and tell him that it is my command that he accompany you to Richmond, there to examine the Cardinal. Take the royal barge, and go you by way of the Palace, where you may both lodge while the good doctor applies his skill. Make no delay, but leave before the sun begins to sink.'

Thomas barely raised his head from the bolster as the two men entered his bedchamber; then he recognised Cromwell and gave a weak smile. 'Good day, Thomas. Did I not sign those latest papers? And who comes with you — Henry's executioner?'

'No, master, it's Henry's physician, Dr. Buttes. He's been sent by Henry himself, such is his concern for your welfare. I'll come back and see you when he's finished.'

'Tell him not to waste his leeches on a dead man,' was the weak response as Cromwell descended the stairs and went in search of George Cavendish and a cup of wine.

'How goes he?' Cromwell enquired nervously as he sat by the fire across from George, who shook his head resignedly.

'It's as if he *wants* to die. He won't eat or drink, he keeps getting out of his warm bed in order to kneel before his altar, and all he will talk about is how he's failed Henry and betrayed God.'

'Will nothing raise his spirits, say you?'

'Only perhaps a visit from Henry himself, and a restoration to his former glory. I think he misses all the adoration and pomp. He's a very proud man, as you probably know for yourself.'

'Indeed, and it must be like a dagger to the heart to be laid this low,' Cromwell replied as he rose to kick a fallen log back into the fire.

After an hour or so, Dr. Buttes descended the stairs with a puzzled look. Cromwell rose in expectation, but the doctor shook his head in a sign of bewilderment.

'He undoubtedly has a malady of the stomach, and to judge by his protests when I prodded certain portions it may well be a canker, in which case he will be dead ere the year's end. But there is also a sickness of the mind that prevents any chance of even a brief recovery. Could his mind be eased in some way, then he might last a little longer, but as I say, in the longer term he is down for death anyway. And in my experience there will be much pain.'

'Is there nothing you can do?' Cromwell pleaded.

The doctor nodded sagely. 'As for the bodily ailment, he should be given a simple of henbane mixed with hemlock and mandrake. It will ease the pain, and may be obtained from any apothecary. It should be taken thrice daily with a little wine. But as for the sickness of the mind, this is not my speciality, and I must leave it with you. Find what eats away at his soul, and you will cure that which is blocking the physical recovery. And I may say privily that should the pain become unbearable, then you should increase the mandrake, although you should require a servant to give it to him, that you may not be blamed for the death that will almost certainly follow. And now I take my leave.'

George was sobbing silently as he took it all in, but Cromwell was angry. 'This is all the making of the Boleyn witch! She has poisoned Henry's mind against the master, and so far bewitched his senses that he has sent a Cardinal to his deathbed. I vow that the day shall come when I will avenge myself of that devil with her child duckies! As for the present, do you know where an apothecary may be found, George?'

'Not at present, but I shall make it my first task to find one.'

'Good. In the meantime I will speak with the master, and see if there is not some way to lift his spirits.'

He tiptoed up the staircase, and was sitting by the bed when Thomas Wolsey opened his eyes.

'Still here, Cromwell? Did not the physician tell you that my days are now numbered? There is nothing you can do except sit with me and watch the sands of my life wash away.'

'If you were not to die,' Cromwell asked quietly, 'if there was one place on this earth that you would wish to visit ere you make your final journey to meet God, where would it be?'

'York,' came the hoarse reply without hesitation. 'In all these years I have never set eyes on my own minster, did you know that?'

'You may leave that small matter with me,' Cromwell assured him.

Cromwell hurried back to Westminster, where he advised Henry privily that his former Lord Chancellor was close to death, and that his last wish was to set eyes on his cathedral of York, and perform one final Mass before God took him, but that there was no money left.

Henry wiped a tear from his eye, and asked, 'How much does he need, say you?'

Cromwell took a deep breath. 'Perhaps a thousand marks?'

Henry nodded. 'It will require the consent of the Council, for such a sum to be voted out of Exchequer.'

'Can you not raise it within the Household accounts?' Cromwell asked, confused.

Henry shook his head. 'I cannot be seen to expend such a sum on one who has been attainted for praemunire, as you yourself can appreciate, Cromwell. To do so would be condoning the offence. And, I may tell you privily, the

238

Household would be sorely pressed to find such a sum at this time.'

'By the same token, would not your Council baulk at such a step, given that my master is not well loved?'

Henry nodded sadly. 'To you falls the task of persuading Norfolk to the matter, since his is likely to be the loudest voice. It is time to discover whether or not your master bequeathed you his filed tongue.'

Cromwell sought audience with Norfolk without delay. He found him in conference with Thomas Boleyn, and seated in the shadows was the Lady Anne, seemingly reading a book, but Cromwell had no illusions that she would not be listening intently to their conversation.

'Have you reconsidered my recent offer, Cromwell?' Norfolk enquired down his nose, 'since it would seem that your former employer is without a groat to his name — not that it is *much* of a name these days.'

Cromwell swallowed his anger and forced a smile to his lips. 'I have indeed, but it comes with one condition.'

'You are in no position to bargain,' Norfolk warned him, as Anne looked up from her book, and Boleyn signed her to silence.

'I might be,' Cromwell offered with what he hoped was a conspiratorial smile. 'In order to be free to join your service, I must needs rid myself of my current obligations, while you, I suspect, have an interest in seeing Thomas Wolsey as far from the King as is possible.'

'So?'

'So he wishes to travel to York, and establish himself within his highest benefice. I have reason to believe that were he once there, he would not choose to return.'

'And the difficulty with this?' Norfolk persisted.

'Finance, My Lord. I have just come from the King, and he has offered one thousand marks to see the Cardinal on his way, subject to Council's approval.'

'And you approach me why, exactly?'

'Forgive me, My Lord, but it is widely rumoured throughout the Court that you have no love for the Cardinal, and might seek to oppose any grant of money to him.'

'As you first service to me, do you know of any wealth of the Cardinal's that might be hidden, in order that the Exchequer might be reimbursed?'

'There is his recent endowment of the grammar school at Ipswich, My Lord. In addition, there is his new college at Oxford.'

Norfolk smiled. 'Very well. Such is my desire to secure the services of a lawyer and drafter of documents with your skill that I will undertake not to oppose the grant of money to see the Archbishop appear in his diocese for the first time since he was granted it. I will also request, as your first duty, that you draft the assignment of the Ipswich endowment into the Exchequer. We will speak again tomorrow forenoon.'

Cromwell wasted no time in carrying the hopeful news back to Richmond, where he found Thomas back on his feet, albeit unsteady, and drinking daily doses of beef tea to build up his strength once the medications from the apothecary had deadened the pains. Cromwell offered to remain for a few days, in order to assist George Cavendish with the task of gathering together the Cardinal's few remaining possessions, ahead of the anticipated journey north, once Thomas was strong enough.

A week or so later, in the early hours of a windy March morning, there was a heavy hammering on the door. Cromwell had been burning the candle late, in an effort to get all his master's papers into some semblance of order, although he had not yet been able to bring himself to announce that he had paid the price of Thomas's release to his diocese by entering Norfolk's service. It felt to him like a terrible act of betrayal, and he was apprehensive as he beat George Cavendish to the door, in case it was some of Norfolk's men come to seek him out and demand the reason for his early absence from his new post.

There were three heavily cloaked men in the doorway, and the glint from the candle that Cromwell held up caught the flash of two sword blades. Cromwell mentally prepared himself for a fight, until the man in the centre demanded entry, and he recognised the voice.

He bowed deeply, scarcely able to believe what was happening, as Henry and his two attendants stepped towards the embers of the fire and shook off their cloaks. Henry looked back at where Cromwell remained in the doorway, still half bowing in amazement.

'Off your mark, man, and get the Cardinal out of his bed.'

Cromwell did as requested, and led a sleepy-eyed and disbelieving Thomas gently down the staircase to meet his visitors. Thomas stood there with an open mouth, convinced that he was still in his bed, and hallucinating.

'Hal?' he murmured weakly, after the longest of stares.

'Who else? I am hungry and thirsty, and they tell me that Thomas Wolsey keeps a good table.'

'Used to, Hal, used to, but unfortunately I am somewhat reduced in circumstances of late. The best I could offer you would be herring and manchet, although I believe we may have some Burgundy left, unless Cromwell here has drunk it all.'

'I am well aware of your reduced circumstances, my dear old friend,' Henry assured him, 'since I was the one whose hand was instrumental in that, during a moment of weakness of which I am now thoroughly ashamed. And as for what we might share together at board, is there not something in the Bible about loaves and fishes?'

'Indeed there is,' Thomas replied with the first smile that Cromwell had seen in weeks, as he gestured to the stools around the table, and nodded to George Cavendish for the late supper to be served.

There was no sign of any reluctance on Thomas's part to eat as the conversation slipped easily from topic to topic, and Thomas assured Henry that although he had been ill, he was now feeling more like his old self, and was looking forward to serving God as loyally as he once served the nation.

'And that nation has not forgotten, my old friend,' Henry replied, as he reached inside his cloak and extracted a drawstring bag which he placed on the table between them.

'A thousand marks, my dear, dear friend, and God speed your journey north.'

XXII

The change in Thomas was immediate, and most noticeable. Although frequently in considerable pain, the regular supplies from the apothecary would usually deaden them sufficiently for Thomas to shrug them off in his enthusiasm for a return to public life, and his apparent reconciliation with Henry seemed to lift his spirits beyond any concern for his bodily ailments. He lost no time in issuing instructions for his household to be prepared to move north by the start of Easter Week 1529, and in a lengthy meeting with Cromwell that might well be his last for some time, if not for ever, Thomas entrusted him with the duty of keeping him fully appraised of events in London, where Cromwell was now assimilated into the administrative service of Thomas Howard, Duke of Norfolk, in his duties as Lord Treasurer of England.

All of Thomas's remaining possessions were loaded into a caravan of twelve carts smuggled out of his Oxford college only days before Norfolk's men descended upon it, the Steward of the College having been warned in advance by Cromwell of the fate that was about to encompass it.

On the first day of Passion Week the procession wound its way east, crossed the Thames via London Bridge, and took the road north, arriving on the evening of the second day at Rye House in Hertfordshire, the home of the Parr family. It was here that Thomas received a hastily written note from the displaced Queen Katherine, who was being temporarily accommodated in Thomas's former manor house of The More, where he had last resided overnight before bidding

243

farewell to Cardinal Campeggio, and which had fallen to Henry following Thomas's acquiescence to the praemunire.

As Katherine had earnestly requested, Thomas, accompanied only by two sturdy grooms, and mounted on his tired old donkey, rode after supper, and under the cover of darkness, to a clandestine meeting with the former Queen. He found her gaunt in the face, plainly dressed, much whiter in the hair than he remembered, and as clearly shattered by the sudden reduction in her fortunes as Thomas was by his. She smiled weakly as she searched his gloved hand for his ring of office, and kissed it gently before easing herself into a chair and offering Thomas the one next to hers.

'We are both the victims of the man we loved and so loyally served,' she observed.

'For myself,' Thomas tactfully replied, 'I do not regard my freedom to serve God in my see of York as a misfortune, Katherine.'

'Ever the diplomat *Tomas*,' she said, 'and where has it led you?'

'On the road to York,' he replied with a weak smile.

Katherine looked at him with her head tilted at an angle of enquiry. 'You know that I am forbidden access to my daughter the Princess Mary?'

Thomas nodded. 'It must bear upon you very hard, My Lady, but I will ever pray that God will ease your heartache, and urge Henry to allow mother and daughter to be reunited.'

'And would you be prepared to lend your assistance to that process by more diplomatic means, *Tomas*?'

'Your meaning, madam?'

'Do you know Eustache Chapuys?'

'I know of him, certainly. He is an Imperial envoy from Savoy, is he not?'

'He is that and more, *Tomas*. He is now the chosen Ambassador of my nephew Charles, and he is here in England to persuade Henry to allow Mary to join me in my exile. He will, in exchange, be prepared to assist Henry's greatest ambition by urging my nephew Charles to bring pressure upon the Pope to grant the annulment of our marriage.'

'You would support that annulment, madam? If so, why not simply tell Henry that?'

'Because, *Tomas*, I fear that my open consent to that outcome will encourage Henry to have Mary declared *bastarda*, which I cannot countenance, even at the cost of remaining separated from her. If the annulment comes from his Holiness directly, I can publicly maintain my denial, and fight for Mary's legitimacy, that she may one day be Queen of England if Henry cannot get a legitimate male heir by that night-crow Boleyn.'

'And why do you tell me all this privily?' Thomas enquired nervously.

Katherine stared intensely at him. 'Can I trust you, *Tomas*, not as your Queen, but simply as a mother whose heart is breaking to know the loving presence of her only child?'

'In either manner, madam, you may trust me as a servant of God first, and a fallen friend of Henry second.'

'Then I may tell you privily that Chapuys will be visiting me here within days, and that when he departs he will carry with him letters to Charles from me, urging upon him those matters of which we spoke just now. I would that he also bear a letter from you, to the same effect. My nephew Charles may no longer trust you, but he respects your judgment, and now that you too have fallen from Henry's favour, he would not see in any letter from you any duplicity or falsehood. And you being a man of God, it would be a natural part of your office to bless and urge the reunion of mother and daughter.'

Thomas thought for a moment. 'I see no harm in that, Katherine. Indeed, given the friendship of many years between us, and in recognition of the happy days that we shared before Henry's will became warped by Norfolk and his niece, I would deem it an honour to be able to perform this very personal service to you.'

Katherine reached out, grasped his hand, and intoned an endearment in her native Spanish that brought a blush to Thomas's face.

'I am not yet a saint, madam, and it is my daily prayer that I become not a blessed martyr either.'

Katherine turned to a groom who had been standing quietly in the corner, who left the chamber briefly and returned with a quill, some ink and a supply of vellum. As Katherine poured him some wine, Thomas sat and wrote a few lines, then shook the ink dry and handed it to Katherine to read. She nodded with satisfaction, and placed it on a pile that was already lying on a side table.

'It will go with all the others,' she told him, nodding to the groom, who collected the papers, bowed, and left the chamber.

A short while later Thomas took his leave and rode back to Rye House, comforted by the fact that he was performing tasks for God and mankind for once, and should perhaps always have done, rather than get in above his head in matters beyond his control.

He was similarly comforted, in the Lady's Chapel of Peterborough Abbey on Maundy Thursday, as he symbolically washed the feet of fifty-nine local poor men to whom he gave small sums of money, cloth for shirts and a modest quantity of simple food. On Easter Sunday he was reminded of more ambitious days as he once again donned his Cardinal's robes in order to lead the Mass, after heading a solemn procession to the Abbey on his donkey, acknowledging the loving and loyal shouts of the crowds that lined his approach to the ancient building.

Thomas and his entourage left the town proper the following Thursday, after ensuring that the local innkeepers and others who had played host to those of his household who could not be accommodated at the Abbey had been paid in full. But this was a short journey, to the nearby house of Sir William Fitzwilliams, who had cause to be grateful to Thomas in his Chancery days, when he had found in his favour against the London civic fathers who wished to prevent Fitzwilliams from establishing the Merchant Taylors Guild.

After a week of convivial company, during which Thomas asked for his host's forgiveness for not being able to eat anything other than a small helping of fish at each of several banquets, on account of his delicate constitution, it was back on the road, via Stamford, Grantham and Newark, to Southwell, where for the first time Thomas was within his Archbishop's diocese of York, where he settled down to enjoy the warmth of an early summer.

Thomas spent his time at Southwell basking in the comforting glow of the love and admiration, bordering upon worship, by which he was surrounded. With little effort on his part, he had become the talking point of the entire region, and the chosen arbiter of long-running disputes between neighbours, rival families and estranged spouses that had been awaiting resolution and arbitration by a skilled mediator such as Thomas, who put into good effect for the common folk of the East Midlands what he had learned among kings and ambassadors. His was also the voice that commanded the worshippers in the Minster to fear God, and the hand that raised the Host, on Sundays and feast-days, when he happily dressed in all his ecclesiastical finery and relived his glory days. Then came a day when he was reminded forcefully of what he had recently escaped.

On Corpus Christi Eve, Thomas had opted for an early night, and a large dose of the simple that kept his pains at bay sufficiently for him to sleep fitfully, dreaming of angry kings and leering executioners armed with blunt axes. George Cavendish was then obliged, with considerable reluctance, to wake him again at the insistence of two messengers who claimed that they came from the King, and could not delay their return to Westminster, even to take food and drink.

Thomas stepped wearily down the stairs and into the chamber, where his two visitors bowed solemnly. Thomas smiled as he recognised them.

'Masters Brereton and Wriothesley, you are welcome. I trust my dear friend Henry is in good health?'

'Indeed, My Lord,' Brereton replied reassuringly.

Thomas then stood there with an enquiring look on his face. Wriothesley had been carrying an ornate box, from which he carefully extracted a parchment and handed it over for Thomas to examine.

'As you can see, My Lord Archbishop, it contains the hands under seal of the entire clergy and nobility of England, petitioning his Holiness the Pope to lose no further time in granting the annulment. It wants only your signature and seal, and we may finally return to London, after several months on the road.'

'And I shall delay you no further than is required to add mine to the collection,' Thomas assured them as he gestured for George to bring him some wax and a candle. In no time at all he had added his signature and seal, and the two men departed. George was alarmed to hear a cry of pain from Thomas as he clutched the edge of the table at which he had been standing.

'What ails you, master?'

'The usual, George. For some reason, the mere sight of those Courtly messengers has brought back my suffering. Please make me up another simple.'

George's face fell. 'The apothecary was most insistent that the dose should not be consumed more than thrice a day, master.'

'The apothecary does not suffer my pains, George. Please do it, and bring it to my bedside.'

When the time came to move north from Southwell, it was decided that they should do so via Scroby, Welbeck, Worksop and Cawood, at all of which there were well appointed houses in which Thomas would be well received. Indeed, the further north they travelled, the more obvious it became that the good people of the northern counties were deeply devout, and so far removed from all knowledge of affairs in London, still less those of mainland Europe, that the toxic complaints of Luther against the Church of Rome had not yet been heard. They knew equally little about the affairs at Court, and for many of them Thomas was the nearest they had ever come to the King himself. This was probably why several local landowners sought to delay him in his progress by laying on hunts, all of which he politely declined as he rode slowly towards his personal Promised Land.

They finally reached Cawood Castle, seven miles south of York, and Thomas said a loud prayer to God as he set eyes on the spires of the fine cathedral in which he would shortly be installed as the practising Primate of England, of which he had hitherto been merely the absentee overlord, enjoying its revenues. He was wondering how he would be received in the circumstances, and was therefore somewhat apprehensive when George Cavendish advised him, shortly after a modest dinner of herring and small beer, that a delegation from the Minster, led by its Dean, Doctor Higden, sought audience with him.

There was a polite exchange of pleasantries, during which Dr Higden tactfully explained to Thomas that he had been absent from his benefice for so long that his fatherless children had slipped into their own ways, while Thomas assured him that this was no curious visit, but the start of a commitment for such of his remaining life as God might, in His infinite grace, grant to him. That being established, Dr Higden got down to the business that had brought him there.

'We look forward to your final installation as orphans being adopted by loving new parents,' he began, 'but until that moment, it is our ancient custom that you not proceed beyond the choir door. This is for the curious, and in your case totally unlikely, reason that should God call you before your installation, you will be buried in the body of the Minster, and not above the choir.'

'This I fully understand, and I shall honour your local custom with a glad heart,' Thomas assured them. 'Touching the matter of my installation, I would that it be conducted on the Monday following the next Sunday when, with your blessing, I shall reside in your house and shall take it upon myself to supply the wherewithal for a grand banquet at which, due to my current frailty, I will, by your leave, consume only some of the fine herring that I have discovered in this part of the country. I also add that whereas it is customary on these occasions for the object of the ceremony to enter the church along a carpet that is thereafter torn up and distributed among the poor, I would fain make the progress along bare ground and in my stockinged feet. This I will do in order to gainsay any word that may have travelled north ahead of me that I am a vain man, or guilty of the sin of pride.'

'It shall be as you wish, *Magister*,' Dr Higden assured him, as the Minster delegation took their leave.

Only one thing dampened Thomas's joy, and feeling of a fulfilled destiny, in the days prior to his planned installation. This was a letter from Thomas Cromwell, urging him to be more circumspect and humbler in his public appearances. He first enquired regarding Thomas's continuing health, then warned him that, at Court, 'Your charitable demeanour is misrepresented here by your enemies. Some allege you keep too great a house and are continually building. However, I think you are happy now that you are at liberty to serve God and banish all vain desires of the world which bring men nothing but trouble and anxiety.'

The warning fell upon deaf ears, but it was accurate, and the outcome of Cromwell's plodding, if unspectacular, activities in the service of Norfolk. From such a position he was able to monitor at least the external manifestations of the plotting that was still taking place, although had he been privy to conversations between Henry and the Lady Anne, the warning he sent to Thomas would have been even more strongly worded.

The guards came for Thomas three days before his planned installation, while he was still at Cawood Castle, although it was some time before Thomas realised that they were there, and even then he mistook their purpose. He was in his bedchamber, trying to force down some fruit sent by a kindly well-wisher, when a large contingent of armed men, led by Henry Percy, Sixth Earl of Northumberland following the death of his war veteran father, arrived at the porter's lodge and demanded the keys to the outer gates in the King's name. Unwilling to take them at their word, the porter send for George Cavendish, who agreed that they could enter as far as the Great Hall to attend upon Thomas, but no further.

Attracted by the noise down below, one of Thomas's serving men tiptoed down the stairs until he reached the bend halfway down, then, goggle-eyed, raced back upstairs and advised Thomas that his Hall was full of strangers. Thomas sent immediately for George Cavendish.

'Who are they below, who caused Gerard such a fright?'

'In truth, master, it is the Earl of Northumberland, with an armed body of his retainers.'

'And you did not see fit to advise me of this earlier, when we might have entertained them more fully? Fie George, bring the Earl up here immediately, that I may offer him my apologies in person. No, on the other hand it is probably better that I do so.'

Thomas clumped down the staircase on legs weak with his advancing years and emerged into the Hall, where he hurried towards Harry Percy with open arms.

'Well met, Harry, and peace be with you. It is many years since we were last together, and if my weak old eyes do not play me false, you have grown as much into a man as you have into your title. It is to be hoped that you honour the name of Northumberland as much as did your father, who was one of my dearest friends — after the King, of course.'

Harry Percy gazed uncomfortably down at the floor, and mumbled to Thomas that he needed to speak with him privily.

Thomas beckoned with his hand for Harry to accompany him up the stairs into his chamber.

Once they were there Harry closed the door gently and with the gentlest touch on Thomas's arm, all but whispered, 'In the name of the King, I arrest you for high treason.'

Thomas's jaw dropped at the same time that Percy seemed to run out of words. The two men stood staring at each other, each locked in their own mind to their last conversation, when the all-powerful Chancellor at the height of his popularity had banished the young page from his household because of his infatuation with a young woman who had taken the King's fancy. The silence was broken by the noisy opening of the chamber door, as Thomas's physician Dr Agostini was roughly shoved into the middle of the chamber by Master Walsh, a royal attendant who Thomas knew only by sight.

'This one's arrested too,' Walsh announced, then checked himself as he became aware of Thomas glaring at him. Walsh had last seen Thomas in better days, and was unsure of the merit of what he had been sent to do, give the high regard in which Thomas had been held by the King not so long ago.

It was Thomas who broke the uneasy silence. 'I cannot conceive of me what grounds the King may have for having me taken up for treason, but no doubt there have been crooked tongues in his ear, and no doubt one or other of you gentlemen has a warrant under the King's hand?'

'We have such,' Walsh explained when Percy seemed to have been struck dumb, 'but we may not show it to you at this time, since it contains further instructions to which you may not be allowed to become privy.'

'Am I for the Tower?' Thomas asked in a wavering voice as he sat down heavily on his bed bolster.

'As I just explained,' Walsh persevered, 'we are not commanded to make you privy to our full instructions. For the moment, it will be sufficient if you yield up the keys to this castle, and prepare yourself and your immediate servants for travel south as soon as this may be accomplished. Your physician here will go ahead of us, under escort of course.'

'I am a very sick man,' Thomas protested, the colour all but gone from his face, 'and I must needs have my physician about me. The King surely cannot desire my death ere we even reach St. Albans?'

'Those are our orders,' Walsh insisted.

Thomas looked for confirmation to Harry Percy, who merely hung his head and nodded.

Two hours later, George Cavendish found Thomas still sitting where he had been when Percy and Walsh had bid him goodnight. His arms were folded around his stomach, and he was crying freely, the tears rolling down his face and splashing onto the collar of his night shirt.

'Have the pains returned, master?' George enquired.

Thomas nodded through his tears. 'But to the physical pains that in truth have never really left me, for all the apothecary's skill, I must now add the pain of betrayal, which burns into me like no other torment. What false tongues have persuaded Henry that I — his staunchest of friends since he was a mere boy — have been guilty of treasonous behaviour? Or have I unwittingly done something, in the service of God, that has so sorely offended him that he takes it to be a threat to his throne? The good Lord knows that if I had served God as diligently as I have done the King, He would not have given me over in this fashion in my grey hairs. It seems that I must become more holy if I am to avoid the wickedness of men.'

Due to an outbreak of flux that kept Thomas on his closed stool for most of that night, and into the following day, it was decided to delay the southward journey until the Sunday morning, when Thomas would be allowed to be accompanied by George Cavendish, his chaplain, his barber and two grooms of his chamber, but no more.

Thomas was aghast. 'There are many in my household who will be left penniless and bereft of any position, and that many miles from their families, such was their loyalty in following me north. May I at least have them gathered in the Hall, that I may explain to them what has happened, and give them some words of comfort?'

'They have been enclosed in your chapel, my lord,' Percy told him uneasily, 'lest their lamentations at your departure should discomfort you further.'

'There will be no departure on my part until I have spoken to them,' Thomas defied him with a lingering vestige of his old determination and single-mindedness. At this point, the clamour of discontent that was audible from the chapel threatened to turn into a full scale riot, and Percy relented.

The servants filed sadly into the Great Hall, many of them wailing and lamenting, and all of them visibly overcome by grief.

Thomas raised his hands in the air, and gave a general blessing before adding, 'I am no more advised of the reason for my forced departure from here than are you, but it is my final instruction to you as your master that you think not ill of the King, who has obviously been overborne by the evil tongues of those who are my enemies. Why they are my enemies I know not, but it is my earnest command that you blame not His Majesty, who was ever my true friend, as was I to him. Rather, put your trust in Him who I serve in my holy office, as do I. God knows the merit of my case, and the King shall know of it ere long, if there be any justice left in this realm. And so I take my loving leave of you all.'

It was necessary for Percy's men to gently urge their horses through the loyal throng that had gathered outside the castle gate to bid Thomas a loving farewell and, to his considerable embarrassment, to call down curses upon those who had falsely accused him of treasonous acts.

The first night was spent at Pontefract, much to Thomas's discomfort, given its reputation for horrible deaths inflicted on noble prisoners, then it was on to Doncaster, where the fading afternoon light was aglow with candles held high in the air by the hundreds who had gathered at the roadside to wish him God speed and a fair trial. It was here that George Cavendish was handed a red buckram bag that Thomas had left in error at Cawood, and which a horseman had been sent back to recover. George opened it in curiosity, and was horrified to discover that it contained nothing other than three hair shirts.

Once they reached Sheffield Park, the home of the Earl of Shrewsbury, Thomas was so weak from lack of food and the lingering flux that it was necessary to delay the progress for over a fortnight, during which Thomas was advised privily by his host that Henry had sent messages ahead that Thomas was to be treated with all due reverence, and that while he had been left with no option but to place Thomas on trial, given the nature of the accusations against him, yet he felt sure in his own mind that Thomas would establish his innocence.

'How can he be assured of that, when I know not even the nature of the accusations against me?' Thomas complained. 'And what if there be those who have been prevailed upon, by torture or by bribe, to give false testimony against me? How then will go my case? I was Chancellor for long enough to know that justice in this realm is handmaiden to expediency, and that the value of a man's oath is measured by the strength of the King's love towards him. Now that I am out of favour, what value *my* oath, pray tell me, my lord?'

'There is heartening news, master,' George told Thomas, as he helped him prepare for bed. 'It seems that a messenger has been sent from the King to hear your defence to the charge laid against you.'

'How can I defend myself against that which I have not yet been apprised of?' Thomas sighed.

'But my Lord Percy assures me that it would be best for you to at least deny any treasonous thoughts or actions.'

'I would have hoped that Henry would know that of me at least,' Thomas argued resignedly, 'but what of Norfolk and his pliant niece? What poison might *they* have poured into his ear? We will perhaps know when I meet with this royal messenger. Do I know him?'

George swallowed hard. 'Probably not, master, since you have never met. He is perhaps known *to* you by name, if not in person.'

Thomas lowered himself, wincing, down the bedcovers. 'We may discuss this further in the morning, since — please God — I feel weary enough for sleep. Have my chaplain attend me for absolution while my head is still in the waking world.'

In the event, it was Thomas's host, the Earl of Shrewsbury, who broke the news as Thomas finished his second Mass of the day, and the chaplain slipped from his bedchamber. The Earl had been waiting in the half-open doorway, and now moved to sit by Thomas's side as he pulled on his hose. 'Today shall be the day when the King learns of your honesty and loyalty, my dear friend. The man is here who shall assure the King that your heart is ever true towards him.'

'So George advises me, but he did not think fit to reveal his identity.'

It fell silent until the Earl said softly, 'Why, it is Sir William Kingston.'

Thomas repeated the name out loud several times, then the colour drained completely from his face. 'The same Sir William who is the Constable of the Tower?'

'Indeed, but what of it? He is here simply to convey your defence to His Majesty.'

'He is here to convey me to the Tower!' Thomas wailed, before clutching his rosary and intoning streams of Latin that were unintelligible to the Earl's ears. Then he looked back at the Earl with an anguished face as he gave the instruction. 'Have Sir William meet me in the Hall within the hour.'

It was necessary for Thomas to take George's arm as his weak legs threatened to collapse under him on the way down the staircase from the bedchamber, and George could feel his master trembling under the Cardinal's robes that he had donned for the meeting.

Kingston rose to meet him, but made no effort to kiss the ring of office that was held out to him. The two men sat across the board staring at each other, until Kingston broke the silence. 'His Majesty commends himself unto you, my Lord Cardinal.'

Thomas narrowed his eyes, almost in defiance, as he replied, 'The important question for this morning, surely Sir William, is whether or not I commend myself to His Majesty.'

'That is why I am here, Your Grace. The King authorises me to tell you that he holds no faith in these scandalous rumours that have been put about, but to avoid all suspicion of partiality, he must deal with you as he deals with all others accused of treason, namely order a trial in which you may prove your innocence to the world.'

Thomas was shaking so hard that he was obliged to grip the edge of the table as he made his next point. 'For over ten years I was the Chancellor of England, as you well know, and in that time it was rumoured that those listed to appear before Star Chamber accused of treason were subjected to all manner of brutalities in order to extract from them confessions that eliminated the need for further trial. Since you, as Constable of that awful place in which such atrocities were committed, must be well aware of what I speak, tell me truly — am I to be racked in order to convince the King of my guilt, in the absence of any other evidence against me?'

'No, My Lord, of that I assure you,' Sir William replied with a shocked expression on his face that was not entirely convincing, since he himself was not entirely convinced. 'To inflict such atrocity on a man of God such as yourself would be a mortal sin that no man's soul could withstand.'

'You have been informed that I am close to death?' Thomas enquired in a croaking voice that was most convincing. 'I doubt that I will make it to London ere God claims my soul, but at least it is a soul clear of all sin such as must cause you nightmares of your own making. I take it that you have orders from the King to convey me to the Tower, assuming that I live that long?'

'To London, certainly. I have no further orders.'

'From the King, or from Norfolk?'

'My orders come from the King's own mouth, your Grace, although clearly I know not of their true origin.'

'To London, and no further, say you?'

'As God is my witness, your Grace.'

Thomas looked up at him, eyes wide with fear. 'And as God is *my* witness, Sir William, I am guilty of no treason against the man who I loyally served for some twenty years. You may inform him of that, but first you must inform me of the nature of my alleged treason. Am I condemned for visiting the Queen Katherine in her misery, as a man of God ministering unto the needy?'

'No, Your Grace, but it is said that there is a letter written by you under your seal inviting Charles of Spain to invade the nation, and promising him an army to support such invasion, in return for which you would be made Pope.'

Thomas burst out laughing, then slowly the laughter turned to tears of self-pity as he shook his head in disbelief. 'I wrote no such letter, but I doubt not that it exists, and I smell the shit of Norfolk in this. But will His Majesty believe me?'

'I cannot tell, your Grace, since mine is the simple task of conveying you to your trial. We must resume the journey on the morrow.'

'By the time we reach Hendon, you will be conveying a corpse,' Thomas assured him.

XXIII

Thomas Cromwell sat staring at the wall. It was late at night in the Drafting Chamber of the Treasury, and in his hand the quill had gone dry from lack of use. The document on the table in front of him was only half complete, but his mind was elsewhere.

He could not for one moment bring himself to believe that the man who had nurtured his career, had promoted him on merit, and had tutored his every action, was guilty of what they were accusing him of. But the evidence was said to be undeniable, in the form of a letter in Thomas's hand, and under his seal. This was surely another slimy underhand deed of Norfolk's, but would the King's trust in Thomas be more powerful than such an incriminating document? And where was it being kept hidden?

He sighed and rose from his stool, stretching his back muscles after hours of cramping them over his work. The assignment deed that he was drafting could wait until the morrow, and everyone else had gone home. But his day had not been idle, and he had several conveyance deeds that required to be copied into a fairer hand than his; these could be left in the adjoining chamber on his way out of the Treasury House, to prove that he had not spent the entire day staring at the wall.

He carried the deeds down the hallway and into the Copying Chamber, where one clerk still remained at his desk. Since that desk was piled high, and the clerk appeared to have plenty to occupy him, Cromwell moved on to one of the desks that had been vacated for the day. It was a mass of disorganised vellum, and as he cleared a space for his latest draft to be copied by the clerk whose desk it was, his eye lit upon a short document that was sticking out from the pile. The writing was all too familiar, and he lifted it out to read it more closely. It was from his disgraced master, to Charles of Spain, seeking his assistance in allowing the Princess Mary to be reunited with her mother.

At a loss as to why this particular document required to be copied by a Treasury clerk, a horrible suspicion began to assail him. He shuffled hurriedly through the rest of the pile, and found a drawing. Not just any old drawing, but a perfect likeness of the seal of the Archbishop of York. Burning with fury, he looked up and addressed the remaining clerk in the chamber. 'Whose position is this? It is quite the most untidy in the entire room.'

The clerk looked up with a malicious grin. 'The new man — Richard Bullmore. A lazy oaf, and likely to be dismissed if he does not change his ways.'

Thanking the clerk for his assistance, Cromwell walked out into the laneway that gave access to King Street, searching his memory for why that name seemed so familiar. Then it came back to him, and his rage was almost ungovernable.

The following evening, as the sun's rays were sliding down behind the turrets of the western side of White Hall, Cromwell stood waiting in an alleyway off the side lane. As the man strode past the narrow entrance to the alleyway in which Cromwell had been hidden from view, he leapt out, grabbed him by the collar, and hauled him into the alleyway with him. With one hand over the man's mouth, Cromwell extracted a wicked looking knife from his tunic belt and held the point to the man's throat as he hissed into his ear.

'Richard Bullmore, by my faith! "Tricky Dick" as we used to call you during my Putney days. You are fortunate indeed that you still have the use of your hands, given your skill in clipping coins and minting new ones from the silver. And now it would seem that you have made a new career of creating false documents. However, this time you have created one too many.'

'Who are you?' Bullmore croaked, as Cromwell removed his hand from his mouth.

'Is the name Thomas Cromwell familiar to you, from your days in Putney?'

'Walter Cromwell's son? He was a violent man, as I recall. Have you inherited his nature?'

'I certainly have, in your case,' Cromwell assured him, fighting the urge to plunge the point of the knife straight into the man's throat, or use it to slit his neck from ear to ear.

'What do you want of me?' the man asked, his voice wavering in abject terror.

'A confession — to the King, no less. In person, on your knees. A confession to having created, no doubt on payment by my lord of Norfolk, a document seemingly under the hand and seal of the Archbishop of York, Thomas Wolsey, inviting Charles of Spain to invade.'

'The King would have me put to death! And Norfolk would have me murdered in some dark alley!'

'A dark alley such as this, perhaps?' Cromwell hissed.

'You intend to murder me?'

'Far too merciful,' Cromwell assured him. 'I will, in due course, should you not agree to confess, do what should have been done to you years ago. In plain, I shall cut off your hands. But prior to that, I shall practice on your bollocks.'

'Have mercy, I beg you!' Bullmore screamed.

263

'The only mercy you can expect of me comes at the price of your confession to the King. Do I have your pledge on that, always keeping in mind that I can seek you out at any time, in any place?'

'I pledge!' Bullmore assured him.

Cromwell removed the knife from the man's throat and kneed him in the small of his back, sending him sprawling out into the laneway with an agonised shriek.

The next sunrise saw Cromwell riding hard through the lanes northward out of Hertfordshire, on his way to wherever Thomas might be found. A few enquiries at wayside hostelries yielded the information that a party of horsemen under the King's orders were expected from Leicester within days, and it did not require a mind trained in Courtly matters to suggest that Leicester Abbey might be the best place to enquire after his old master.

George Cavendish embraced him warmly as a groom took off his heavily soiled riding cape, but Cromwell was the first to speak. 'How goes your master?'

George shook his head, and tears appeared in the corners of his eyes. 'He is near to death and will be unlikely to make London. Just before we reached Leicester, on the road from Nottingham, he slid from his mule, and had to continue the journey with his legs tied under it, like some common criminal. He is in his bedchamber, and from time to time we hear his screams of agony.'

'Has he the services of a physician?'

'At Sheffield Park, at the house of my lord of Shrewsbury, he was attended by one Dr. Nicholas, who examined the black stools that he was then voiding. They were wondrous black, and the good physician gave them some Latin name that I do not recall, but which presages death within days. It is a canker, and it causes him great agonies.'

'Has he been shriven?'

'Every hour, the last not many minutes since. He is not just prepared for death, Thomas — he is praying for it.'

'Have you a supply of that mandrake simple?'

'An adequate supply until we reach London. I fear that I have been obliged to increase the dose, such has been my distress to see the pain he undergoes.'

'And does the master still prefer Rhenish?'

'In truth, while he does, he has not been able to stomach anything other than small beer since we left Cawood some weeks since.'

Cromwell placed a hand on each of Cavendish's shoulders and looked him intently in the eye. 'Do you bring me a supply of Rhenish, and as much mandrake as you have. Then retire to your pantry, and I wish you a good night. I will keep vigil in the master's chamber, and will sleep on the floor wrapped in my cloak.'

A few minutes later Cromwell crept up to Thomas's bedside with the draught in his hand. Thomas looked up. Cromwell tried not to show his distress at what he was witnessing, and what he must do, as he placed the draught on the side table and took Thomas's cold hand in his.

'I bring the greatest news possible, Master. I have found the villain who drafted the pernicious deed that Norfolk would seek to employ for your downfall, and he has pledged to confess his part in it.'

Thomas screamed as a wave of burning agony ran through his innards, leaving another stinking stool among the bedsheets. 'The man will be dead ere he can testify. I am done for, Cromwell, and only you can clear my good name now, by swearing on your oath what the man confessed to you. But I will be dead ere that happens, should God ease my sufferings in His infinite mercy.'

'Perhaps not God, Master, but there are others who can ensure that you do not die with your name sullied.'

Thomas turned his head to look at the draught sitting on the side table. 'They say I may not take more of the simple to ease my pain.'

'I am no physician, Master,' Cromwell replied, his head bowed. 'Will you grant me absolution for what I must do?'

'Gladly, Thomas. *Te absolvo*. There, it is done. Your penance shall be to prove my innocence once I am gone. Tell me, Thomas, have you ever taken a man's life?'

'Once, master. In Italy. On the field of battle. I was a soldier then.'

'Give me the draught, my dearest Thomas, then leave me in God's hands.'

Cromwell stumbled down the staircase, his eyes blurred by tears, before reclaiming his horse and riding hard to London, cursing loudly into the night air.

Four days later, Cromwell bent the knee before Henry, who sat in his Audience Chamber at Westminster with the Lady Anne at his side. She was smirking, and Thomas wanted to strangle her with his bare hands.

'Did he confess at the end?' Henry asked him fearfully.

'Only to his confessor, and even then not to those matters most recently libelled against him, of which he was innocent, as I have a witness to attest.'

'Who is this witness?' Henry enquired eagerly.

'A man in the employ of your Treasurer, your Highness. A man named Richard Bullmore, a skilled forger of coins and documents beside. It was his hand that created the document of which my late master was accused.'

'Bullmore is dead,' Anne announced gloatingly.

Cromwell's eyebrows shot upwards, and Henry looked suspiciously back at Anne, who looked momentarily confused, then explained.

'My uncle informs me that the man accused by Master Cromwell was found floating in the river at Whitehall steps two days ago.'

'I had not then publicly named him,' Cromwell said ominously.

Henry looked back at him. 'It is of no matter now, since my old friend is dead. Do you arrange his funeral, Master Cromwell?'

'He was buried in Leicester Abbey, Your Majesty. A simple ceremony.'

'I shall ensure that his name is cleared of any suggestion of treason,' Henry promised. 'It is the least I can do, for such a loyal and steadfast friend.'

'He will no doubt look down from Heaven and bless you for that,' Cromwell assured him.

'If indeed he be in Heaven,' Anne added.

Cromwell bowed from the presence, and looked up at a grinning Anne before departing the chamber, with an oath burning through his head that he would one day bring her down even lower than she had worked towards the downfall of Cardinal Archbishop Thomas Wolsey — the ambitious and tragically proud victim of a noble-dominated society that could not tolerate his lowly origins.

A NOTE TO THE READER

Dear Reader,

Thank you for sharing the life and times of Thomas Wolsey with me.

Cardinal Thomas Wolsey, Lord Chancellor of England and Archbishop of York, was in his time the most influential figure in early Tudor England. His rise to power was dramatic, and his fall from royal preferment even more dramatic, and yet he remains a shadowy figure in traditional accounts of the Courts of Henry VII and his son Henry VIII.

I was very fortunate to have access to *Thomas Wolsey — his life and death*, written by George Cavendish, Wolsey's former and loyal gentleman usher, who gives us a first-hand account of the final years of his master's life. During his middle years, in quiet conversations around the board, Wolsey told Cavendish something of his early life, but even then left out enough for an historical novelist like me to colour in the outlines. I admit to artistic licence in making Wolsey and Thomas Howard schoolboy enemies, but it is not implausible, since they were the same age, and grew up in the same county of East Anglia. And how else to explain the obvious mutual dislike other than in terms of the fact that Wolsey was a greatly gifted commoner thrust into high office that the likes of Norfolk regarded as theirs solely by right of birth?

As for Wolsey's death, it is even more obscure in its precise cause, even though Cavendish was there to witness it. But his somewhat prudish pen spared us the gory detail, and we know only that in his declining days Wolsey was reaping the consequences of his former rich lifestyle, and in particular his love of fine food and wine, in the form of some sort of stomach ailment. Again I plead guilty to adding the detail that seemed to me both appropriate and realistic.

Finally, the matter of Wolsey's relationship with his Secretary, Thomas Cromwell. I am not the first historical speculator to ascribe Cromwell's dedication to the downfall of Anne Boleyn to his anger and pain at the humiliating end inflicted on his mentor. Cromwell was another lowly-born man of outstanding ability who owed everything to the man who had raised him up, in his case from the gutters of Putney, and the England of Henry VIII was a prime location for the settling of old scores by underhand means.

But the central character in what I have written remains the butcher's boy from Ipswich who broke through the class ceiling and demonstrated that ability by itself could secure a man a comfortable lifestyle. As a former educator myself, I can only read in awe of how 'Tom Wulcy', as he then was, graduated from Oxford at the age of fifteen, even allowing for the somewhat lax academic rigour of those times. His grasp of most of languages of Europe leaves me with a profound belief that in Thomas Wolsey, the comparatively unlettered Henry VIII was blessed to have such a talented envoy at his command at a time when England was seeking to assert its influence on the European stage.

But let's not forget the man's failings as well. Venality was as much his style as piety, and it's a matter of historical record that Wolsey sired two children on his resident mistress. His sins of gluttony were only exceeded by the sin of pride, of which Thomas Wolsey was guilty to an astonishing degree. No doubt scarred by noble 'put-downs' regarding his origins, he over-reacted by amassing wealth to a degree that almost exceeded that of Henry himself, and his extravagance in the conversion of York Place into York Palace, and the creation of Hampton Court, gave his enemies at Court an obvious cheap shot.

All in all, a worthy subject for an historical novel, and I sincerely hope that you enjoyed reading it as much as I did writing it. So much so that I was tempted back into print to speculate on how Cromwell sought his revenge for a man long dead by the time that Anne Boleyn's head left the block and landed in the blood-splattered mud of Tower Green.

As ever, I look forward to receiving feedback from you, whether in the form of a review on **Amazon** or **Goodreads**. Or, of course, you can try the more personal approach on my website, and my Facebook page: **DavidFieldAuthor**.

Happy reading!

David

davidfieldauthor.com

Sapere Books is an exciting new publisher of brilliant fiction and popular history.

To find out more about our latest releases and our monthly bargain books visit our website: **saperebooks.com**

Manufactured by Amazon.ca
Bolton, ON